# A Bride of the Plains

Baroness Emmuska Orczy

**A Bride of the Plains**

ISBN: 978-1-64799-101-2

# CONTENTS

# CHAPTER I

## "God bless them all! they are good lads"

It was now close on eight o'clock and more than two hours ago since first the dawn broke over that low-lying horizon line which seems so far away, and tinged the vast immensity of the plain first with grey and then with mauve and pale-toned emerald, with rose and carmine and crimson and blood-red, until the sun—triumphant and glorious at last—woke the sunflowers from their sleep, gilded every tiny blade of grass and every sprig of rosemary, and caused every head of stately maize to quiver with delight at the warmth of his kiss.

The plain stretched its limitless expanse as far as human eye can reach—a sea of tall straight stems, with waves of brilliant green and plume-crowned crests shimmering like foam in the sunlight.

As far as human eye can see!—and further, much further still!—the sea of maize, countless upright stems, hundreds of thousands of emerald green sheaths crowned with flaxen tendrils like a maiden's hair; down on the ground—a carpet for the feet of the majestic corn—hundreds and thousands of orange-coloured pumpkins turning their huge shiny carcases to the ripening rays of the sun, and all around in fantastic lines, rows of tall sunflowers, a blaze of amber, with thick velvety hearts laden with seed.

And all of it stretching out apparently to infinity beyond that horizon line which is still hidden by a silvery haze, impalpable womb that cradles the life-giving heat.

Stately stems of maize—countless as the pebbles on a beach, as the specks of foam upon the crest of a wave, limitless as the sea and like the sea mutable, ever-changing, restless—bending to every breath of the summer breeze, full of strange, sweet sounds, of moanings and of sighs, as the emerald sheaths tremble in the wind, or down below the bright yellow carcases of the pumpkins crack and shiver in the growing heat.

An ocean of tall maize and gaily-coloured pumpkins as far as the eye can reach, and long, dividing lines of amber-coloured sunflowers, vivid and riotous, flaunting their crude colouring in the glowing sunlight.

Here and there the dull, dark green of hemp breaks the unvarying stretches of maize, and far away there is a tanya (cottage) with a group of stunted acacias near it, and a well whose tall, gaunt arm stretches weirdly up to the sky, whilst to the south the sluggish Maros winds its slow course lazily toward the parent stream.

1

An ocean of maize and of pumpkins and of sunflowers, with here and there the tall, crested stems of hemp, and above it the sky—blue and already glowing through the filmy mist which every minute grows more ethereal and more impalpable as veil upon veil of heat-holding vapours are drawn from before its face.

A beautiful morning in mid-September, and yet in all this vast immensity of fertile land and ripening fruit there is no sign of human toil, no sound of beast or creaking waggon, no sign of human life around that distant tanya.

The tiny lizard in his comfortable position on the summit of a gigantic pumpkin can continue his matutinal sleep in peace; the stork can continue undisturbed his preparations for his impending long voyage over seas. Man has not yet thought to break by travail or by song the peaceful silence of the plain.

And yet the village lies not very far away, close to the Maros; the small, low, hemp-thatched houses scarcely peep above the sea of tall-stemmed maize, only the white-washed tower of the church with its red-painted roof stands out clear and abrupt against the sky.

And now the sharp, cracked sound of the Elevation bell breaks the silence of the summer's morning. The good Pater Bonifácius is saying Mass; he, at any rate, is astir and busy with his day's work and obligations. Surely it is strange that at so late an hour in mid-September, with the maize waiting to be gathered in, the population of Marosfalva should still be absent from the fields.

Hej! But stranger, what would you! Such a day is this fourteenth of September.

What? You did not know it? The fourteenth of September, the ugliest, blackest, most God-forsaken day in the whole year!

You did not know? You cannot guess? Then what kind of a stranger are you if you do not know that on this hideous fourteenth of September all the finest lads of Marosfalva and the villages around are taken away by the abominable government? Away for three years to be made into soldiers, to drill and to march, to carry guns and bayonets, to obey words of command that they don't understand, to be packed off from place to place—from Arad to Bistricz, from Kecskemét to Nagyvárad, aye? and as far as Bosnia too—wherever that may be!

Yes, kind Sir! the lads of Marosfalva and of Fekete, of Kender and of Görcz, are taken away just like that, in batches every year, packed into one of those detestable railways like so many heads of cattle and separated from their mothers, their sisters, their sweethearts, all because a hateful government for which the people of Marosfalva do not care one brass fillér, has so decreed it.

2

Mind you, it is the same in all the other villages, and in every town in Hungary—so at least we have been given to understand—but we have nothing to do with other villages or with the towns: they do just as the good God wills them to do. It is our lads—the lads of Marosfalva and Kender and Fekete and Görcz—who have to be packed off in train-loads to-day and taken away from us for three years.

Three years! Why, the lad is a mere child when he goes—one-and-twenty on his last birthday, bless him!—still wanting a mother's care of his stomach and his clothes, and a father's heavy stick across his back from time to time to keep him from drink and too much love-making.

Three years! When he comes back he is a man, has notions of his own, has seen the world and cares no more about his native village and the narrow cottage where he used to run in and out bare-footed, bare-chested, bare-headed and comfortably dirty from head to foot.

Three years! And what are the chances that he come back at all? Bosnia? Where in the world is that? And if you are a soldier, why then you go to war, you get shot at, killed may be, or at any rate maimed. Three years! You may never come back! And when you do you are not the same youngster whom your mother kissed, your father whacked, and your sweetheart wept over.

Three years! Nay, but 'tis a lifetime. Mother is old, she may never see her son again. Girls are vain and fickle, they will turn their thoughts in other directions—there are the men who have done their military service, who have paid their toll to the abominable government up at Budapest and who are therefore free to court and free to marry.

Aye! Aye! That's how it is. They must go through with it, though they hate it all—every moment of it. They hate to be packed into railway carriages like so many dried heads of maize in a barn, they hate to wear the heavy cloth clothes, the hard boots, the leather pouches and belts. My God, how they hate it!

And the rude alien sergeant, with his "Vorwärts!" and "Marsch!" and "Rechts" and "Links"—I ask you in the name of the Holy Virgin what kind of gibberish is that?

But they must all go!—all those, at least, who are whole and sound in body. Bless them! They are sound enough when they go! It is when they come back! . . .

Yes! They must all go, those who are sound in eyes and wind and limb, and it is very difficult to cheat the commission who come to take our lads away. There was Benkó, for instance; he starved himself for three months this summer, hoping to reduce his chest

3

measurements by a few needful centimètres; but it was no use. The doctor who examined him said that with regular food and plenty of exercise he would soon put on more flesh, and he would get both for the next three years. And János—you remember?—he chopped off one of his toes—thinking that would get him off those hated three years of service; but it seems there is a new decree by which the lads need not be possessed of all ten toes in order to serve the hateful government.

No, no! It is no use trying to get out of it. They measure you, and bang your chest and your back, they look at your eyes and make you open your mouth to look at your teeth, but anyhow they take you away for three years.

They make you swear that you will faithfully serve your country and your King during that time, that you will obey your superiors, and follow your leader wherever he may command, over land and by water. By water! I ask you! When there was Albert and Jenö who could not bear even the sight of water; they would not have gone in a boat on the Maros if you had offered them a gold piece each! How could they swear that they would follow some fool of a German officer on water?

They could not swear that. They knew they could not do it. But they were clapped in prison like common malefactors and treated like brigands and thieves until they did swear. And after that—well! they had once to cross the Theiss in a ferry-boat—they were made to do it!

Oh, no! Nothing happened to them then, but Albert came back after his three years' service, with two of his front teeth gone, and we all know that Jenö now is little better than an idiot.

So now you know, stranger, why we at Marosfalva call the fourteenth day of September the very blackest in the whole calendar, and why at eight o'clock in the morning nobody is at work in the fields.

For the fourteenth day being such a black one, we must all make the most of the few hours that come before it. At nine o'clock of that miserable morning the packing of our lads into the train will commence, but until then they are making merry, bless them! They are true Hungarians, you know! They will dance, and they will sing, they will listen to gipsy music and kiss the girls so long as there is breath in their body, so long as they are free to do it.

At nine o'clock to-day they cease to be free men, they are under the orders of corporals and sergeants and officers who will command them to go "Vorwärts" and "Rechts" and "Links" and all that God-forsaken gibberish, and put them in irons and on bread and water if they do not obey. But yesterday, on the thirteenth of

4

September that is, they were still free to do as they liked: they could dance and sing and get drunk as much as they chose.

So the big barn that belongs to Ignácz Goldstein, the Jew, is thrown open for a night's dancing and music and jollification. At five o'clock in the afternoon the gipsies tuned up; there was a supper which lasted many hours, after which the dancing began. The first csárdás was struck up at eight o'clock last evening, the last one is being danced now at eight o'clock in the morning, while the whole plain lies in silence under the shimmering sky, and while Pater Bonifácius reads his mass all alone in the little church, and prays fervently for the lads who are going away to-day for three years: away from his care and his tender, paternal attention, away from their homes, their weeping mothers and sorrowing sweethearts.

God bless them all! They are good lads, but weak, impulsive, easily led toward good or evil. They are dancing now, when they should be praying, but God bless them all! They are good lads!

# CHAPTER II

## "Money won't buy everything"

Inside the barn the guttering candles were burning low. No one thought of blowing them out, so they were just left to smoke and to smoulder, and to help render the atmosphere even more stifling than it otherwise would have been.

The heat has become almost unbearable—unbearable, that is, to anyone not wholly intent on pleasure to the exclusion of every other sensation, every other consciousness. The barn built of huge pine logs, straw-thatched and raftered, is filled to overflowing with people—men, women, even children—all bent upon one great, all-absorbing object—that object, forgetfulness.

The indifferent, the stolid, may call it what he will, but it is the common wish to forget that has brought all these people—young and old—together in Ignácz Goldstein's barn this night—the desire to forget that hideous, fateful fourteenth of September which comes with such heartrending regularity year after year—the desire to forget that the lads, the flower of the neighbouring villages, are going away to-day ... for three years?—nay! very likely for ever!—

5

three years! and all packed up like cattle in a railway truck! and put under the orders of some brutal sergeant who is not Hungarian, and can only say "Vorwärts!" or "Marsch!" and is backed in his arbitrary commands by the whole weight of government, King and country.

For three years!—and there is always war going on somewhere—and that awful Bosnia! wherever it may be—lads from Hungarian villages go there sound in body and in limb and come back bent with ague, halt, lame or blind.

Three years! More like for ever!

And therefore the whole population of Marosfalva and of the villages round spends its last happy four-and-twenty hours in trying to forget that nine o'clock of the fourteenth day of September is approaching with sure and giant strides; everyone has a wish to forget; the parents and grandparents, the sisters, the sweethearts, the lads themselves! The future is so hideous, let the joy of the present kill all thoughts of those coming three years.

Marosfalva is the rallying-point, where this final annual jollification takes place. They all come over on the thirteenth from Fekete and Görcz, and Kender, in order to dance and to sing at Marosfalva in the barn which belongs to Ignácz Goldstein the Jew. Marosfalva boasts of a railway station and it is from here that at nine o'clock in the morning the lads will be entrained; so all day on the thirteenth there has been a pilgrimage along the cross-roads from the outlying villages and hamlets round Marosfalva—a stream of men and women and young children all determined to forget for a few hours the coming separation of the morrow; by five o'clock in the afternoon all those had assembled who had meant to come and dancing in the barn had begun.

Ignácz Goldstein's barn has always been the setting in which the final drama of the happy year is acted. After that night spent there in dancing and music and merry-making, down goes the curtain on the comedy of life and the tragedy of tears begins.

Since five o'clock in the afternoon the young people have been dancing—waltzing, polkaing, dancing the csárdás—mostly the csárdás, the dance of the nation, of the people, the most exhilarating, most entrancing, most voluptuous dance that feet of man have ever trod. The girls and lads are indefatigable, the slow and languorous Lassu (slow movement) alternates with the mad, merry csárdás, they twirl and twist, advance, retreat, separate and reunite in a mad, intoxicating whirl. Small booted feet stamp on the rough wooden floor, sending up clouds of dust. What matter if the air becomes more and more stifling? There are tears and sighs to be stifled too.

6

"Ho, there, czigány! Play up! Faster! Faster! 'Tis not a funeral dirge you are playing."

The gipsy musicians, hot and perspiring, have blown and scraped and banged for fifteen solid hours; no one would ever think of suggesting that a gipsy needed rest; the clarinetist, it is true, rolled off his seat at one time, and had to be well shaken ere he could blow again, but the leader—as good a leader, mind you, as could be found in the kingdom—had only paused when the dancers were exhausted, or when bite and sup were placed before him. There they were, perched up on a rough platform made up of packing-cases borrowed from the station-master; the czimbalom player in the centre, his fat, brown hands wield the tiny clappers with unerring precision, up and down the strings, with that soft, lingering tone which partakes of the clavecins and the harp alike. At the back the double-bass, lean and dark, with jet-black eyes that stare stolidly at his leader.

There is a second fiddle, and the fat clarinetist and, of course, the leader—he whose match could not be found in the kingdom. He stands on the very edge of the rough platform, his fiddle under his chin, and he stoops well forward, so that his hands and instrument almost touch the foremost of the dancing pairs.

They—the dancers—crowd closely round the gipsy band, for so must the csárdás be danced, as near the musicians as possible, as close together as the wide, sweeping petticoats of the girls will allow.

Such petticoats! One on the top of the other, ten or a dozen or more, and all of different colour: the girls are proud of these petticoats—the number of them is a sign of prosperity; and now as they dance and swing from the hips these petticoats fly out, caught by the currents of air until they look like gargantuan showers of vividly-coloured petals shaken by giant hands.

Above the petticoats the girls' waists look slim in the dark, tight-fitting corslet, above which again rises the rich, olive-tinted breast and throat; full white sleeves of linen crown the bare, ruddy arms, and ribbons of national colours—red, white and green—float from the shoulders and the waist.

The smooth, thick hair is closely plaited, from the crown of the head in two long, tight plaits; it is drawn rigidly away from the forehead, giving that quaint, hard finish to the round, merry face which is so characteristic of the Asiatic ancestry.

Each one of them a little picture which seems to have stepped straight out of a Velasquez canvas, the bell-shaped skirt, the stiff corslet, the straight, tight hair and round eyes full of vitality.

The men wear their linen shirt and full trousers with fringed, embroidered ends, the leather waistcoat and broad belt covered

7

with metal bosses and wrought with bright-coloured woollen threads. They get very excited in the mazes of the dance, they shout to the gipsies to play faster and ever faster; each holds his partner tightly round the slim waist and swings her round and round, till she stumbles, giddy and almost faint in his arms.

And round the dancers in a semicircle the spectators stand in a dense crowd—the older folk and the girls who have not secured partners—they watch and watch, indefatigable like the dancers, untiring like the musicians. And behind this semicircle, in the dark corners of the barn, the children foot it too, with the same ardour, the same excitement as their elders.

The last csárdás of this memorable night! It is eight o'clock now, and through the apertures in the log wall the brilliant light of this late summer's morning enters triumphant and crude.

Andor is dancing with Elsa—pretty, fair-haired Elsa, the daughter of old Kapus Benkó,[1] an old reprobate, if ever there was one. Such a handsome couple they look. Is it not a shame that Andor must go to-day—for three years, perhaps for ever?

The tears that have struggled up to Elsa's tender blue eyes, despite her will to keep them back, add to the charm of her engaging personality, they help to soften the somewhat serious expression of her young face. Her cheeks are glowing with the excitement of the dance, her graceful figure bends to the pressure of Andor's arm around her waist.

Ten or a dozen cotton petticoats are tied round that slim waist of hers, no two of a like colour, and as she twists and twirls in Andor's arms the petticoats fly out, till she looks like a huge flower of many hues with superposed corollas, blue, green, pink and yellow, beneath which her small feet shod in boots of brilliant leather look like two crimson stamens.

The tight-fitting corslet bodice and the full, white sleeves of the shift make her figure appear peculiarly slim and girlish, and her bare throat and shoulders are smooth and warmly tinted like some luscious fruit.

No wonder that Andor feels this dance, this movement, the music, the girl's sweet, quick breath, going to his head like wine. Elsa was always pretty, always dainty and gentle, but now she is excited, tearful at the coming parting, and by all the saints a more exquisite woman never came out of Paradise!

The semicircle of spectators composed of older folk draws closer round the dancers, but the other couples remain

---

[1] In Hungary the surname precedes the Christian name.

8

comparatively unheeded. It is Elsa and Andor whom everyone is watching.

He is tall and broad-shouldered, with the supple limbs of a young stag, and the mad, irresponsible movements of a colt. His dark eyes shine like two stars out of his sun-burnt face; his muscular arms encircle Elsa's fine waist with a grip that is almost masterful. The wide sleeves of his linen shirt flutter above his shoulders till they look like wings and he like some messenger of the gods come to carry this exquisite prey off from the earth.

"What a well-matched couple!" murmur the older women as they watch.

"Elsa will be the beauty of the village within the next year, mark what I say!" added a kindly old soul, turning to her neighbour—a slatternly, ill-kempt, middle-aged woman, who was casting looks on Andor and Elsa that were none too kind.

"Hm!" retorted the latter, with sour mien, "then 'tis as well that that good-for-nothing will be safely out of the way."

"I would not call Andor good-for-nothing, Irma néni,"[2] said one of the men who stood close by, "he has not had much chance to do anything for himself yet. ..."

"And he never will," snapped the woman, with a click of her thin jaws, "I know the sort—always going to do wonderful things in a future which never comes. Well! at any rate while he is a soldier they will teach him that he is no better than other lads that come from the same village, and not even as good, seeing that he has never any money in his wallet."

"Andor will be rich some day," suggested the kindly old soul who had first spoken, "don't you forget it, Irma néni."

"I have no special wish to remember it, my good Kati," retorted Irma dryly.

"I thought," murmured the other, "seeing that Andor has really courted Elsa this summer that ... perhaps ..."

"My daughter has plenty of admirers," said Irma, in her bitter-toned, snappish way, "and has no reason to wait for one who only may be rich some day."

"Bah! Lakatos Pál cannot live for ever. Andor will have every fillér of his money when he dies, and Pál will cut up very well."

"Lakatos Pál is a youngish man—not fifty, I imagine," concluded Irma with a sneer. "He may live another thirty years, and Elsa would be an old woman herself by then."

---

[2] Aunt Irma—the words aunt (néni) and uncle (bácsi) are used indiscriminately in Hungary when addressing elderly people, and do not necessarily imply any relationship.

The other woman said nothing more after that. It was no use arguing the point. Irma was the wife of old Kapus—both of them as shiftless, thriftless, ill-conditioned a pair as ever stole the daylight from God in order to waste it in idleness. How they came to be blessed with such a pretty, winning daughter as Elsa an all too-indulgent God only knew.

What, however, was well known throughout the village was that as Kapus and his wife never had a crown to bless themselves with, and had never saved enough to earn a rest for themselves in their old age, they had long ago determined that their daughter should be the means of bringing prosperity to them as soon as she was old enough for the marriage-market.

Elsa was beautiful! Thank the good God for that! Kapus had never saved enough to give her a marriage-portion either, and had she been ugly, or only moderately pretty, it would have been practically impossible to find a husband for her. But if she became the beauty of Marosfalva—as indeed she was already—there would be plenty of rich men who would be willing to waive the question of the marriage-portion for the sake of the glory of having captured the loveliest matrimonial prize in the whole countryside.

"Leave Irma néni alone, mother," said the man who had first taken up the cudgels in favour of Andor; "we all know that she has very ambitious views for Elsa. Please God she may not be disappointed."

From more than one group of spectators came similar or other comments on pretty Elsa and her partner. The general consensus of opinion seemed to be that it was as well Andor was going away for three years. Old Kapus and his wife would never allow their daughter to marry a man with pockets as empty as their own, and it was no use waiting for dead men's shoes. Lakatos Pál, the rich uncle, from whom Andor was bound to inherit some day, was little past the prime of life. Until he died how would Andor and a penniless wife contrive to live? For Lakatos Pál was a miser and hoarded his money—moreover, he was a confirmed bachelor and woman-hater; he would do nothing for Andor if the young man chose to marry.

Ah, well! it was a pity! for a better-looking, better-matched pair could not be found in the whole county of Arad.

"Lucky for you, Béla, that Andor goes off to-day for three years," said a tall, handsome girl to her neighbour; "you would not have had much chance with Elsa otherwise."

The man beside her made no immediate reply; he was standing with legs wide apart, his hands buried in the pockets of his trousers. At the girl's words, which were accompanied by a provocative glance from her large, dark eyes, he merely shrugged his wide shoulders, and jingled some money in his pockets.

The girl laughed.

"Money won't buy everything, you know, my good Béla," she said.

"It will buy most things," he retorted.

"The consent of Irma néni, for instance," she suggested.

"And a girl's willingness to exchange the squalor of a mud hut for comfort, luxury, civilization."

Unlike most of the young men here to-night, who wore the characteristic costume of the countryside—full, white linen shirt and trousers, broad leather belt, embossed and embroidered and high leather boots, Béla was dressed in a town suit of dark-coloured cloth, cut by a provincial tailor from Arad. He was short of stature, though broad-shouldered and firmly knit, but his face was singularly ugly, owing to the terrible misfortune which had befallen him when he lost his left eye. The scar and hollow which were now where the eye had once been gave the whole face a sinister expression, which was further accentuated by the irregular line of the eyebrows and the sneer which habitually hovered round the full, hard lips.

Béla was not good to look on; and this is a serious defect in a young man in Hungary, but he was well endowed with other attributes which made him very attractive to the girls. He had a fine and lucrative position, seeing that he was his Lordship's bailiff, and had an excellent salary, a good house and piece of land of his own, as well as the means of adding considerably to his income, since his lordship left him to conclude many a bargain over corn and plums, and horses and pigs. Erös Béla was rich and influential. He lived in a stone-built house, which had a garden round it, and at least five rooms inside, with a separate kitchen and a separate living-room, therefore he was a very eligible young man and one greatly favoured by mothers of penniless girls; nor did the latter look askance on Béla despite the fact that he had only one eye and that never a pleasant word escaped his lips.

Even now he was looking on at the dancing with a heavy scowl upon his face. The girl near him—she with the dark, Oriental eyes and the thin, hooked nose, Klara Goldstein the Jewess—gave him a nudge with her brown, pointed elbow.

"I wouldn't let Andor see the temper you are in, my friend," she said, with a sarcastic little laugh; "we don't want any broken bones before the train goes off this morning."

"There will be broken bones if he does not look out," muttered

11

the other between his teeth, as he drew a tightly clenched fist from his pocket.

"Bah! why should you care?" retorted Klara, who seemed to take an impish delight in teasing the young man, "you are not in love with Elsa, are you?"

"What is it to you?" growled Béla surlily.

"Nothing," she replied, "only that we have always been friends, you and I—eh, Béla?"

And she turned her large, lustrous eyes upon him, peering at him through her long black lashes. She was a handsome girl, of course, and she knew it—knew how to use her eyes, and make the men forget that she was only a Jewess, a thing to be played with but despised—no better than a gipsy wench, not for a Hungarian peasant to look upon as an equal, to think of as a possible mate.

Béla, whose blood was hot in him, what with the wine which he had drunk and the jealous temper which was raging in his brain, was nevertheless sober enough not to meet the languorous glances which the handsome Jewess bestowed so freely upon him.

"We are still friends—are we not, Béla?" she reiterated slowly.

"Of course—why not?" he grunted, "what has our friendship to do with Andor and Elsa?"

"Only this: that I don't like to see a friend of mine make a fool of himself over a girl who does not care one hairpin for him."

Béla smothered a curse.

"How do you know that?" he asked.

"Everyone knows that Elsa is over head and ears in love with Andor, and just won't look at anyone else."

"Oho!" he sneered, "everyone knows that, do they? Well! you can tell that busy-body everyone from me that before the year is out Kapus Elsa will be tokened to me, and that when Andor comes back from having marched and drilled and paced the barrack-yard he will find that Kapus Elsa is Kapus no longer, but Erös, the wife of Erös Béla, the mother of his first-born. To this I have made up my mind, and when I make up my mind to anything, neither God nor the devil dares to stand in my way."

"Hush! hush! in Heaven's name," she protested quickly, "the neighbours will hear you."

He shrugged his shoulders, and murmured something very uncomplimentary anent the ultimate destination of those neighbours.

Some of them certainly had heard what he said, for he had not been at pains to lower his voice. His riches and his position had made him something of an oracle in Marosfalva, and he held all the peasantry in such contempt that he cared little what everyone thought of him. He therefore remained indifferent and sulky now whilst many glances of good-humoured mockery were levelled upon him.

No one, of course, thought any the worse of Erös Béla for desiring the beauty of the village for himself—he was rich and could marry whom he pleased, and that he should loudly and openly proclaim his determination to possess himself of the beautiful prize was only in accordance with the impulsive, hot-headed, somewhat bombastic temperament of the Magyars themselves.

Fortunately those chiefly concerned in Erös Béla's loudly spoken determination had heard nothing of the colloquy between him and the Jewess. The wild, loud music of the csárdás, their own gyrations and excitement, shut them out entirely from their surroundings.

Their stamping, tripping, twirling feet had carried them into another world altogether; Ignácz Goldstein's barn had become a fairy bower, they themselves were spirits living in that realm of bliss; there was no longer any impending separation, no military service, no blank and desolate three years! Andor, his arm tightly clasped round Elsa's waist, his head bowed till his lips touched her bare shoulder, contrived to whisper magic words in her ear.

Magic words?—simple, commonplace words, spoken by myriads of men before and since into myriads of willing ears, in every tongue this earth hath ever known. But to Elsa it seemed as if the Magyar tongue had never before sounded so exquisite! To her the words were magic because they wrought a miracle in her. She had been a girl—a child ere those words were spoken. She liked Andor, she liked her father and her mother, little Emma over the way, Mari néni, who was always kind. She had loved them all, been pleased when she saw them, glad to give them an affectionate kiss.

But now, since that last csárdás had begun, a strange and mysterious current had gone from Andor's arm right through her heart; something had happened, which caused her cheeks to glow with a fire other than that produced by the heat of the dance and made her own hands tremble when they rested on Andor's shoulder. And there was that in his look which made her eyes burn and fill with tears.

"You are beautiful, Elsa! I love you!"

She could not answer him, of course; how could she, when she felt that her throat was choked with sobs? Yet she felt so happy, so happy that never since the day of her first communion, when Pater Bonifácius had blessed her and assured her that her soul was as white as that of an angel—never since then had she known such perfect, such absolute happiness. She could not speak, she almost

13

thought once that she was going to faint, so strange was the thrill of joy which went right through her when Andor's lips rested for one brief, sweet moment upon her shoulder.

And now the lights are burning low, the gipsies scrape their fiddles with a kind of wild enthusiasm, which pervades them just as much as the dancers. Round and round in a mad twirl now, the men hold the girls with both hands by the waist, the girls put a hand on each of their partner's shoulders; thus they spin round and round, petticoats flying, booted feet stamping the ground.

The young faces are all hot and streaming, quick breaths come in short, panting gasps from these young chests. The spectators join in the excitement, the men stamp and clap their heels to the rhythm of the dance, the women beat their hands one against the other to that same wild, syncopated measure. Old men grasp middle-aged women round the waist; smiling, self-deprecatingly they too begin to tread; Hej! 'Tis not so long ago we were young too, and that wild Hungarian csárdás fires the blood until it glows afresh.

Everyone moves, every body sways, it is impossible to keep quite still while that intoxicating rhythm fills the air.

Only Klara the Jewess stands by, stolid and immovable; the Magyar blood is not in her, hers is the languorous Oriental blood, the supple, sinuous movements of the Levant. She watches this bacchanalian whirligig with a sneer upon her thin, red lips. Beside her Erös Béla too is still, the scowl has darkened on his face, his one eye leers across the group of twirling dancers to that one couple close to the musicians' platform.

In the noise that goes on around him he cannot, of course, hear the words which Andor speaks, but he sees the movements of the young man's lips, and the blush which deepens over Elsa's face. That one eye of his, keener than any pair of eyes, has seen the furtive kiss, quick and glowing, which grazed the girl's bare shoulder, and noted the quiver which went right through the young, slender body and the look that shot through the quickly-veiled blue eyes.

He was only a peasant, a rough son of the soil, whose temperament was hot with passion and whose temper had never known a curb. He had never realized until this moment how beautiful Elsa was, and how madly he loved her. For he called the jealous rage within by the sacred name of love, and love to a Magyar peasant is his whole existence, the pivot round which he frames his life, his thoughts of the present, his dreams of the future.

The soil and the woman!—they are his passions, his desires, his religion—to own a bit of land—of Hungarian land—and the woman whom he loves. Those two possessions will satisfy him—

14

beyond these there is nothing worth having—a plough, of course—a hut wherein to sleep—an ox or two, perhaps—a cow—a horse.

But the soil and the woman on whom he has fixed his love—we'll call it love ... he certainly calls it so—those two possessions make the Hungarian peasant more contented than any king or millionaire of Western civilization.

Erös Béla had the land. His father left him a dozen kataszter (land measure about two and three-quarter acres) or so; Elsa was the woman whom he loved, and the only question was who—he or Andor—would be strong enough to gain the object of his desire.

# CHAPTER III

## "You will wait for me?"

But now it is all over, the final bar of the csárdás has been played, the last measure trodden. From the railway station far away the sharp clang of a bell has announced the doleful fact that in half an hour the train will start for Arad, thence to Brassó, where the recruits will be enrolled, ticketed, docketed like so many heads of cattle—mostly unwilling—made to do service for their country.

In half an hour the train starts, and there is so much still to say that has been left unsaid, so many kisses to exchange, so many promises, protestations, oaths.

The mothers, fearful and fussy, look for their sons in among the crowd like hens in search of their chicks; their wizened faces are hard and wrinkled like winter apples, they carry huge baskets on their arms, over-filled with the last delicacies which their fond, toil-worn hands will prepare for the beloved son for the next three years:—a piece of smoked bacon, a loaf of rye bread, a cake of maize-flour.

The lads themselves—excited after the dance, and not quite as clear-headed as they were before that last cask of Hungarian wine was tapped in Ignácz Goldstein's cellar—feel the intoxication of the departure now, the quick good-byes, the women's tears. A latent spirit of adventure smothers their sorrow at leaving home.

The gipsies have struck up a melancholy Magyar folksong; the crowd breaks up in isolated groups, mothers and fathers with their sons whisper in the dark corners of the barn. The father who did his

15

service thirty years ago gives sundry good advice—no rebellion, quiet obedience, no use complaining or grumbling, the three years are quickly over. The mother begs her darling not to give way to drink, and not to get entangled with one of the hussies in the towns; women and wine, the two besetting temptations that assail the Magyar peasant—let the darling boy resist both for his sorrowing mother's sake.

But the lad only listens with half an ear, his dark eyes roam around the barn in search of the sweetheart; he wants one more protestation of love from her lips, one final oath of fidelity.

Andor has neither father to admonish him, nor mother to pray over him; the rich uncle Lakatos Pál, with whom he has lived hitherto, does not care enough about him to hang weeping round his neck.

And Elsa has given her father and mother the slip, and joined Andor outside the barn.

Her blue eyes—tired after fifteen hours of pleasure—blink in the glare of the brilliant sun. Andor puts his arm round her waist and she, closing her aching eyes, allows him to lead her away.

And now they are wandering down the great dusty high road, beneath the sparse shade of the stunted acacias that border it. They feel neither heat, nor dust, and say but little as they walk. From behind them, muffled by louder sounds, come the sweet, sad strains of the Magyar love-song, "Csak egy kis lány van a világon."

> "There is but one girl in all the world,
> And she is my own white dove.
> Oh! How great must God's love be for me!
> That He thought of giving you to me."

"Elsa, you will wait for me?" asked Andor, with deep, passionate anxiety at last.

"I will wait for you, Andor," replied the girl simply, "if the good God will give me the strength."

"The strength, Elsa, will be in yourself," he urged, "if only you love me as I love you."

"Three years is such a long time!" she sighed.

"I will count the weeks that separate us, Elsa—the days—the hours——"

"I, too, will be counting them."

"When I come back I will at once talk with Pali bácsi—he is getting tired of managing his property—I know that at times lately he has felt that he needed a rest, and that he means to ask me to see to everything for him. He will give me that nice little house on the

16

Fekete Road, and the mill to look after. We can get married at once, Elsa—when I come back."

He talked on somewhat ramblingly, at times incoherently. It was easy to see that he was trying to cheat sorrow, to appear cheerful and hopeful, because he saw that Elsa was quite ready to give way to tears. It was so hard to walk out of fairyland just when she had entered it, and found it more beautiful than anything else in life. The paths looked so smooth and so inviting, and fairy forms beckoned to her from afar; it all would have been so easy, if only the good God had willed it so. She thought of the many sins which—in her innocent life—she had committed, and for which Pater Bonifácius had given her absolution; perhaps if she had been better—been more affectionate with her mother, more forbearing with her father, the good God would have allowed her to have this happiness in full which now appeared so shadowy.

She fell to wishing that Andor had not been quite so fine and quite so strong, that his chest had been narrower, or his eyesight less keen. Womanlike, she felt that she would have loved him just as much and more, if he were less vigorous, less powerful; and in that case the wicked government would not want him; he could stay at home and help Pali bácsi to look after his lands and his mills, and she could marry him before the spring.

Then the pressure of his arm round her waist recalled her to herself; she turned and met his glowing, compelling eyes, she felt that wonderful vitality in him which made him what he was, strong in body and strong in soul; his love was strong because his body was strong, as was his soul, his spirit and his limbs, and she no longer wished him to be weak and delicate, for then it would no longer be Andor—the Andor whom she loved.

The clang of the distant bell chased away Elsa's last hovering dreams. Andor did not hear it; he was pressing the girl closer and closer to him, unmindful of his surroundings, unmindful that he was on the high road, and that frequently ox-carts went by laden with people, and that passers-by were hurrying now toward the railway station.

True that no one took any notice of this young man and maid; everyone was either too much absorbed in the business of the morning, or too much accustomed to these final scenes of farewell and tenderness ere the lads went off for their three years' service, to throw more than a cursory glance on these two.

"I love you, Elsa, my dove, my rose," Andor reiterated over and over again; "you will wait for my return, will you not?"

"I will wait, Andor," replied the girl through her sobs.

"The thought of you will lighten my nights, and bring

17

sunshine to my dreary days. Every morning and every evening when I say my prayers, I shall ask my guardian angel to fly over to yours, and to tell him to whisper in your ear that I love you beyond all else on earth."

"We must part now, Andor," she said earnestly, "the second bell has gone long ago."

"Not yet, Elsa, not yet," he pleaded; "just walk as far as that next acacia tree. There no one will see us, and I want one more kiss before I go."

She never thought to resist him, since her own heart was at one with his wish, and he was going away so soon and for so long. So they walked as far as the next acacia tree, and there he took her in his arms and kissed her on the cheeks, the eyes, the lips.

"God alone knows, Elsa," he said, and now his own voice was choked with sobs, "what it means to me to leave you. You are the one woman in the world for me, and I will thank the good God on my knees every day of my life for the priceless blessing of your love."

After that they walked back hand in hand. They had wandered far, and in a quarter of an hour the train would be starting. It meant a week in prison in Arad for any recruit to miss the train, and Andor did mean to be brave and straight, and to avoid prison during the three years.

The gipsy musicians had carried their instruments over to the railway station; here they had ensconced themselves in full view of the train and were playing one after the other the favourite songs of those who were going away.

When Andor and Elsa reached the station the crowd in and around it was dense, noisy and full of animation and colour. A large batch of recruits who had come by the same train from more distant villages had alighted at Marosfalva and joined in the bustle and the singing. They had got over the pang of departure from home half an hour or an hour ago; they had already left the weeping mothers and sweethearts behind, so now they set to with a will in true Hungarian fashion to drown regrets and stifle unmanly tears by singing their favourite songs at the top of their rough voices, and ogling those girls of Marosfalva who happened to be unattached.

The captain in command, with his lieutenant, was pacing up and down the station platform. He now gave a command to a couple of sergeants, and the entraining began. Helter-skelter now, for it was no use losing a good seat whilst indulging in a final kiss or tear. There was a general stampede for the carriages and trucks; the recruits on ahead, behind them the trail of women, the mothers with their dark handkerchiefs tied round their heads, the girls with

18

pale, tear-stained faces, their petticoats of many colours swinging round their shapely hips as they run, the fathers, the brothers.

Here comes Pater Bonifácius, who has finished saying his mass just in time to see the last of his lads. He has tucked his soutane well up under his sash, and he is running across the platform, his rubicund, kindly face streaming with excitement.

"Pater! Pater! Here!"

A score of voices cry to him from different carriages, and he hurries on, grasping each rough, hot hand as it is extended out to him.

"Bless you, my children," he cries, and the large, red cotton handkerchief wanders surreptitiously from his nose to his eyes. "Bless you and keep you."

"Be good lads," he admonishes earnestly, "remember your confession and the holy sacraments! No drinking!"

"Oh, Pater!" comes in protesting accents all around him.

"Well! not more than is good for you. Abstinence on Fridays— a regular confession and holy communion and holy mass on Sundays will help to keep you straight before the good God."

There's the last bell! Clang! clang! In two minutes comes the horn, and then we are off. The gipsies are playing the saddest of sad songs, it seems as if one's heartstrings were being wrenched out of one's body.

"There is but one girl in all the world!"

For each lad only one girl!—and she is there at the foot of the carriage-steps, a corner of her ribbon or handkerchief or cotton petticoat stuffed into her mouth, to keep her from bursting into sobs. The mothers now are dry-eyed and silent. They look with dull, unseeing gaze on this railway train, the engine, the carriages, which will take their lads away from them. Many have climbed up on the steps of the carriages, hanging on to the handrails, so as to be near the lads as long as possible. Their position is a perilous one, the sergeants as well as the railway officials have to take hold of them by the waist and to drag them forcibly down to the ground before they will give way.

It is the mothers who are the most obstinate. They cling to the handrails, to the steps, even to the wheels—there will be a fearful accident if they are not driven off by force. And they will yield only to force; guards and porters take hold of them by the waist and drag them away from their perilous positions.

They fight with stolid obstinacy; they will hang on to the train—they are the mothers, you see!—and yet from where they are they cannot always see their sons, herded in with forty or fifty other lads in a truck, some standing, some squatting on the ground, or on

19

the provision baskets. But if you cannot see your son, it is always something to be on the step of the train which is about to take him away.

The lads are all singing now at the top of their voices, but down below on the platforms there is but little noise; the mothers do not speak, because they are fighting for places on the steps of the railway-carriages, where the boys are; they press their lips tightly together, and when a guard or a porter comes to drag them away they just hit out with their elbows—stolidly, silently.

The fathers and the other older men stand about in groups, leaning on their sticks, talking in whispers, recounting former experiences of entraining, or recruiting, of those abominable three years; and the young girls—the sweethearts, the sisters, the friends—dare not speak for fear they should break down and help to unman the lads.

Andor, by dint of fighting and obstinacy, has kept his place in the door of one of the carriages; he sits on the floor, with his feet down on the step below, and refuses to quit his position for anyone. Several lads from the rear have tried to throw him out or to drag him in, but Andor is mightily strong—you cannot move him if he be not so minded.

Elsa, sitting on the step lower down, is resting her elbow on his knee. There is no thought of hiding their love for one another; let the whole village know it, or the whole countryside, they do not care; they are not going to deprive themselves of these last few minutes—these heaven-born seconds, whilst their hands can still meet, their eyes can speak the words which their lips no longer dare frame.

"I love you!"

"You will wait for me?"

In those few words lies all the consolation for the present, all the hope of the future. With these words engraved upon heart and memory they can afford to look more serenely upon these blank and dreary three years.

It was as well to have spoken them; as well to have actually put into words what they had already known in their hearts long ago. Now they can afford to wait, and Andor will do it with confidence, he is a man and he is free. He viewed the future as a master views his slave; the future is his to do with what he likes, to mould, to shape in accordance with his will.

The land which must one day be his, and Elsa his already! Andor almost fell to wishing that the train would start quickly—so many seconds would have been lived of those three intervening years.

20

Elsa tries to look as full of hope as he does; she is only a woman, and the future is not hers to make at will. She is not the conqueror, the lord and king of her own destiny; there are so many difficulties in the path of her life which she would like to forget at this moment, so as not to embitter the happiness which has come to her; there is her shiftless mother and vagabond father, there is the pressure of poverty and filial duty—it is easy for Andor—he is a man!

"You will wait for me, Elsa?" Andor asks for the twentieth time, and for the twentieth time her lips murmur an assent, even though her heart is heavy with foreboding.

There goes the horn!

"Elsa, my love, one more kiss," cries Andor, as he presses her closely, ever more closely to his heart. "God bless you, my rose! You will wait for me?"

The engine gives a shrill whistle. All the men now—realizing the danger—drag their women-folk away from the slowly-revolving wheels. The gipsy musicians strike up the first spirited bars of the Rákóczy March, as with much puffing and ponderous creakings and groanings the heavily-laden train with its human freight steams away from the little station.

"My son! my son!"

"Benkó! my son!"

"János!"

"Endre!"

A few heartrending cries as each revolution of the wheels takes the lads a little further away from their homes.

"Elsa, you will wait for me?" comes as a final, appealing cry from Andor.

He stands in the door of the carriage, which he holds wide open, and through a mist of tears which he no longer tries to suppress he sees Elsa standing there, quite still—a small image of beauty and of sorrow. The sun glints upon her hair, it shines and sparkles like living gold; her hands are clasped tightly together, and with her full, many-hued petticoats round her slim waist and tiny red-shod feet she looks like a flower.

The crowd below moves alongside of the train—for the first minute or so they all keep up with it, close to the carriage at the door of which can still be seen the head of son or brother or sweetheart. But now the engine puts on more speed, the wheels revolve more quickly—some of the crowd fall away, unable to run so fast.

Only the mothers try to keep up—the old women, some of them bare-footed, stolid, looking straight before them—hardly

21

looking at the train, just running ... alongside the train first of all, then they must needs fall back—but still they run along the metals, even though the train moves away so quickly now that soon even a mother could not distinguish her son's head, like a black pin-point leaning out of the carriage window.

So they run:—one or two women run thus for over a kilomètre, they run long after the train has disappeared from view.

But Elsa stood quite still. She did not try to run after the train.

Through the noise of the puffing engine, the final cries of farewell, through all the noise and the bustle, Andor's cry rose above all, his final appeal to her to be true:

"Elsa! you will wait for me?"

# CHAPTER IV

### "Now that he is dead"

Stranger, if you should ever be driving on the main road between Szeged and Arad, tell your driver to pull up at the village of Marosfalva; its one broad street runs inland at right angles from the road; you will then have on your right two or three bits of meadowland overshadowed by willow trees, which slope down to the Maros; beyond the Maros lies the great plain—the fields of maize and pumpkin, of hemp and sunflower. And who knows what lies beyond the fields?

But on your left will be the village of Marosfalva with the wayside inn and public bar, kept by Ignácz Goldstein, standing prominently at the corner immediately facing you. Two pollarded acacias are planted near the door of the inn, above the lintel of which a painted board scribbled over with irregular lettering invites the traveller to enter. A wooden verandah, with tumble-down roof and worm-eaten supporting beams, runs along two sides of the house, and from the roof hang a number of gaily-coloured and decorated earthenware pots and jars.

The open space in front of the inn and the whole of the length of the one street of Marosfalva are very dusty and dry in the summer, in the autumn and spring they are a sea and river of mud, and in the winter the snow hides the deep, frozen crevasses; but place and street are as God made them, and it is not man's place to interfere. To begin with, the cattle and geese and pigs must all pass this way on their way to the water, so of course it is impossible to do anything with the ground even if one were so minded.

The inn is the only house in Marosfalva which boldly faces the street, all the others seem to be looking at it over their shoulders, the front of one house facing the back of its neighbour, with a bit of garden or yard between, and so on, the whole kilomètre length of the street.

But each house has its wooden verandah, which shields the living rooms against the glare of the sun in summer, and shelters them from snow and rain in winter. These wooden verandahs are in a greater or lesser state of repair and smartness, and under the roof of every verandah hang rows of the same quaintly-decorated and picturesque earthenware jars.

Round every house, too, there are groups of gay sunflowers and of dull green hemp, and the roofs, thatched with maize-stalks, are ornamented along the top with wooden carvings which stand out clear and fantastic against the intense blue of the sky.

Then, stranger, if you should alight at the top of the street and did wander slowly down its dusty length, you will presently see it widen out just in front of the church. It stands well there, doesn't it?—at one end of this open place, with its flat, whitewashed façade and tower—red-roofed and crowned with a metal cross that glints in the sun—the whole building so like in shape to a large white hen, with head erect and crimson comb and wings spread out flat to the ground.

The presbytery is close by—you cannot miss it. It is a one-storied house, with a row of green-shuttered windows along the front and at the side a low gate which leads to a small garden at the back, and over which appears a vista of brilliant perennials and a stiff row of purple asters.

There is the tiny school-house, too, which in the late summer is made very gay in front with vividly coloured dahlias—an orgy of yellow and brick-red, of magenta and orange.

If your driver has come along with you down the street, he will point out to you the house of Barna Jenö—mayor of the Commune of Marosfalva—a personage of vast consideration in the village—a consideration which he shares with Hóhér Aladár, who is the village justice of the peace, and with Erös Béla, who is my lord the Count's bailiff.

Then lower down, beyond the church, is the big barn belonging to Ignácz Goldstein, where on special occasions, as well

23

as on fine Sunday afternoons, the young folk meet for their simple-hearted, innocent amusements—for their dancing, their singing and their courtships, and further on still are the houses of the poorer peasants—of men like Kapus Benkó who has never saved a fillér and until lately, when he was stricken down with illness, had to work as a day labourer for wage, instead of owning a bit of land of his own and planting it up for his own enjoyment. Here the houses are much smaller and squalid-looking: they have no verandahs—only a narrow door and tiny, diminutive windows which are not made to open and shut. The pieces of ground around them are also planted, like the others, with hemp and with sunflowers, but even these look less majestic, less prosperous than those which surround the houses higher up the streets; their brown heads are smaller, more sparsely laden with the good oil-bearing seeds, and the stems of the hemp do not look as if they ever would make a thatch.

The street itself is wide and a regular heat-trap in summer: in the autumn and the spring it is ankle-deep in mud, and of course in the winter it is buried in snow. But in the late summer it is at its best, one or two heavy showers of rain have laid the dust, and the sunflowers and dahlias round the little school-house and by the presbytery are very gay—such a note of crude and vivid colour which even puts the decorated jars to shame.

Also the sun has lost some of its unbearable heat; after four o'clock in the afternoon it is pleasant to sit or stand outside one's house for a bit of gossip with a neighbour. The brown-legged, black-eyed children, coolly clad in loose white shifts, bare-footed and bare-headed, can play outside now; the little girls, with bright-coloured kerchiefs tied round their heads, and pink or blue petticoats round their waists, vie with the dahlias in hue.

On Sunday afternoons it is cool enough to dance in Ignácz Goldstein's barn. The black day in the calendar—the fourteenth of September—has come and gone, and the lads have gone with it: except for the weeping mothers and sweethearts the ordinary village life has resumed its peaceful course. But then, there are every year a few weeping mothers and sweethearts in Marosfalva or Kender or Görcz, just as there is everywhere else: the lads have to go and do their military service as soon as they come of age.

And then others come back about this time, those who have completed their three years, and they must be made welcome with dancing and music—the things which a Hungarian peasant loves best in all the world.

And as the days are still long and the evenings warm there are the strolls hand-in-hand, arm-in-arm—after the dancing—up the village street as far as the slowly-flowing Maros. One or two of the lads who have come home after three years have found their sweethearts waiting for them—but only one or two. Three years is a long, long time! Girls cannot afford to wait for husbands while their youth and good looks fly away so quickly. And the lads, too, are fickle; some of them have apparently forgotten amongst the more showy, more lively beauties of garrison towns, the doe-eyed girl to whom they had promised faith. They are ready, as soon as they come back, for new courtships, fresh love-making, another girl—with blue eyes this time, and fair hair instead of brown.

Then, of course, there are those who never will come back. That awful, mysterious place called Bosnia has swallowed them up. There was fighting, it seems, in Bosnia, and many were killed: two lads from Marosfalva, one from Fekete and two from Kender.

Bosnia must belong to the Crown of Hungary—whatever that may mean—the politicians say so, anyhow, and in order that the Crown of Hungary should have what rightly belongs to it the lads from our villages have to fight and get killed.

"Is that just, I ask you?" so the mothers argue.

The sweethearts weep for awhile and then cast about for fresh fish out of the waters of Life. Sometimes there are mistakes: lads who have been reported killed turn up at the village on the appointed day, either hale and hearty or maimed and crippled. In either case they are welcome. But at times the mistake is the other way: no black report has come; the mothers, the fathers, the sweethearts, expect the young soldier home—he does not come. The others return on a given day—they arrive by train—Laczi or Benkó or Pál is not amongst them. Where is he? Well! they were not all in the same regiment; they have seen little or nothing of one another during these three years.

The anxious mothers rush to Barna Jenö—the mayor—and he drafts a letter of inquiry which is duly sent off to the proper authorities at Budapest. In the course of time—not very promptly—the reply comes. A letter of condolence, curtly worded: the name of Laczi or Benkó or Pál, as the case may be, was inadvertently omitted from the list of killed after the skirmish near Banialuka.

Sometimes also the young soldier having received his discharge, does not care to return to his native village: he has lost his taste for pigs and geese, for digging and sowing; he has had a glimpse of life and wants to see some more; the emigration agents at Budapest are active and persuasive. "America is a land of gold," they say; "no further trouble but to stoop and pick up the gold just where it lies."

And the lad listens and ponders. He will not go home, for he is afraid that his mother's tears will deter him from his purpose: he

25

follows the advice of the emigration agent, expends his last fillér, sells his spare shirt and takes passage at Fiume on a big ship which conveys him to the land of riches.

Oh! Those lads who go away like that come back sure enough! Broken in health and spirits, dying of that relentless and mysterious disease called "homesickness," they drift back after a few years to their villages, having amassed a little money perhaps, but having lost that vitality, that love of life and of enjoyment which is the characteristic of these sons of Hungary—the land of warmth and of sunshine, of generous wines and luscious corn.

And Erös Béla, walking arm-in-arm with Kapus Elsa on that warm Sunday afternoon, had talked much of Andor and of his untoward fate.

The two young people had met outside the church after Benediction, they had strolled down as far as the Maros and back again into the village.

The warm late September sunshine shed a golden glow upon the thatched roofs of the cottages and made every bright-coloured pot that hung under the verandahs gleam with many-hued and dazzling reflections. It touched the red roof of the little church with an additional coat of glittering crimson and caused the metal cross upon the spire to throw out vivid sparks of light.

The festive air of a Sunday afternoon hung upon the village street, men and maids walked by arm-in-arm, the girls in their finery with cotton petticoats swinging out, and high-heeled boots clinking as they walked, the men with round felt hats tilted rakishly over one eye, their bronzed faces suffused in smiles, the song never for long absent from their lips.

From the top of the street a flock of geese in charge of a diminutive maiden of ten was slowly waddling down toward the stream, shaking their grey and white feathers under the hot kiss of the sun, and behind them, in slow majesty, a herd of cows and oxen—snow-white, with graceful, tall horns, lyre-shaped and slender—ambled lazily along.

Elsa and Béla had paused outside the house of Hóhér Aladár— who was the village justice of the peace and husband to Ilona, Béla's only sister.

A mightily rich man was Hóhér Aladár, and Ilona was noted for being the most thrifty housewife in a country where most housewives are thrifty, and for being a model cook in a land where good cooks abound.

Her house was a pattern of orderliness and cleanliness: always immaculately whitewashed outside and the little shutters painted a vivid green, it literally shone with dazzling brightness on these hot summer afternoons. The woodwork of the verandah was elaborately carved, the pots that hung from the roof had not a chip or crack in them.

No wonder that Erös Béla was proud of these housewifely qualities in his only sister, and that he loved to make a display of them before his fiancée whose own mother was so sadly lacking in them.

Now he pushed open the front door and stood aside to allow Elsa to enter, and as she did so the sweet scent of rosemary and lavender greeted her nostrils; she looked round her with unfeigned appreciation, and a little sigh—hardly of envy but wholly wistful—escaped her lips. The room was small and raftered and low, but little light came through the two small windows, built one on each side of the front door, but even in the dim light the furniture shone with polish, and the wooden floor bore every sign of persistent and vigorous scrubbing. There was a cloth of coloured linen upon the centre table, beautifully woven in a chess-board pattern of red and blue by Ilona's deft hands. The pewter and copper cooking utensils on and about the huge earthenware stove were resplendently bright, and the carved oak dower-chest—with open lid—displayed a dazzling wealth of snow-white linen—hand-woven and hand-embroidered—towels, sheets, pillow-cases, all lying in beautiful bundles, neatly tied with red ribbons and bows.

Again Elsa sighed—in that quaint, wistful little way of hers. If her mother had been as thrifty and as orderly as Ilona, then mayhap her own marriage with Erös Béla need never have come about. She could have mourned for Andor quietly by herself, and the necessity of a wealthy son-in-law would probably never have presented itself before her mother's mind.

But now she followed Ilona into the best bedroom, the sanctum sanctorum of every Hungarian peasant home—the room that bears most distinctly the impress of the housewifely character that presides over it. And as Elsa stood upon the threshold of her future sister-in-law's precious domain, she forgot her momentary sadness in the hope of a brighter future, when she, too, would make her new home orderly and sweet-scented, with beautifully-polished furniture and floors radiant with cleanliness. The thought of what her own best bedroom would be like delighted her fancy. It was a lovely room, for Béla's house was larger by far than his sister's, the rooms were wider and more lofty, and the windows had large, clear panes of glass in them. She would have two beautiful bedsteads in the room, and the bedspreads would be piled up to the ceiling with down pillows and duvets covered in scarlet twill; she would have two beautiful spreads of crochet-work, a washstand with marble

27

top, and white crockery, and there would be a stencilling of rose garlands on the colour-washed walls.

So now her habitual little sigh was not quite so wistful as it had been before; the future need not after all be quite so black as she sometimes feared, and surely the good God would be kind to her in her married life, seeing that she obeyed His commandment and honoured her mother by doing what her mother wished.

Ilona in the best bedroom was busy as usual with duster and brush. She did not altogether approve of Béla's choice of a wife, and her greetings of Elsa were always of a luke-warm character, and were usually accompanied by lengthy lectures on housewifery and the general management of a kitchen.

Elsa always listened deferentially to these lectures, with eyes downcast and an attitude of meekness; but in her own heart she was thankful that her future home would lie some distance out of the village and that Ilona would probably have but little time to walk out there very often.

In the meanwhile, however, she hated these Sunday afternoon visits, with their attendant homilies from Ilona first, then from Aladár—who was self-important and dictatorial, and finally from Béla, who was invariably disagreeable and sarcastic whenever he saw his sister and his fiancée together.

Fortunately, to-day Béla had said that she need not stay more than a few minutes.

"We'll just pay our respects to Ilona and Aladár," he had said pompously, "and take another walk before the sun goes down."

And Elsa—taking him at his word—had made but a meteoric appearance in her future sister-in-law's cottage—a hasty greeting, a brief peck on Ilona's two cheeks, and one on Aladár's bristly face, then the inevitable homily; and as soon as Ilona paused in the latter, in order to draw breath, Elsa gave her another peck, by way of farewell, explained hastily that her mother was waiting for her, and fled incontinently from the rigid atmosphere of the best bedroom.

Béla and his brother-in-law had started on politics, and it took a little time before Elsa succeeded in persuading him to have that nice walk with her before the sun went down. But now they were out again in the sunshine at last, and Elsa was once more able to breathe freely and with an infinity of relief.

"I wonder," said Béla dryly, "if you are really taking in all the good advice which Ilona so kindly gives you from time to time. You can't do better than model yourself on her. She is a pattern wife and makes Aladár perfectly happy. I wonder," he reiterated, with something of a sneer, "if you will learn from her, or if your mother's influence will remain with you for ever?"

Then, as with her accustomed gentleness she chose to remain silent, rather than resent his sneer, he added curtly:

"If you want to make me happy and comfortable you will follow Ilona's advice in all things."

"I will do my best, Béla," she said quietly.

Then for some reason which the young man himself could not perhaps have explained he once more started talking about Andor.

"It was very hard on him," he said, with a shrug of his wide shoulders, "to die just when he was on the point of getting his discharge."

And after an almost imperceptible moment of hesitation he added with studied indifference: "Of course, all that talk of his being still alive is sheer nonsense. I have done everything that lay in my power to find out if there was the slightest foundation for the rumour, but now I—like all sensible people—am satisfied that Andor is really dead."

Elsa was walking beside him, her hand resting lightly on his arm, as was fitting for a girl who was tokened and would be a bride within the week: she walked with head bent, her eyes fixed upon the ground. She made no immediate reply to her fiance's self-satisfied peroration, and her silence appeared to annoy him, for he continued with some acerbity:

"Don't you care to hear what I did on Andor's behalf?"

"Indeed I do, Béla," she said gently, "it was good of you to worry about him—and you so busy already."

"I did what I could," he rejoined mollified. "Old Lakatos Pál has hankered after him so, though he cared little enough about Andor at one time. Andor was his only brother's only child, and I suppose Pali bácsi[3] was suddenly struck with the idea that he really had no one to leave his hoardings to. He was always a fool and a lout. If Andor had lived it would have been all right. I think Pali bácsi was quite ready to do something really handsome for him. Now that Andor is dead he has no one; and when he dies his money all goes to the government. It is a pity," he added, with a shrug of the shoulders. "If a peasant of Marosfalva had it it would do good to the commune."

"I am sure if Andor had lived to enjoy it he would have spent it freely and done good with it to everyone around," she said quietly.

"He would have spent it freely, right enough," he retorted dryly, "but whether he would have done good to everyone around with it—I doubt me ... to Ignácz Goldstein, perhaps ..."

---

3 See footnote on p. 22.

29

"Béla, you must not say that," she broke in firmly; "you know that Andor never was a drunkard."

"I never suggested that he was," retorted Béla, whose square, hard face had become a shade paler than before, "so there is no reason for my future wife to champion him quite so hotly as you always do."

"I only spoke the truth."

"If someone else spoke of me a hundred times more disparagingly than I ever do of Andor would you defend me as warmly, I wonder, as you do him?"

"Don't let us quarrel about Andor," she rejoined gently, "it does not seem right now that he is dead."


# CHAPTER V

## "Love will follow"


They had reached the small cottage where old Kapus and his wife and Elsa lived. It stood at the furthest end of the village, away from the main road, and the cool meadows beside the Maros, away from the church and the barn and all the brightest spots of Marosfalva. Built of laths and mud, it had long ago quarrelled with the whitewash which had originally covered it, and had forcibly ejected it, showing deep gaps and fissures in its walls; the pots and jars which hung from the overhanging thatch were all discoloured and broken, and the hemp which hung in bundles beside them looked uneven and dark in colour, obviously beaten with a slipshod, careless hand.

Such a contrast to the house of Hóhér Aladár—the rich justice of the peace and of Ilona his wife! Elsa knew and expected that the usual homily on the subject would not fail to be forthcoming as it did on every Sunday afternoon; she only wondered what particular form it would take to-day, whether Béla would sneer at her and her mother for the tumble-down look of the verandah, for the bad state of the hemp, or the coating of dirt upon the earthenware pots.

But it was the hemp to-day.

"Why don't you look after it, Elsa?" said Béla roughly, as he pointed to the tangled mass of stuff above him, "your mother ruins even the sparse crop which she has."

"I can't do everything," said Elsa, in that same gentle, even voice which held in its tones all the gamut of hopeless discouragement; "since father has been stricken he wants constant attention. Mother won't give it him, so I have to be at his beck and call. Then there is the washing ..."

"I know, I know," broke in Béla with a sneer, "you need not always remind me that my future wife—the bride of my lord the Count's own bailiff—does menial work for a village schoolmistress and a snuffy old priest!"

Elsa made no reply. She pushed open the door of the cottage and went in; Béla followed her, muttering between his teeth.

The interior of Kapus Benkó's home was as squalid, as forlorn looking as its approach; everywhere the hand of the thriftless housewife was painfully apparent, in the blackened crockery upon the hearth, in the dull, grimy look of the furniture—once so highly polished—in the tattered table-cloth, the stains upon the floor and the walls, but above all was it apparent in the dower-chest—that inalienable pride of every thrifty Hungarian housewife—the dower-chest, which in Ilona's cottage was such a marvel of polish outside, and so glittering in its rich contents of exquisite linen. But here it bore relentless if mute testimony to the shiftless, untidy, disorderly ways of the Kapus household. For instead of the neat piles of snow-white linen it was filled with rubbish—with husks of maize and mouldy cabbage-stalks, thrown in higgledy-piggledy with bundles of clothes and rags of every sort and kind.

It stood close to the stove, the smoke of which had long ago covered the wood with soot. The lid was thrown open and hung crooked upon a broken hinge.

When Elsa entered the cottage with Erös Béla her mother was busy with some cooking near the hearth, and smoke and the odour of gulyás (meat stew) filled the place. Close to the fire in an armchair of polished wood sat old Kapus Benkó, now a hopeless cripple. The fate which lies in wait in these hot countries for the dissolute and the drunkard had already overtaken him. He had had a stroke a couple of years ago, and then another last summer. Now he could not move hand or foot, his tongue refused him service, he could only see and hear and eat. Otherwise he was like a log: carried from his palliasse on which he slept at night to the armchair in which he sat all day. Elsa's strong young arms carried him thus backwards and forwards, she ministered to him, nursed him, did what cheering she could to brighten his days that were an almost perpetual night.

31

At sight of Elsa his wrinkled face, which was so like that of a corpse, brightened visibly. She ran to him and said something in his ear which caused his dulled eyes to gleam with momentary pleasure.

"What did you bring Béla home with you for?" said the mother ungraciously, speaking to her daughter and rudely ignoring the young man, who had thrown his hat down and drawn one of the chairs close to the table. At Kapus Irma's inhospitable words he merely laughed and shrugged his shoulders.

"Well, Irma néni!" he said, "this is the last Sunday, anyhow, that you will be troubled with my presence. After Wednesday, as I shall have Elsa in my own home, I shall not need to come and visit here."

"No!" retorted Irma, with a snap of her lean jaws, "you will take good care to alienate her from her duty to her father and to her mother, won't you?"

Then, in answer to a further sneer from him, she added, more viciously: "You will teach her to be purse-proud like yourself—vain, and disdainful of her old home."

Béla's one eye—under the distorted brow—wandered with a sullen expression of contempt over every individual piece of furniture in the room.

"It's not a home to be proud of, anyway," he said dryly; "is it, Irma néni?"

"You chose your future wife out of it," retorted Irma; "and 'tis from here that you will have to fetch her on Wednesday, my friend."

She was always ready to quarrel with Béla, whose sneering ways she resented, all the more that she knew they were well-deserved. But her last words had apparently poured oil over the already troubled waters of the young man's wrath, for now his sullen expression vanished, and a light of satisfaction and of pride lit up his ungainly face:

"And I will fetch my future wife in a style befitting her new position, you may be sure of that," he said, and brought his clenched fist down upon the table with a crash, so that pots and pans rattled upon the hearth and started the paralytic from his torpor.

Then he threw his head back and began to talk still more arrogantly and defiantly than he had done hitherto.

"Forty-eight oxen," he said, "shall fetch her in six carts! Aye! even though she has not one stick of furniture wherewith to endow her future husband. Forty-eight oxen, I tell you, Irma néni! Never has there been such a procession seen in Marosfalva! But Erös Béla is the richest man in the Commune," he added, with an aggressive laugh, "and don't you forget it."

But the allusion to Elsa's poverty and his own riches had exasperated the old woman.

"With all your riches," she retorted, in her turn, with a sneer, "you had to court Elsa for many years before she accepted you."

"And probably she would not have accepted me at all if you had not bullied and worried her, and ordered her to say 'Yes' to me," he rejoined dryly.

"Children must obey their parents," she said, "it is the law of God."

"A law which you, for one, apply to your own advantage, eh, Irma néni?"

"Have you any cause for complaint?"

"Oh, no! Elsa's obedience has served me well. And though I dare say," he added, suddenly casting a sullen look upon the young girl, "she has not much love for me now, she will do her duty by me as my wife, and love will follow in the natural course of things."

Elsa had taken no part in this wordy warfare between her mother and her future husband. It seemed almost as if she had not heard a word of it. No doubt her ears were trained by now no longer to heed these squabbles. She had drawn a low stool close to the invalid's chair, and sitting near him with her hand resting on his knee, she was whispering and talking animatedly to him, telling him all the gossip of the village, recounting to him every small event of the afternoon and of the morning: Pater Bonifácius' sermon, the behaviour of the choir boys, Patkós Emma's new kerchief; when the stock of gossip gave out she began to sing to him, in a low, sweet voice, one of those innumerable folk-songs so dear to every Hungarian peasant's heart.

Irma intercepted the look which Béla cast upon his fiancée. She, too, turned and looked at her daughter, and seeing her there, sitting at the feet of that miserable wreck of humanity whom she called "father!" ministering to him, for all the world like the angels around the dying saints, a swift look of pity softened for a moment the mother's hard and pinched face.

"You cannot expect the girl to have much love for you now," she said, once more turning a vicious glance upon her future son-in-law; "your mode of courtship was not very tender, you will admit."

"I don't believe in all that silly love-making," he rejoined roughly, "it is good enough for the loutish peasants of the alföld (lowlands); they are sentimental and stupid: an educated man does not make use of a lot of twaddle when he woos the woman of his choice."

"All men act very much in the same way when they are in

33

love," said Irma sententiously. "But I don't believe that you are really in love with Elsa."

He shrugged his shoulders, and laughed, a short, sarcastic, almost cruel laugh.

"Perhaps not," he said. "But I want her for my wife all the same."

"Only because she is the noted beauty of the countryside, and because half the village wanted her."

"Precisely," he said with a sneer; "there was a good deal of bidding for Elsa, eh, Irma néni? So you elected to give her to the highest bidder."

"You had been courting her longer than anybody," rejoined Irma, who this time chose to ignore his taunt.

"And I would have won her sooner—on my own—even without your help, if it had not been for that accursed Andor."

"Well! he is dead now, anyway. All doubts, I suppose, are at rest on that point."

"There are a few fools still left in the village who maintain that he will turn up some day."

"We all hope he will, because of Lakatos Pál. The poor man is fretting himself into his grave, since he has realized that when he dies his money and land must all go to the Government."

"He can sell his land and distribute his money while he lives," retorted Béla; "but you won't catch him doing that—the old miser."

"Can't anything more be done?—about Andor, I mean."

"Of course not," he said impatiently; "everything that could be done has been done. It's no use going on having rows by post with the War Office about the proofs of a man's death who has been food for worms these past two years."

"Well! you know, Béla, people here are not satisfied about those proofs. I, for one, never held with those who would not believe in Andor's death; there are plenty of folk in the village—and Pater Bonifácius is one of them—who swear that he will come home one of these days—perhaps when Pali bácsi is dead. And then he would find himself the richest man in the Commune," she added, not without a point of malice, "richer even than you, my good Béla."

"Hold your tongue, you old fool!" broke in Béla savagely, as once more the sinister leer which hovered round his sightless eye was turned toward Elsa.

"Didn't I say that I, for one, never believed that rubbish?" retorted Irma sullenly; "and haven't I preached to her about it these past two years? But you needn't be afraid," she added, as she turned once more to her stewing-pot, "she didn't hear what I said. When she talks or sings to her father you might shoot off a cannon—she wouldn't hear it. You may say what you like just now, Béla, she'll not listen."

"Oho!" said Béla, even as a curious expression of obstinacy, not unmixed with cruelty, crept into his colourless face, "you seem to forget, Irma néni, that the rest of Elsa's life will have to be spent in listening to me. We'll soon see about that."

"Elsa!" he called peremptorily.

Then, as indeed the girl appeared not to hear, but went on softly crooning and singing to the helpless invalid like a mother to its babe, the young man worked himself up into a passion of fury. The veins in his pale forehead and temples swelled up visibly, the glitter in his one eye became more cruel and more menacing, finally he brought his clenched fist once more crashing down upon the table, even while he rose to his feet, as if to give fuller meaning to his future marital authority.

"Elsa!" he shouted once more, hoarsely. "Elsa, do you hear what I say?"

# CHAPTER VI

## "I don't wish to marry; not yet"

The girl thus roughly apostrophized turned slowly round. She seemed neither hurt nor even surprised at the young man's exhibition of temper. In her blue eyes there was a strange look—one which had lately been habitual to her, but which neither her mother nor Béla were able to interpret: it was a look which conveyed the thought of resignation or indifference or both, but also one which was peculiarly lifeless, as of a soul who had touched the cold hand of despair.

Far be it from me to seek complexity in so simple a soul as was that of this young Hungarian peasant girl. Elsa Kapus had no thought of self-analysis; complicated sex and soul problems did not exist for her; she would never have dreamed of searching the deep-down emotions of her heart and of dragging them out for her mind to scrutinize. The morbid modern craze for intricate and composite emotions was not likely to reach an out-of-the-way Hungarian village that slept peacefully on the banks of the sluggish Maros, cradled in the immensity of the plain.

Elsa had loved Lakatos Andor—the handsome, ardent young lover whose impetuous courtship of her five years ago had carried her on the wings of Icarus to a region so full of brightness and of sunlight that it was no wonder that the wings—which had appeared god-like—turned out to be ephemeral and brittle after all, and that she was soon precipitated back and down into the ordinary sea of everyday life.

Elsa had never heard of Icarus, but she had felt herself soaring upwards on heavenly wings when Andor—his lips touching her neck—had whispered with passionate ardour: "Elsa, I love you!"

She had never heard of Icarus' fall, but she had experienced her own from the giddy heights of heavenly happiness, down to the depths of dull, aching despair. The fall had been very gradual—there had been nothing grand or heroic or soul-stirring about it: Andor had gone away, having told her that he loved her, and adjured her to wait for him. She had waited for three years, patiently, quietly, obstinately, despite the many and varied sieges laid to her heart and her imagination by the inflammable, eligible youth of the countryside. Elsa Kapus—the far-famed beauty of half the county, counted her suitors by the score. Patiently, quietly, obstinately she kept every suitor at bay—even though many were rich and some in high positions—even though her mother, with the same patience, the same quietude, and the same obstinacy worked hard to break her daughter's will.

But Andor was coming back. Andor had adjured her to wait for him: and Elsa was still young—just sixteen when Andor went away. She was in no hurry to get married.

No one, of course, guessed the reason of her obstinate refusal of all the best matrimonial prizes in the county. No one guessed her secret—the depth of her love for Andor—her promise to wait for him—her mother guessed it least of all. Everyone put her stubbornness down to conceit and to ambition, and no one thought any the worse of her on that account. When she refused young Barna—the mayor's eldest son, and Nagy Lajos, the rich pig merchant from Somsó, people shrugged their shoulders and said that mayhap Elsa wanted to marry a shopkeeper of Arad or even a young noble lord. Irma néni said nothing for the first year, and even for two. She saw Nagy Lajos go away, and young Barna court another girl. That was perhaps as it should be. Elsa was growing more beautiful every year—and there was a noble lord who owned a fine estate and a castle close by, who had taken lately to riding over

36

on Sunday afternoons to Marosfalva, and paid marked attention to Elsa.

Noble lords had been known to marry peasant girls—at least in books, so Irma néni had been told, and, of course, one never knows! God's ways were wonderful sometimes.

But when two years had gone by, when a rich shopkeeper from Arad had come and courted and been refused, and when the noble lord had suddenly ceased his Sunday afternoon visits to Marosfalva, Irma became more anxious. She had a long and serious talk with her daughter, which led to no good.

To all her mother's wise counsels and sound arguments Elsa had opposed the simple statement of facts:

"I do not wish to marry, mother dear; not just yet."

This, of course, would never do. Irma realized that she had allowed her ambition for her daughter to run away with her common-sense. Elsa must have got some queer notion or other in her head; that intimacy with the schoolmistress—who came from Budapest and talked a vast amount of sentimental stuff which she had imbibed out of books—must be stopped at once, and Elsa be taken in hand by her own mother.

To aim high was quite one thing, but to let every chance, however splendid, slip through one's fingers was the work of a fool.

The work of taking Elsa in hand was thus promptly undertaken. Fate favoured the mother's intentions: old Kapus was stricken with paralysis, and Elsa had, from that hour forth, to spend most of her time with her father in the house, and immediately under her mother's eye.

Though young Barna was married by now, and the pig merchant, the noble lord and the rich shopkeeper all gone to seek a sweetheart elsewhere, there were still plenty of suitors dangling round the beauty of the country-side: in fact her well-known pride and aloofness had brought a surfeit of competitors in the lists. Foremost among these was Erös Béla, who was not only young and in a high position as my lord the Count's chief bailiff, but was also reputed to be the richest man for miles around.

Erös Béla had long ago made public his determination to win Elsa for wife, and he had carried his courtship unostentatiously but persistently all along, despite the many rivals in the field. Elsa never disliked him, she accepted his attentions just as she did those of everyone else. Periodically Béla would make a formal proposal of marriage, which Irma néni, in her own name and that of Elsa's paralytic father, invariably accepted. But to his sober and well-worded proposals Elsa gave the same replies that she gave to her more impetuous adorers.

"I don't want to marry. Not yet!"

When the work of taking Elsa in hand began in earnest, Irma used Erös Béla as her chief weapon of attack. He was very rich, young enough to marry, my lord the Count looked upon him as his right hand—moreover Béla had made Irma néni a solemn promise that if Elsa became his wife, his father and mother-in-law should receive that fine house in the Kender Road to live in, with a nice piece of garden, three cows and five pigs, and a little maid-of-all-work to wait upon them.

Backed with such a bargain, Béla's suit was bound to prosper.

And yet, for another whole year, Elsa was obstinate. Irma had to resort to sterner measures, and in a country like Hungary, where much of the patriarchal feeling toward parents still exists, a mother's stern measures become very drastic indeed. A child is a child while she is under her parents' roof. If she be forty she still owes implicit obedience, unbounded respect to them. If she fail in these, she becomes an unnatural creature, denounced to her friends as such, under a cloud of opprobrium before her tiny, circumscribed world.

Kapus Irma brought out the whole armoury of her parental authority, her parental power: and her methods could be severe when she chose. I will not say that she ill-treated the girl, though it was more than once that Elsa's right cheek and ear were crimson when the left were quite pale, and that often, on the hot Sundays in July and August, when the girls go in low-necked corslets and shifts to church, Elsa wrapped a kerchief over her shoulders—the neighbours said in order to hide the corrections dealt by Irma néni's vigorous hand. But it was morally that her mother's authority weighed most heavily upon the girl. Her commands became more defined, and presently more peremptory. Elsa was soon placed in the terrible alternative of either being faithless to Andor or disobedient to her mother.

And it is characteristic of that part of the world that of the two sins thus in prospect, the latter seemed by far the more heinous.

Yet Andor was due back at the end of the summer. The fourteenth of September came and went and the new recruits went with it—another week, and those who had completed their three years would be coming home. Andor would, of course, be among them. There had come no adverse report about him, and no news during those three years is always counted to be good news. No letters or sign of life had come from him, but, then, many of the lads never wrote home while they did their three years, and Andor had no one to write to. He would not be allowed to write to Elsa, or, rather, Elsa would never be allowed to receive letters from him, and his uncle Lakatos Pál, the old miser, would only be furious with him for spending his few fillérs on note-paper and stamps. But Elsa had waited patiently during three years, knowing that though she had no news of him, he would not forget her. She never mistrusted him, she never doubted him.

She waited for him, and he did not return. At first, his non-appearance excited neither surprise nor comment in the village. Andor had no relations except his uncle Lakatos Pál, who did not care one brass fillér about him: there had been no one to count the years, the months, the days when he would return: there was only Elsa who cared, and she dared not say anything at first, for fear of making her mother angry.

But at the turn of the year Lakatos Pál became ill, and when he got worse and worse and the doctor seemed unable to do anything to make him well, he began to talk of his nephew, Andor.

That is to say, he bewailed the fact that his only brother's only child was dead, and that he—a poor sick man—had no one to look after him.

He first spoke of this to Pater Bonifácius, who was greatly shocked and upset to hear such casual news of Andor's death, and it was only bit by bit that he succeeded in dragging fuller particulars out of the sick man. It seems that when the lad's regiment was out in Bosnia there was an outbreak of cholera among the troops. Andor was one of those who succumbed. It had all occurred less than a month before his discharge was actually due, in fact these discharges had already been distributed to those who were sick, in the hope that the lads would elect to go home as soon as they could be moved, and thus relieve the Government of the burden and expense of their convalescence.

But Lakatos Andor had died in the hospital of Slovnitza. An official letter announcing his demise was sent to Lakatos Pál, his uncle and sole relative, but Lakatos only threw the letter into a drawer and said nothing about it to anybody.

It was nobody's business, he said. The Government would see to the lad's burial, no doubt, but some busy-bodies at Marosfalva might think that it was his—Lakatos'—duty to put up a stone or something to the memory of his nephew: and that sort of nonsense was very expensive.

So no one in Marosfalva knew that Andor had died of cholera in the hospital of Slovnitza until Lakatos Pál became sick, and in his loneliness spoke of the matter to Pater Bonifácius.

Then there was universal mourning in the village. Andor had always been very popular: good-looking, as merry as a skylark and a splendid dancer, he was always the life and soul of every

39

entertainment. Girls who had flirted with him wept bitter tears, the mothers who thought how rich Andor would have been now that old Lakatos was sure to die very soon—sighed deep sighs of regret.

Many there were who never believed that Andor was dead. He was not the lad to die of cholera: he might break his neck one day—riding or driving—for he was always daring and reckless—but to lie sick of cholera and to die in a hospital?—no, no, that did not seem like Andor.

Presently it became known that the official letter—announcing the death—had not been quite in order; it was only a rumour—but the rumour quickly gained credence, it fitted in with popular sentiment. Pater Bonifácius himself, who had seen the letter, declared that the wording of it was very curt and vague—much more curt and vague than such letters usually were. It seems that there were a great many cases of cholera in the isolation hospital at Slovnitza and lists were sent up daily from there to Budapest of new cases, of severe cases, of discharges and of deaths. In one of these lists Andor's name certainly did appear among the dead, and a brief note to that effect had been officially sent to Lakatos. But surely the news should have had confirmation!

Where was the lad buried?

Who was beside him when he died?

Where were the few trinkets which he possessed; his mother's wedding-ring which he always wore on his little finger?

Pater Bonifácius wrote to the War Office at Budapest asking for a reply to these three questions. He received none. Then he persuaded Barna Jenö—the mayor—to write an official document. The War Office up at Budapest sent an equally official document saying that they had no knowledge on those three points: Lakatos Andor was one of those whose names appeared on the list of deaths from cholera at Slovnitza, and that was quite sufficient proof to offer to any reasonable human being.

Pater Bonifácius sighed in bitter disappointment, Lakatos Pál continued to bemoan his loneliness until he succeeded in persuading himself that he had always loved Andor as his own son, and that the lad's supposed death would presently cause his own.

And the neighbours—especially the women—held on to the belief that Andor was not dead; they declared that he would return one day to enjoy the good-will of his rich uncle now, to marry a girl of Marosfalva, and to look forward to a goodly legacy from Pali bácsi by and by.

# CHAPTER VII

## "They are Jews and we are Hungarians"

But what of Elsa during this time? What of the sorrow, the alternating hope and despair of those weary, weary months? She did not say much, she hardly ever cried, but even her mother—hard and unemotional as she was—respected the girl's secret for awhile, after the news was brought into the cottage that Andor was really dead.

Erös Béla had brought the news, and Elsa, on hearing it thus blurted out in Béla's rough, cruel fashion, had turned deathly pale, ere she contrived to run out of the room and hide herself away in a corner, where she had cried till she had made herself sick and faint.

"Have you been blind all these years, Irma néni?" Erös Béla had said with his habitual sneer, when Irma threw up her bony hands in hopeless puzzlement at her daughter's behaviour. "Did you not know that Elsa has been in love with Andor all along?"

"No," said Irma in her quiet, matter-of-fact tone, "I did not know it. Did you?"

"Of course I did," he replied dryly; "but I have also known for the past six months that Andor was dead."

"You knew it?" exclaimed Irma with obvious incredulity.

"I have told you so, haven't I?" he retorted, "and I am not in the habit of lying."

"But how did you come to know it?"

"When he did not return last September I marvelled what had happened; I wonder no one else did. Then, when Lakatos Pál first became ill—long even before he confided in Pater Bonifácius—I made inquiries at the War Office and found out the truth."

"Whatever made you do that?" asked Irma, with a shrug of the shoulders. "Andor wasn't anything to you."

"Perhaps not," replied Béla curtly; "but, you see, I was afraid that Pali bácsi would die and that Andor would come back and find himself a rich man. I should have lost Elsa then, so I was in a hurry to know."

Irma once more shrugged her shoulders in her habitual careless, shiftless way—shelving, as it were, the whole responsibility of her life, her fate, and her daughter upon some other power than her own will. She cared nothing about these intrigues of Béla's or of anyone else; she only wanted Elsa to make a rich marriage, so that she—the mother—might have a happy, comfortable, above all leisurely, old age.

But she had enough common sense to see that Elsa laboured under the weight of a very great sorrow, and while the girl was in such a condition of grief it would be worse than useless to worry her with suggestions of matrimony. Girls had been known to do desperate things if they were overharassed, and Kapus Irma was no fool; she knew what she wanted, and her instinct, coupled with her greed and cupidity, showed her the best way to get it.

So she left Elsa severely alone for a time, left her to pursue her household duties, to look after her father, to wash and iron the finery of the more genteel inhabitants of Marosfalva—the schoolmistress' blouses, Pater Bonifácius' surplices. Erös Béla continued in his unemotional attentions to her—he was more sure of success than ever. His words of courtship were the drops of water that were ultimately destined to wear away a stone.

Elsa, lulled into security by her mother's placidity and Béla's apparent simple friendship, hardly was conscious of the precise moment when the siege against her passive resistance was once more resumed. It was all so gradual, so kind, so persuasive: and she had so little to look forward to in the future. What did it matter what became of her?—whom she married or where her home would be? She saw more of Erös Béla than she did of anyone else, for Erös Béla was undoubtedly Irma's most favoured competitor. Elsa knew that he was of violent temperament, dictatorial and rough; she knew that he was fond of drink, and of the society of Klara Goldstein, the Jewess, but she really did not care.

She had kept her promise to Andor, she had waited for him until she knew that he never, never could come back; now she might as well obey her mother and put herself right with God, since she cared so little what became of her.

And the beauty of Marosfalva was tokened to Erös Béla in the spring of the following year, and presently it was given out that the wedding would take place on the feast of Holy Michael and All Angels at the end of September. Congratulations poured in upon the happy pair, rejoicings were held in every house of note in the village. Everyone was pleased at the marriage, pleased that the noted beauty would still have her home in Marosfalva, pleased that Erös Béla's wealth would all remain in the place.

And Elsa received these congratulations and attended these rejoicings with unvarying equanimity and cheerfulness. There was nothing morbid or self-centred in the girl's attitude. People who did not know—and no one really did—and who saw her at mass on Sundays or walking arm-in-arm with Béla in the afternoons would say that she was perfectly happy. Not a radiant bride certainly, not a typical Hungarian menyecske whose laughter echoes from end to end of the village, whose merry voice rings all the day, and whose pretty bare feet trot briskly up and down from her cottage to the river, or to the church, or to a neighbour's house, but an equable, contented bride, a fitting wife for a person of such high consideration as was Erös Béla.

Her manner to him was always equally pleasant, and though the young pair did not exchange very loving glances—at any rate not in public—yet they were never known to quarrel, which was really quite remarkable, seeing that Béla's temper had not improved of late.

He was giving way to drink more than he used to, and there were some ugly rumours about my lord the Count's dissatisfaction with his erstwhile highly-valued bailiff. Many people said that Béla would get his dismissal presently if he did not mend his ways; but then he very likely wouldn't care if he did get dismissed, he was a rich man and could give his full time to cultivating his own land.

This afternoon, while he was talking with Irma and sullenly watching his future wife, he appeared to be quite sober, until a moment ago when unreasoning rage seized hold of him and he shouted to Elsa in a rough and peremptory manner. After that, his face, which usually was quite pallid, became hotly flushed, and his one seeing eye had a restless, quivering look in it.

Nor did Elsa's placid gentleness help to cool his temper. When he shouted to her she turned and faced him, and said with a pleasant—if somewhat vague smile:

"Yes, Béla, what is it you want?"

"What is it I want?" he muttered, as he sank back into his chair, and resting his elbows on the table he buried his chin in his hands and looked across at the girl with a glowering and sullen look; "what is it I want?" he reiterated roughly. "I want to know what has been the matter with you these last two days?"

"Nothing has been the matter with me," she replied quietly, "nothing unusual, certainly. Why do you ask?"

"Because for the last two days you have been going about with a face on you fit for a funeral, rather than for a wedding. What is it? Let's have it."

"Nothing, Béla. What should it be?"

"I tell you there is something," he rejoined obstinately, "and what's more I can make a pretty shrewd guess what it is, eh?"

"I don't know what you mean," she said simply.

"I mean that the noted beauty of Marosfalva does me the honour of being jealous. Isn't that it, now? Oh! I know well enough, you needn't be ashamed of it, jealousy does your love for me credit, and flatters me, I assure you."

"I don't know what you mean, Béla," she reiterated more firmly. "I am neither jealous nor ashamed."

"Not ashamed?" he jeered. "Oho! look at your flaming cheeks! Irma néni, haven't you a mirror? Let her see how she is blushing."

"I don't see why she should be jealous," interposed Irma crossly, "nor why you should be for ever teasing her. I am sure she has no cause to be ashamed of anything, or of being jealous of anyone."

"But I tell you that she is jealous of Klara Goldstein!" he maintained.

"What nonsense!" protested the mother, while the blush quickly fled from the young girl's cheeks, leaving them clear and bloodless.

"I tell you she is," he persisted, with wrathful doggedness; "she has been sullen and moody these last two days, ever since I insisted that Klara Goldstein shall be asked to-morrow to the farewell banquet and the dance."

"Well, I didn't see myself why you wanted that Jewess to come," said Irma dryly.

"That's nobody's business," he retorted. "I pay for the entertainment, don't I?"

"You certainly do," she rejoined calmly. "We couldn't possibly afford to give Elsa her maiden's farewell, and if you didn't pay for the supper and the gipsies, and the hire of the schoolroom, why, then, you and Elsa would have to be married without a proper send-off, that's all."

"And a nice thing it would have been! Whoever heard of a girl on this side of the Maros being married without her farewell to maidenhood. I am paying for the supper and for everything because I want my bride's farewell to be finer and grander than anything that has ever been seen for many kilomètres round. I have stinted nothing—begrudged nothing. I have given an ox, two pigs and a calf to be slaughtered for the occasion. I have given chickens and sausages and some of the finest flour the countryside can produce. As for the wine ... well! all I can say is that there is none better in my lord's own cellar. I have given all that willingly. I did it because I liked it. But," he added, and once again the look of self-satisfaction and sufficiency gave way to his more habitual sinister expression, "if I pay for the feast, I decide who shall be invited to eat it."

Irma apparently had nothing to say in response. She shrugged her shoulders and continued to stir the stew in her pot. Elsa said nothing either; obedient to the command of her future lord, she had faced him and listened to him attentively and respectfully all the while that he spoke, nor did her face betray anything of what went

44

on within her soul, anything of its revolt or of its wounded pride, while the storm of wrath and of sneers thus passed unheeded over her head.

But Béla, having worked himself up into a fit of obstinate rage, was not content with Elsa's passive obedience. There had from the first crept into his half-educated but untutored and undisciplined mind the knowledge that though Elsa was tokened to him, though she was submissive, and gentle and even-tempered, her heart did not belong to him. He knew but little about love, believed in it still less: in that part of the world a good many men are still saturated with the Oriental conception of a woman's place in the world, and even in the innermost recesses of their mind with the Oriental disbelief in a woman's soul; but in common with all such men he had a burning desire to possess every aspiration and to know every thought of the woman whom he had chosen for his wife.

Therefore now, when in response to his rage and to his bombast Elsa had only silence for him—a silence which he knew must hide her real thoughts, he suddenly lost all sense of proportion and of prudence; for the moment he felt as if he could hate this woman whom he had wooed and won despite her resistance, and in the teeth of strenuous rivalry; he was seized with a purely savage desire to wound her, to see her cry, to make her unhappy—anything, in fact, to rouse her from this irritating apathy.

"I suppose," he said at last, making a great effort to recover his outward self-control, "I suppose that you object to my asking Klara Goldstein to come to your farewell feast?"

Thus directly appealed to by her lover, Elsa gave a direct reply.

"Yes, I do," she said.

"May I ask why?"

"A girl's farewell on the eve of her wedding-day," she replied quietly, "is intended to be a farewell to her girl friends. Klara Goldstein was never a friend of mine."

"She belongs to this village, anyway, doesn't she?" he queried, still trying to speak calmly. He had risen to his feet and stood with squared shoulders, legs wide apart, and hands buried in the pockets of his tightly-fitting trousers. An ugly, ill-tempered, masterful man, who showed in every line of his attitude that he meant to be supreme lord in his own household.

"Klara Goldstein belongs to this village," he reiterated with forced suavity, "she is my friend, is she not?"

"She may be your friend, Béla," rejoined Elsa gently, "and she certainly belongs to this village; but she is not one of us. She is a Jewess, not a Hungarian, like we all are."

45

"What has her religion to do with it?" he retorted.

"It isn't her religion, Béla," persisted the girl, with obstinacy at least as firm as his own; "you know that quite well. Though it is an awful thing to think that they crucified our Lord."

"Well! that is a good long while ago," he sneered; "and in any case Klara and Ignácz Goldstein had nothing to do with it."

"No, I know. Therefore I said that religion had nothing to do with it. I can't explain it exactly, Béla, but don't we all feel alike about that? Hungarians are Hungarians, and Jews are Jews, and there's no getting away from that. They are different to us, somehow. I can't say how, but they are different. They don't speak as we do, they don't think as we do, their Sunday is Saturday, and their New Year's day is in September. Jewesses can't dance the csárdás and Jews have a contempt for our gipsy music and our songs. They are Jews and we are Hungarians. It is altogether different."

He shrugged his shoulders, unable apparently to gainsay this unanswerable argument. After all, he too was a Hungarian, and proud of that fact, and like all Hungarians at heart, he had an unexplainable contempt for the Jews. But all the same, he was not going to give in to a woman in any kind of disagreement, least of all on a point on which he had set his heart. So now he shifted his ground back to his original dictum.

"You may talk as much as you like, Elsa," he said doggedly, "but Klara Goldstein is my friend, and I will have her asked to the banquet first and the dance afterwards, or I'll not appear at it myself."

"That's clear, I hope?" he added roughly, as Elsa, in her habitual peace-loving way, had made no comment on that final threat.

"It is quite clear, Béla," she now said passively.

"Of course the girl shall be asked, Béla," here interposed Irma néni, who had no intention of quarrelling with her wealthy son-in-law. "I'll see to it, and don't you lose your temper about it. Here! sit down again. Elsa, bring your father's chair round for supper. Béla, do sit down and have a bite. I declare you two might be married already, so much quarrelling do you manage to get through."

But Béla, as sulky now as a bear with a sore head, refused to stay for supper.

"I can't bear sullen faces and dark looks," he said savagely. "I'll go where I can see pleasant smiles and have some fun. I must say, Irma néni," he added by way of a parting shot, as he picked up his hat and made for the door, "that I do not admire the way you have brought up your daughter. A woman's place is not only to obey

46

her husband, but to look cheerful about it. However," he added, with a dry laugh, "we'll soon put that right after to-morrow, eh, my dove?"

And with a perfunctory attempt at a more lover-like attitude, he turned to Elsa, who already had jumped to her feet, and with a pleasant smile was holding up her sweet face to her future lord for a kiss.

She looked so exquisitely pretty then, standing in the gloomy half-light of this squalid room, with the slanting golden sunshine which peeped in through the tiny west window outlining her delicate silhouette and touching her smooth fair hair with gold.

Vanity, self-satisfaction, and mayhap something a little more tender, a little more selfless, stirred in the young man's heart. It was fine to think that this beautiful prize—which so many had coveted—was his by right of conquest. Even the young lord whose castle was close by had told Erös Béla that he envied him his good luck, whilst my lord the Count and my lady the Countess had of themselves offered to be present at the wedding and to be the principal witnesses on behalf of the most beautiful girl in the county.

These pleasant thoughts softened Béla's mood, and he drew his fiancée quite tenderly to him. He kissed her on the forehead and on the cheeks, but she would not let him touch her lips. He laughed at her shyness, the happy triumphant laugh of the conqueror.

Then he nodded to Irma and was gone.

"He is a very good fellow at heart," said the mother philosophically, "you must try and humour him, Elsa. He is very proud of you really, and think what a beautiful house you will have, and all those oxen and pigs and a carriage and four horses. You must thank God on your knees for so much good fortune; there are girls in this village who would give away their ears to be standing in your shoes."

"Indeed, mother dear, I am very, very grateful for all my good fortune," said Elsa cheerfully, as with vigorous young arms she pulled the paralytic's chair round to the table and then got him ready for his meal.

After which there was a moment's silence. Elsa and her mother each stood behind her own chair: the young girl's clear voice was raised to say a simple grace before a simple meal.

The stew had not been put on the table, since Béla did not stay for supper. It would do for to-morrow's dinner, and for to-night maize porridge and rye bread would be quite sufficient.

Elsa looked after her father and herself ate with a hearty, youthful appetite. Her mother could not help but be satisfied that the child was happy.

The philosophy of life had taught Kapus Irma a good many lessons, foremost among these was the one which defined the exact relationship between the want of money and all other earthly ills. Certainly the want of money was the father of them all. Elsa in future would never feel it, therefore all other earthly ills would fall away from her for lack of support.

It was as well to think that the child realized this, and was grateful for her own happiness.

# CHAPTER VIII

### "I put the bunda away somewhere"

Kapus Irma went out after supper to hold a final consultation with the more influential matrons of Marosfalva over the arrangements for to-morrow's feast. Old Kapus had been put to bed on his paillasse in the next room and Elsa was all alone in the small living-room. She had washed up the crockery and swept up the hearth for the night; cloth in hand, she was giving the miserable bits of furniture something of a rub-down and general furbishing-up: a thing she could only do when her mother was away, for Irma hated her to do things which appeared like a comment on her own dirty, slatternly ways.

Cleanliness, order and a love of dainty tidiness in the home are marked characteristics of the true Hungarian peasantry: the cottages for the most part are miracles of brightness, brightly polished floors, brightly polished pewter, brightly covered feather pillows. Kapus Irma was a notable exception to the rule, and Elsa had often shed bitter tears of shame when one or other of her many admirers followed her into her home and saw the squalor which reigned in it—the dirt and untidiness. She was most ashamed when Béla was here, for he made sneering remarks about it all, and seemed to take it for granted that she was as untidy, as slovenly as her mother. He read her long lectures about his sister's fine qualities and about the manner in which he would expect his own wife to keep her future home, and made it an excuse for some of his most dictatorial pronouncements and rough, masterful ways.

But to-night even this had not mattered—though he had

48

spoken very cruelly about the hemp—nothing now mattered any more. To-day she had been called for the third time in church, to-morrow evening she would say good-bye to her maidenhood and take her place for the last time among her girl-friends: after to-morrow's feast she would be a matron—her place would be a different one. And on Tuesday would come the wedding and she would be Erös Béla's wedded wife.

So what did anything matter any more? After Tuesday she would not even be allowed to think of Andor, to dream that he had come back and that the past two dreadful years had only been an ugly nightmare. Once she was Erös Béla's wedded wife, it would be no longer right to think of that last morning five years ago, of that final csárdás, and the words which Andor had whispered: above all, it would no longer be right to remember that kiss—his warm lips upon her bare shoulder, and later on, out under the acacia tree, that last kiss upon her lips.

She closed her eyes for a moment; a sigh of infinite regret escaped through her parted lips. It would have been so beautiful, if only it could have come true! if only something had been left to her of those enchanted hours, something more tangible than just a memory.

Resolutely now she went back to her work; for the past two years she had found that she could imagine herself to be quite moderately happy, if only she had plenty to do; and she did hope that Béla would allow her to work in her new home and not to lead a life of idleness—waited on by paid servants.

She had thrown the door wide open, and every now and then, when she paused in her work, she could go and stand for a moment under its narrow lintel; and from this position, looking out toward the west, she could see the sunset far away beyond where the plain ended, where began another world. The plumed heads of the maize were tipped with gold, and in the sky myriads and myriads of tiny clouds lay like a gigantic and fleecy comet stretching right over the dome of heaven above the plain to that distant horizon far, far away.

Elsa loved to watch those myriads of clouds through the many changes which came over them while the sun sank so slowly, so majestically down into the regions which lay beyond the plain. At first they had been downy and white, like the freshly-plucked feathers of a goose, then some of them became of a soft amber colour, like ripe maize, then those far away appeared rose-tinted, then crimson, then glowing like fire ... and that glow spread and spread up from the distant horizon, up and up till each tiny cloud was suffused with it, and the whole dome of heaven became one

49

fiery, crimson, fleecy canopy, with peeps between of a pale turquoise green.

It was beautiful! Elsa, leaning against the frame-work of the door, gazed into that gorgeous immensity till her eyes ached with the very magnificence of the sight. It lasted but a few minutes—a quarter of an hour, perhaps—till gradually the blood-red tints disappeared behind the tall maize; they faded first, then the crimson and the rose and the gold, till, one by one, the army of little clouds lost their glowing robes and put on a grey hue, dull and colourless like people's lives when the sunshine of love has gone down—out of them.

With a little sigh Elsa turned back into the small living-room, which looked densely black and full of gloom now by contrast with the splendour which she had just witnessed. From the village street close by came the sound of her mother's sharp voice in excited conversation with a neighbour.

"It will be all right, Irma néni," the neighbour said, in response to some remark of the other woman. "Klara Goldstein does not expect our village girls to take much notice of her. But I will say that the men are sharp enough dangling round her skirts."

"Yes," retorted Irma, "and I wish to goodness Béla had not set his heart on having her at the feast. He is so obstinate: once he has said a thing ..."

"Béla's conduct in this matter is not to be commended, my good Irma," said the neighbour sententiously; "everyone thinks that for a tokened man it is a scandal to be always hanging round that pert Jewess. Why didn't he propose to her instead of to Elsa, if he liked her so much better?"

"Hush! hush! my good Mariska, please. Elsa might hear you."

The two women went on talking in whispers. Elsa had heard, of course, what they said: and since she was alone a hot blush of shame mounted to her cheeks. It was horrid of people to talk in that way about her future husband, and she marvelled how her own mother could lend herself to such gossip.

Irma came in a few minutes later. She looked suspiciously at her daughter.

"Why do you keep the door open?" she asked sharply, "were you expecting anybody to come in?"

"Only you, mother, and Pater Bonifácius is coming after vespers," replied the girl.

"I stopped outside for a bit of gossip with Mariska just now. Could you hear what she said?"

"Yes, mother. I did hear something of what Mariska said."

"About Béla?"

"About him—yes."

"Hej, child! you must not take any notice of what folks say—it is only tittle-tattle. You must not mind it."

"I don't mind it, mother. I am sure that it is only tittle-tattle."

"Your father in bed?" asked Irma abruptly changing the subject of conversation.

"Yes."

"And you have been busying yourself, I see," continued the mother, looking round her with obvious disapproval, "with matters that do not concern you. I suppose Béla has been persuading you that your mother is incapable of keeping her own house tidy, so you must needs teach her how to do it."

"No, mother, nothing was further from my thoughts. I had nothing to do after I had cleared and washed up, and I wanted something to do."

"If you wanted something to do you might have got out your father's bunda" (big sheepskin cloak worn by the peasantry) "and seen if the moth has got into it or not. It is two years since he has had it on, and he will want it to-morrow."

"To-morrow?"

"Why, yes. I really must tell you because of the bunda, Jankó and Móritz and Jenö and Pál have offered to carry him to the feast in his chair just as he is. We'll put his bunda round him, and they will strap some poles to his chair, so that they can carry him more easily. They offered to do it. It was to be a surprise for you for your farewell to-morrow: but I had to tell you, because of getting the bunda out and seeing whether it is too moth-eaten to wear."

While Irma went on talking in her querulous, acid way, Elsa's eyes had quickly filled with tears. How good people were! how thoughtful! Was it not kind of Móritz and Jenö and the others to have thought of giving her this great pleasure?

To have her poor old father near her, after all, when she was saying farewell to all her maidenhood's friends! And what a joy it would be to him!—one that would brighten him through many days to come.

Oh! people were good! It was monstrously ungrateful to be unhappy when one lived among these kind folk.

"Where is the bunda, mother?" she asked eagerly. "I'll see to it at once. And if the moths are in it, why I must just patch the places up so that they don't show. Where is the bunda, mother?"

Irma thought a moment, then she frowned, and finally shrugged her shoulders.

"How do I know?" she said petulantly; "isn't it in your room?"

"No, mother. I haven't seen it since father wore it last."

51

"And that was two years ago—almost to a day. I remember it quite well. It was quite chilly, and your father put on his bunda to go down the street as far as the Jew's house. It was after sunset, I remember. He came home and went to bed. The next morning he was stricken. And I put the bunda away somewhere. Now wherever did I put it?"

She stood pondering for a moment.

"Under his paillasse?" she murmured to herself. "No. In the cupboard? No."

"In the dower-chest, mother?" suggested Elsa, who knew of old that that article of furniture was the receptacle for everything that hadn't a proper place.

"Yes. Look at the bottom," said Irma placidly, "it might be there."

It was getting dark now. Through the open door and the tiny hermetically closed windows the grey twilight peeped in shyly. The more distant corner of the little living-room, that which embraced the hearth and the dower-chest, was already wrapped in gloom.

Elsa bent over the worm-eaten piece of furniture: her hands plunged in the midst of maize-husks and dirty linen of cabbage-stalks and sunflower-seeds, till presently they encountered something soft and woolly.

"Here is the bunda, mother," she said.

"Ah, well! get it out now, and lay it over a chair. You can have a look at it to-morrow—there will be plenty of time before you need begin to dress," said Irma, who held the theory that it was never any use doing to-day what could conveniently be put off until to-morrow.

"Mayn't I have a look at it now, mother?" asked Elsa, as she struggled with the heavy sheepskin mantle and drew it out of the surrounding rubbish; "the light will hold out for another half-hour at least, and to-morrow morning I shall have such a lot to do."

"You may do what you like while the light lasts, my girl, but I won't have you waste the candle over this stupid business. Candle is very dear, and your father will never wear his bunda again after to-morrow."

"I won't waste the candle, mother. But Pater Bonifácius is coming in to see me after vespers."

"What does he want to come at an hour when all sensible folk are in bed?" queried Irma petulantly.

"He couldn't come earlier, mother dear; you know how busy he is always on Sundays ... benediction, then christenings, then vespers. ... He said he would be here about eight o'clock."

"Eight o'clock!" exclaimed the woman, "who ever heard of

such a ridiculous hour? And candles are so dear—there's only a few centimètres of it in the house."

"I'll only light the candle, mother, when the Pater comes," said Elsa, with imperturbable cheerfulness; "I'll just sit by the open door now and put a stitch or two in father's bunda while the light lasts: and when I can't see any longer I'll just sit quietly in the dark, till the Pater comes. I shall be quite happy," she added, with a quaint little sigh, "I have such a lot to think about."

"So have I," retorted Irma, "and I shall go and do my thinking in bed. I shall have to be up by six o'clock in the morning, I expect, and anyhow I hate sitting up in the dark."

She turned to go into the inner room, but Elsa—moved by a sudden impulse—ran after her and put her arms round her mother's neck.

"Won't you kiss me, mother?" she said wistfully. "You won't do it many more times in my old home."

"A home you have often been ashamed of, my child," the mother said sullenly.

But she kissed the girl—if not with tenderness, at any rate with a curious feeling of pity which she herself could not have defined.

"Good-night, my girl," she said, with more gentleness than was her wont. "Sleep well for the last time in your old bed. I doubt if to-morrow you'll get into it at all, and don't let the Pater stay too long and waste the candle."

"I promise, mother," said Elsa, with a smile; "good-night!"

# CHAPTER IX

### "Then, as now, may God protect you"

The bunda was very heavy. Elsa dragged it over her knee, and sat down on a low stool in the open doorway. She had pulled the table a little closer, and on it were her scissors, needles and cotton, as well as the box of matches and the candle which she would be allowed to light presently when Pater Bonifácius came.

The moth certainly had caused many ravages in the sheepskin cloak—there were tiny holes everywhere, and the fur when you

53

touched it came out in handfuls. But as the fur would be turned inwards, that wouldn't matter so much. The bunda was quite wearable: there was just a bad tear in the leather close to the pocket, which might show and which must be mended.

Elsa threaded her needle, and began to hum her favourite song under her breath:

"Nincsen annyi tenger csillag az égen
Mint a hányszor vagy eszembe te nékem."

"There are not so many myriads of stars in the sky as the number of times that my thoughts fly to thee!"

She was determined not to think any more of the past. In a few hours now that chapter in her life would be closed, and it was useless and wicked to be always thinking of the "might-have-been." Rather did she set herself resolutely to think of the future, of that part of it, at any rate, which was bright. There would be her mother installed in that comfortable house on the Kender Road, and with a nice bit of land and garden round in which to grow vegetables and keep some poultry. There would be her three cows and the pigs which Béla was giving her, and which he would graze on his own land.

Above all, there would be the comfortable bed and armchair for the sick man, and the little maid to wait upon him.

There was so much, so much to be thankful for! And since God chose to take Andor away, what else was there to live for, save to see her mother and father contented?

The light was going fast. Elsa had made a splendid job of that one pocket. The other, too, wanted a stitch. It was very badly torn—if only the feeble light would hold out another ten minutes ... that hole, too, would be securely mended.

With the splendid disregard of youth for its most precious gift, Elsa strained her eyes to thread her needle once more.

She tackled the second pocket of the shabby bunda. There was a long tear at the side, as if the wearer's hand had missed the actual pocket and been thrust carelessly or roughly through the leather.

Elsa put her hand through the hole, too, to see the extent of the mischief. Yes! that was it, her father must more than once have missed the pocket and put his hand into the hole, making it bigger and bigger. Why! there was a whole lot of rubbish deep down inside the lining. Elsa drew out an empty tobacco-pouch, a bit of string, a length of tinder, and from the very bottom, where it lay in a crinkled mass, a ball of crumpled paper.

This she smoothed out, holding it over her knee. It was a letter—one which must have been delivered on the very day when her father last wore the bunda. The envelope had not been broken: old Kapus hadn't had time to read his letter, the last which he had received before living death encompassed him. The tears gathered in Elsa's eyes at thought of her father handling this very letter with shaking yet still living hands: now they were incapable even of gripping this tiny piece of paper.

But then—two years ago, her mother said it was, almost to a day when last he wore the bunda—then he had received the letter from the postman and evidently thrust it into his pocket, meaning to read it at some more convenient time.

The peasants of that part of the world have never quite lost their distrust of railways, of telegrams, and even of letters—they are half-afraid of them all, afraid with that vague, unreasoning fear which animals have for things they see yet cannot understand.

Elsa handled this unopened letter with something of that same fear. She did not think at first of looking at the superscription. Who could have been writing to her father two years ago? He had no rich friends who could afford to spend money on note-paper and stamps. There was no news in the great outer world which someone could have wished to impart to him. The light indeed was very dim before Elsa, sitting here with the old bunda on her knee, thought of looking more closely at the envelope.

She bent down and out toward the light, trying to decipher the writing.

The letter was addressed to her.

Oh! it was quite clear!

"Tekintetes Kapus Elsa kisasszonynak."

It was quite, quite clearly written. The letter was addressed to her. The postman had brought it here two years ago: her father had taken it from him and thrust it into the pocket of his bunda, meaning to give it presently to his daughter.

But that evening perhaps he forgot it altogether: he had been drinking rather heavily of late. And the next day he was stricken down with paralysis, his tongue refused him service, and he no longer could tell his daughter—as no doubt he wanted to do—that a letter had come for her and that it was in the pocket of his bunda.

And the bunda was thrust away into the dower-chest with the husks of maize and the cabbage-stalks, and it had never been taken out until to-night—the eve of Elsa's wedding-day.

She tore open the envelope now with fingers that trembled slightly. The light was very dim, and where the glorious sunset had been such a little while ago there was only the dull grey canopy of an overcast sky. But Elsa could just make out the writing: already her eye had wandered to the signature, "your ever-devoted Andor." The message seemed to come to her as from the grave, for she thought that these were probably Andor's last words to her, penned just before he died in that awful hospital in Bosnia.

"My sweet dove!" she read. "This is to tell you that I am well: although it has been a close fight between life and death for me. But I did so want to live, my sweetheart, for I have you to look forward to in life. I have been at death's door, and I believe that the doctor here, before he went away one evening, signed the paper to say that I was dead. But that same night I took a turn for the better, and it was wonderful how soon I was up again. I'll tell you all about it some day, my love, some day when I come to claim your promise that you would wait for me. Because, dear heart, while I have been ill I have been thinking very seriously. I have not a silver florin to bless myself with: how can I come and dare to ask you to be my wife? Your father and mother would kick me out of their house, they would forbid me to see you; they would part you from me, my dear, beautiful angel, and I should feel that it was just. I—a good-for-nothing, penniless lout, daring to approach the queen of beauty, the most exquisite girl on God's earth. I have thought it all over, dear heart, and all will be well if you will be true to me—if you will wait for me another two years. Oh! I do not ask you to do it, I am not worthy of your love. Who am I, that you should keep yourself for me?—but I will pray to God night and day that He may not take away your love from me. I am going to America, dear heart, with an English gentleman who has been very kind to me. He was the English Consul at Cettinje, and when there were so many of us—Hungarian lads—lying sick of that awful cholera in the hospital at Slovnitza, his wife, a sweet, kind lady, used to come and visit us and cheer us up. She was very ugly and had big teeth and no waist, but she was an angel of goodness. She took some interest in me, and once when I was still very weak and ill I told her about you, about our love and what little hope I had of ever winning you, seeing that I was penniless. She was greatly interested, and when I was finally allowed to leave the hospital, she told me to come and see her husband, the English Consul. Well! dear heart, this kind gentleman is sending me out to a farm which he possesses in a place called Australia—I think that it is somewhere in America, but I am not sure. When I get there I shall receive more wage in one week than our alföld labourers get in three months, and it will all be good money, of which I can save every fillér, because my food and housing will be given to me free, and the kind English lady—may the Virgin protect her, despite her large teeth and flat chest—gave me a whole lot of clothes to take with me. So every fillér which I earn I can save, and I reckon that in two years I shall have saved two thousand florins" (about £160) "and then I shall come home. If I still find you free, my dove—which I pray to God I may do—we can get married at once. Then we'll rent the Lepke farm from Pali bácsi, as I shall have plenty of money for the necessary security, and if we cannot make that pay and become rich folk within three years, then I am not the man whom I believe myself to be.

"But, my darling love, do not think for a moment that I want to bind you to me against your will. God only knows how deeply I love you; during the last three years the thought of you has been the sunshine of my days, the light of my nights. If, when you have received and pondered over this letter, you send me a reply to say that you still love me, that you will be true to me and will wait for my return, then you will change my world into a paradise. No work will be too hard, no difficulty too great to surmount, if it will help me the sooner to come back to you. But if, on the other hand, you tell me or leave me to guess that I am a fool for thinking that you would waste your beauty and your sweetness on waiting for a good-for-nothing scamp like me, why, then, I shall understand. I shall go out to America—or wherever that place called Australia may be—but maybe I shall never come back. But I should never curse you, dear heart, I should never cease to love you: I should quite understand.

"I have got one of the nurses at the hospital to write this letter for me, to put my rough words into good Hungarian and to write down my thoughts in a good, clear hand. That is how it comes to be so well written. You know I was never much of a hand with a pen and paper, but I do love you, my dove! My God, how I love you.

"The nurse says that Australia is not in America at all—that it is a different place altogether. Well! I do not care where it is. I am going there because there I can earn one hundred florins a month, and save enough in two years to marry you and keep you in comfort. But I shall not see you, my dove, before I go: if I saw you again, if I saw

57

Hungary again, our village, our alföld, Heaven help me! but I don't think I would have the heart to go away again.

"Farewell, dear heart, I go away full of hope. We go off next week in a big, big ship from here. I go full of sadness, but if you do want me to come back just write me a little letter with the one word 'Yes,' and address it as above. Then will my sadness be changed to heavenly joy and hope. But if it is to be 'No,' then tell me so quite truly, and I will understand.

"Then, as now, may God protect you, my dove, my heart,

"Your ever-devoted
"Andor."

The letter fell out of Elsa's hands on to her knee. She took no heed of it, she was staring out into the immensity far away, into the fast-gathering gloom. Two years ago! Two years of sorrow and vain regrets which never need have been. One word from her father or from the postman, the feel of crisp paper in her father's bunda when it was put away two years ago, and the whole course of her life would have been changed.

The village street behind her was silent now, even the footsteps of belated folk hurrying to their homes sent up no echo from the soft, sandy ground. And before her the fast-gathering night was slowly wrapping the plain in its peace-giving shroud. Inside the cottage all was still: mother and father lay either asleep or awake thinking of the morrow.

A great, heavy sob shook the young girl's vigorous young frame. It seemed too wantonly cruel, this decree of Fate which had withheld from her the light of her life. How easy it would have been to wait! How swiftly these two years would have flown past. Her heart would have kept young—waiting for Andor and for happiness, whereas now it was numb and unsentient, save for a feeling of obedience and of filial duty, of pity for her mother and father, and of resignation to her future state.

Indeed Fate was being wantonly cruel to her to the last in thus putting before her eyes a picture of the might-have-been just when it was too late. In a few hours from now the great vow would be spoken, the irrevocable knot tied which bound her to another man. Her troth was already plighted, her confession made to Pater Bonifácius—in a few hours from now she would be Béla's wife, and if Andor did come back now, she must be as nothing to him, he as a mere distant friend.

But probably he never would come back. He received no reply

to his fond letter of farewell, not one word from her to cheer him on his way. No doubt by now he had made a home for himself in that far distant land. Another woman—a stranger—revelled in the sunshine of his love, while Elsa, whose whole life had been wrapped up in him, was left desolate.

For a moment a wild spirit of revolt rose in her. Was it too late, after all? Was any moment in life too late to snatch at fleeing happiness? Why shouldn't she run away to-night—now?—find that unknown country, that unknown spot where Andor was? Surely God would give her strength! God could not be so unjust and so cruel as men and Fate had been!

Pater Bonifácius, turning from the street round the angle of the cottage, found her in this mood, squatting on the low stool, her elbows on her knees, her face buried in her hands. He came up to her quite gently, for though his was a simple soul it was full of tenderness and of compassion for the children of these plains whom God had committed into his charge.

"Elsa, my girl," he asked softly, "what is it?"

# CHAPTER X

## "The best way of all"

Pater Bonifácius had placed his kindly hand on the girl's hunched-up shoulders, and there was something in his touch which seemed to soothe the wild paroxysm of her grief. She raised her tear-stained face to his, and without a word—for her lips were shaking and she could not have spoken then—she handed him Andor's letter.

"May I go in," he asked, "and light the candle? It is too dark now to read."

She rose quickly, and with an instinctive sense of respect for the parish priest she made hasty efforts to smooth her hair and to wipe her face with her apron. Then she turned into the room, and though her hand still trembled slightly, she contrived to light the candle.

The old priest adjusted his horn-rimmed spectacles on his nose and drew a chair close to the light.

He sat down and read Andor's letter through very slowly. When he had finished, he handed it back to Elsa.

"God's ways, my child, are mysterious," he said, with a short sigh; "it is not for us to question them."

"Mysterious?" exclaimed the girl, with passionate wrath; "I call them cruel and unjust, pater! What have I done, that He should have done this to me? Andor loved me and I loved him, he wrote me a letter full of love, begging for a word from me to assure him that I would always love him and that I would wait for him. Why was that letter kept from me? Why was I not allowed to reply to it? My father would not have kept the letter from me, had he not been stricken down with paralysis on the very day when it came. It is God who kept my happiness away from me. It is God who has spoilt my life and condemned me to regrets and wretchedness, when I had done nothing to deserve such a cruel fate!"

"It is God," interposed the priest gently, "who even at this moment forgives an erring child all the blasphemy which she utters."

Then, as Elsa, dry-eyed and with quivering lips, still looked the personification of revolt, he placed his warm, gentle hands upon hers and drew her a little closer to him.

"Are we, then," he asked softly, "such very important things in the scheme of God's entire creation that everything must be ordered so as to suit us best?"

"I only wanted to be happy," murmured Elsa, in a quivering voice.

"You only wanted to be happy in your own way, my child," rejoined the priest, as he patted her hands tenderly, "but it does not happen to have been God's way. Now who shall say which is the best way of being happy? Who knows best? You or God?"

"If the postman had given me the letter, and not to father," she murmured dully, "if father had not been stricken down with illness the very next day, if I had only had this letter two years ago, instead of to-day ..."

And the sentence was left unfinished, broken by a bitter sigh of regret.

"If it all had been as you say, my child," said Pater Bonifácius kindly, "then you might perhaps have been happy according to your own light, whereas now you are going to be happy in accordance with that of God."

She shook her head and once more her eyes filled with tears.

"I shall never be happy again," she whispered.

"Oh, yes, you will, my dear," retorted the kindly old man, whose rugged face—careworn and wrinkled—was lit up with a half-humorous, wholly indulgent smile; "it is wonderful what a capacity for happiness the good God has given to us all. The only thing is that we can't always be happy in our own way; but the other ways—if they are God's ways—are very much better, believe me. Why He chose to part you from Andor," he added, with touching simplicity, "why He chose to withhold that letter from you until to-night, we shall probably never know. But that it was His way for your future happiness, of that I am convinced."

"There could have been no harm this time, Pater, in Andor and I being happy in our way. There could be no wrong in two people caring for one another, and wanting to live their lives together."

"Ah! that we shall never know, my child. The book of the 'might-have-been' is a closed one for us. Only God has the power to turn over its pages."

"Andor and I would have been so happy!" she reiterated, with the obstinacy of a vain regret; "and life would have been an earthly paradise."

"And perhaps you would have forgotten heaven in that earthly paradise; who knows, your happiness might have drawn you away from God, you might have spent your life in earthly joys, you might have danced and sung and thought more and more of pleasure, and less and less of God. Who knows? Whereas now you are just going to be happy in God's way: you are going to do your duty by your mother and your father, and, above all, by your husband. You are going to fill your life by thoughts of God first and then of others, instead of filling it with purely selfish joys. You are going to walk up the road of life, my child, with duty to guide you over the roughnesses and hard stones that will bestrew your path: and every roughness which is surmounted, every hardship which is endured, every sacrifice of self which is offered up to One who made the greatest possible sacrifice for us all, will leave you happier than before ... happier in God's way, the best way of all."

He talked on for a long while in this gentle, heartfelt way, and gradually, as the old man spoke, the bitterness and revolt died out of the simple-minded child's heart. Hers, after all, was a simple faith—but as firmly rooted within her as her belief in the sunshine, the alternating days and nights, the turns of the season. And the kind priest, who after life's vicissitudes had found anchorage in this forlorn village in the midst of the plains, knew exactly how to deal with these childlike souls. Like those who live their lives upon the sea, the Hungarian peasant sees only immensity around him, and above him that wonderful dome which hides its ineffable mysteries behind glorious veils of sunset and sunrise, of storm and of fantastic clouds. The plain stretches its apparently limitless expanse to a distance which he—its child—has never reached. Untutored and unlearned, he does not know what lies beyond that low-lying horizon into whose arms the sun sinks at evening in a pool of fire.

Everything around him is so great, so vast, so wonderful—the rising and setting of the sun, the stars and moon at nights, the gathering storms, the rainfalls, the sowing of the maize and the corn, the travail of the earth and the growing and developing of the stately heads of maize from one tiny, dried, yellow grain—that he has no inclination for petty casuistry, for arguments or philosophy. God's work is all that he ever sees: the book of life and death the only one he reads.

And because of that simple faith, that sublime ignorance, Elsa found comfort and peace in what Pater Bonifácius said. I will not say that she ceased to regret, nor that the grief of her heart was laid low, but her heart was soothed, and to her already heavy sorrow there was no longer laid the additional burden of a bitter resentment.

Then for awhile after he had spoken the priest was silent. No one knew better than he did the exact value of silence, whilst words had time to sink in. So they both remained in the gloom side by side—he the consoler and she the healed. The flickering candle light played curious and fantastic tricks with their forms and faces, lighting up now and then the wrinkled, wizened face of the old man, with the horn-rimmed spectacles perched upon his nose, and now and then the delicate profile of the girl, the smooth, fair tresses and round, white neck.

"Shall we not say a little prayer together?" whispered Pater Bonifácius at last, "just the prayer which our dear Lord taught us— Our Father which art in heaven ..."

Slowly the young girl sank on her knees beside the gentle comforter; her fair head was bowed, her face hidden in her hands. Word for word now she repeated after him the sublime invocation taught by Divine lips.

And when the final whispered Amen ceased to echo in the low, raftered room, Pater Bonifácius laid his hand upon the child's head in a gesture of unspoken benediction.

62

# CHAPTER XI

## "After that, happiness will begin"

Pater Bonifácius' kindliness, his gentle philosophy and unquestioning faith exercised a soothing influence over Elsa's spirits. The one moment of rebellion against Fate and against God, before the arrival of the old priest, had been the first and the last.

There is a goodly vein of Oriental fatalism still lurking in the Hungarians: "God has willed it!" comes readily enough to their lips. Though this unsophisticated child of the plains suffered none the less than would her more highly-cultured sisters in the West, yet she was more resigned—in her humble way, more philosophical—accepting the inevitable with an aching heart, mayhap, but with a firm determination to make the best of the few shreds of happiness which were left to her.

Elsa had promised before God and before the whole village that she would marry Erös Béla on the feast of St. Michael and All Angels, and after that single thought of rebellion, she knew that on the following Tuesday this would have to be just as surely as the day follows the night and the night the day.

Even that selfsame evening, after the Pater had gone and before she went to bed, she made her final preparations for the next three days, which were the turning-points of her life. To-morrow her farewell banquet: a huge feast in the big schoolroom, hired expressly for the occasion. Fifty people would sit down to that, they were the most intimate friends of the contracting parties, hers and Béla's, and her mother's. It is the rule that the bride's parents provide this entertainment, but Kapus Benkó and his wife had not the means for it, and Erös Béla, insisting upon a sumptuous feast, was ready enough to pay for this gratification of his own vanity.

After the banquet, dancing would begin and would be kept up half the night. Then the next morning was the wedding-day. The wedding Mass in the morning, then the breakfast, more dancing, more revelling, more jollification, also kept up throughout the night. For it is only on the day following, that the bridegroom goes to fetch his bride out of her home, to conduct her to his own with all the pomp and circumstance which his wealth allows. So many carts, so many oxen, so many friends in the carts, and so many gipsies to make music while the procession slowly passes up the village street.

All that was, of course, already arranged for. The banquet for to-morrow was prepared, the ox roasted whole, the pigs and the

63

capons stuffed. Erös Béla had provided everything, and provided most lavishly. Fifty persons would sit down to the farewell banquet, and more like two hundred to the wedding-breakfast; the village was agog with excitement, gipsies from Arad had been engaged, my lord the Count and the Countess were coming to the wedding Mass! ... how could one feeble, weak, ignorant girl set her will against this torrent?

Elsa, conscious of her helplessness, set to with aching heart, but unwavering determination to put the past entirely behind her.

What was the good of thinking, since Fate had already arranged everything?

She went to bed directly after the Pater went away, because there was no more candle in the house, and because her mother kept calling querulously to her; and having stretched her young limbs out upon the hard paillasse, she slept quite peacefully, because she was young and healthy and did not suffer from nerves, and because sorrow had made her very weary.

And the next morning, the dawn of the first of those all-important three days, found her busy, alert, quite calm outwardly, even though her cheeks had lost something of their rosy hue, and her blue eyes had a glitter in them which suggested unshed tears.

There was a lot to do, of course: the invalid to get ready, the mother's dressing to see to, so that she should not look slovenly in her appearance, and call forth some of those stinging remarks from Béla which had the power to wound the susceptibilities of his fiancée.

Irma was captious and in a tearful humour, bemoaning the fact that she was too poor to pay for her only daughter's farewell repast.

"Whoever heard of a bridegroom paying for his fiancée's farewell?" she said. "You will despise your poor parents now, Elsa."

It was certainly an unusual thing under the circumstances; the maiden's farewell to the friends of her girlhood, to their parents and belongings, is a great event in this part of the world in connection with the wedding festivities themselves, of which it is the precursor. The parents of the bride invariably provide the entertainment, and do so in accordance with their means.

But Erös Béla was a proud man in the county: he would not hear of any festival attendant upon his marriage being less than gorgeous and dazzling before the eyes of the whole countryside. He chose to pay the piper, so that he might call the tune, and though Elsa—wounded in her own pride—did her best to protest, she was overruled by her mother, who was only too thankful to see this expensive burden taken from off her shoulders.

Kapus Irma was a proud mother to-day, for as Elsa finally stood before her, arrayed in all her finery for the coming feast, she fully justified her right to be styled "the beauty of the county."

A picture she looked from the top of her small head, with its smooth covering of fair hair, yellow as the ripening corn, to the tips of her small, arched feet, encased in the traditional boots of bright crimson leather.

Her fair hair was plaited closely from the crown of her head and tied up with strands of red, white and green ribbons, nor did the hard line of the hair drawn tightly away from the face mar the charm of its round girlishness. It gave it its own peculiar character— semi-oriental, with just a remaining soupçon of that mysterious ancestry whose traditions are lost in the far-off mountains of Thibet.

The tight-fitting black corslet spanned the girlish figure, and made it look all the more slender as it seemed to rise out of the outstanding billows of numberless starched petticoats. Necklace and earrings made of beads of solid gold—a present from Béla to his fiancée—gave a touch of barbaric splendour to this dainty apparition, whilst her bare shoulders and breast, her sturdy young arms and shapely, if toil-worn, hands made her look as luscious a morsel of fresh girlhood as ever gladdened the heart of man.

Irma surveyed her daughter from head to foot with growing satisfaction. Then, with a gesture of unwonted impulse, she took the young girl by the shoulders and, drawing her closely to her own bony chest, she imprinted two sounding kisses on the fresh, pale cheeks.

"There," she said lustily, "your mother's kiss ought to put some colour in those cheeks. Heigho, child!" she added with a sigh, as she wiped a solitary tear with the back of her hand, "I don't wonder you are pale and frightened. It is a serious step for a girl to take. I know how I felt when your father came and took me out of my mother's house! But for you it is so easy: you are leaving a poor, miserable home for the finest house this side of the Maros and a life of toil and trouble for one of ease! To-day you are still a maid, to-morrow you will be a married woman, and the day after that your husband will fetch you with six carts and forty-eight oxen and a gipsy band and all his friends to escort you to your new home, just as every married woman in the country is fetched from her parents' home the day after she has spoken her marriage vows. After that your happiness will begin: you will soon forget the wretched life you have had to lead for years, helping me to put maize into a helpless invalid's mouth."

"I shall never forget my home, dear mother," said Elsa

65

earnestly, "and every fillér which I earned and which helped to make my poor father comfortable was a source of happiness to me."

"Hm!" grunted the mother dryly, "you have not looked these past two years as if those sources of happiness agreed with you."

"I shall look quite happy in the future, mother," retorted Elsa cheerily; "especially when I have seen you and father installed in that nice house in the Kender Road, with your garden and your cows and your pigs and a maid to wait on you."

"Yes," said Irma naïvely, "Béla promised me all that if I gave you to him: and I think that he is honest and will keep to his promise."

Then, as Elsa was silent, she continued fussily:

"There, now, I think I had better go over to the schoolroom and see that everything is going on all right. I don't altogether trust Ilona and her parsimonious ways. Such airs she gives herself, too! I must go and show her that, whatever Béla may have told her, I am the hostess at the banquet to-day, and mean to have things done as I like and not as she may choose to direct. ... Now mind you don't allow your father to disarrange his clothes. Móritz and the others will be here by about eleven, and then you can arrange the bunda round him after they have fixed the carrying-poles to his chair. We sit down to eat at twelve o'clock, and I will come back to fetch you a quarter of an hour before that, so that you may walk down the street and enter the banqueting place in the company of your mother, as it is fitting that you should do. And don't let anyone see you before then: for that is not proper. When you fix the bunda round your father's shoulders, make all the men go out of the house before you enter the room. Do you understand?"

"Yes, mother."

"You know how particular Béla is that everything should be done in orderly and customary style, don't you?"

"Yes, mother," replied Elsa, without the slightest touch of irony; "I know how much he always talks about propriety."

"Though you are not his wife," continued Irma volubly, "and won't be until to-morrow, you must begin to-day to obey him in all things. And you must try and be civil to Klara Goldstein, and not make Béla angry by putting on grand, stiff airs with the woman."

"I will do my best, mother dear," said Elsa, with a quick short sigh.

"Good-bye, then," concluded Irma, as she finally turned toward the door, "don't crumple your petticoats when you sit down, and don't go too near the hearth, there is some grease upon it from this morning's breakfast. Don't let anyone see you and wait quietly for my return."

Having delivered herself of these admonitions, which she felt were incumbent upon her in her interesting capacity as the mother of an important bride, Irma at last sailed out of the door. Elsa—obedient to her mother and to convention, did not remain standing beneath the lintel as she would have loved to do on this beautiful summer morning, but drew back into the stuffy room, lest prying eyes should catch sight of the heroine of the day before her state entry into the banqueting hall.

With a weary little sigh she set about thinking what she could do to kill the next two hours before Móritz and Jenö and those other kind lads came to take her father away. With the door shut the room was very dark: only a small modicum of light penetrated through the solitary, tiny window. Elsa drew a chair close beside it and brought out her mending basket and work-box. But before settling down she went back into the sleeping-room to see that the invalid was not needing her.

Of course he always needed her, and more especially to-day, one of the last that she would spend under his roof. He was not tearful about her departure—his senses were too blunt now to feel the grief of separation—he only felt pleasantly excited, because he had been told that Móritz and Jenö and the others were coming over presently and that they meant to carry him in his chair, just as he was, so that he could be present at his daughter's "maiden's farewell." This had greatly elated him: he was looking forward to the rich food and the luscious wine which his rich future son-in-law was providing for his guests.

And now, when Elsa came to him, dressed in all her pretty finery, he loved to look on her, and his dulled eyes glowed with an enthusiasm which had lain atrophied in him these past two years.

He was like a child now with a pretty doll, and Elsa, delighted at the pleasure which she was giving him, turned about and around, allowed him to examine her beautiful petticoats, to look at her new red boots and to touch with his lifeless fingers the beads of solid gold which her fiancé had given her.

Suddenly, while she was thus displaying her finery for the benefit of her paralytic father, she heard the loud bang of the cottage door. Someone had entered, someone with a heavy footstep which resounded through the thin partition between the two rooms.

She thought it must be one of the young men, perhaps, with the poles for the carrying-chair; and she wondered vaguely why he had come so early.

She explained to the invalid that an unexpected visitor had come, and that she must go and see what he wanted; and then, half ashamed that someone should see her contrary to her mother's express orders and to all the proprieties, she went to the door and opened it.

The visitor had not closed the outer door when he had entered, and thus a gleam of brilliant September daylight shot straight into the narrow room; it revealed the tall figure of a man dressed in town clothes, who stood there for all the world as if he had a perfect right to do so, and who looked straight on Elsa as she appeared before him in the narrow frame of the inner door.

His face was in full light. She recognized him in the instant.

But she could not utter his name, she could not speak; her heart began to beat so fast that she felt that she must choke.

The next moment his arms were round her, he kicked the outer door to with his foot, and then he dragged her further into the room; he called her name, and all the while he was laughing—laughing with the glee of a man who feels himself to be supremely happy.

# CHAPTER XII

## "It is too late"

And now there he was, as of old, sitting, as was his wont, on the corner of the table, his two strong hands firmly grasping Elsa's wrists. She held him a little at arm's length, frightened still at the suddenness of his apparition here—on this day—the day of her farewell feast.

When first he drew her to him, she had breathed his name—softly panting with excitement, "Andor!"

The blood had rushed to her cheeks, and then flowed back to her heart, leaving her pale as a lily. She did not look at him any more after that first glance, but held her head bent, and her eyes fixed to the ground. Slowly the tears trickled down her cheeks one by one.

But he did not take his glowing, laughing eyes away from her, though he, too, was speechless after that first cry of joy:

"Elsa!"

He held her wrists and in a happy, irresponsible way was

swinging her arms out and in, all the while that he was drinking in the joy of seeing her again.

Surely she was even more beautiful than she had ever been before. He did not notice that she was dressed as for a feast, he did not heed that she held her head down and that heavy tears fell from her eyes. He had caught the one swift look from her blue eyes when she first recognized him: he had seen the blush upon her cheeks then; the look and the blush had told him all that he wanted to know, for they had revealed her soul to him. Manlike, he looked no further. Happiness is such a natural thing for wretched humanity to desire, that it is so much easier to believe in it than in misery when it comes.

At last he contrived to say a few words.

"Elsa! how are you, my dove?" he said naïvely.

"I am quite well, thank you, Andor," she murmured through her tears.

Then she tried to draw her wrists out of his tenacious clutch.

"May I not kiss you, Elsa?" he asked, with a light, happy laugh—the laugh of a man sure of himself, and sure of the love which will yield him the kiss.

"If you like, Andor," she replied.

She could not have denied him the kiss, not just then, at any rate, not even though every time that his warm lips found her eyes, her cheeks, her neck, she felt such a pain in her heart that surely she thought that she must die of it.

After that he let her wrists go, and she went to sit on a low stool, some little distance away from him. Her cheeks were glowing now, and it was no use trying to disguise her tears. Andor saw them, of course, but he did not seem upset by them: he knew that girls were so different to men, so much more sensitive and tender: and so now he was only chiding himself for his roughness.

"I ought to have prepared you for my coming, Elsa," he said. "I am afraid it has upset you."

"No, no, Andor, it's nothing," she protested.

"I did want to surprise you," he continued naïvely. "Not that I ever really doubted you, Elsa, even though you never wrote to me. I thought letters do get astray sometimes, and I was not going to let any accursed post spoil my happiness."

"No, of course not, Andor."

"You did not write to me, did you, Elsa?" he asked.

"No, Andor. I did not write."

"But you had my letter? ... I mean the one which I wrote to you before I sailed for Australia."

"The postman," she murmured, "gave it to father when it

69

came. Then the next day father was stricken with paralysis; he never gave it to me. Only last night ..."

"My God," he broke in excitedly, "and yet you remained true to me all this while, even though you did not know if I was alive or dead! Holy Mother of God, what have I done to deserve such happiness?"

Then as she did not speak—for indeed the words in her throat were choked by her tears—he continued talking volubly, like a man who is intoxicated with the wine of joy:

"Oh! I never doubted you, Elsa! But I had planned my home-coming to be a surprise to you. It was not a question of keeping faith, of course, because you were never tokened to me, therefore I just wanted to read in your dear eyes exactly what would come into them in the first moment of surprise ... whether it would be joy or annoyance, love or indifference. And I was not deceived, Elsa, for when you first saw me such a look came into your eyes as I would not exchange for all the angels glances in Paradise."

Elsa sighed heavily. She felt so oppressed that she thought her heart must burst. Andor's happiness, his confidence made the hideous truth itself so much more terrible to reveal. And now he went on in the same merry, voluble way.

"I went first to Goldstein's this morning. I thought Klara would tell me some of the village gossip to while away the time before I dared present myself here. I didn't want Pali bácsi or anybody to see me before I had come to you. I didn't want anybody to speak to me before I had kissed you. The Jews I didn't mind, of course. So I got Klara to walk with me by a round-about way through the fields as far as this house; then I lay in wait for a while, until I saw Irma néni go out. I wanted you all to myself at once ... with no one by to intercept the look which you would give me when first you recognized me."

"And ... did Klara tell you anything?" she murmured under her breath.

"She told me of uncle Pali's illness," he said, more quietly, "and how he seemed to have fretted about me lately ... and that everyone here thought that I was dead."

"Yes. What else?"

"Nothing else much," he replied, "for you may be sure I would not do more than just mention your sweet name before that Jewess."

"And ... when you mentioned my name ... did she say anything?"

"No. She laughed rather funnily, I thought. But of course I

would not take any notice. She had always been rather jealous of you. And now that I am a rich man ..."

"Yes, Andor?"

"When I say a rich man," he said, with a careless shrug of his broad shoulders, "I only mean comparatively, of course. I have saved three thousand crowns"—(about £120)—"not quite as much as I should have liked; but things are dear out there, and there was my passage home and clothes to pay for. Still! three thousand crowns are enough to pay down as a guarantee for a really good farm, and if Klara Goldstein spoke the truth, and Pali bácsi is really so well disposed toward me, why, I need not be altogether ashamed to present myself before your parents. Need I, my dove?"

"Before my parents?" she murmured.

"Why, yes," he said, as he rose from the table now and came up quite close to her, looking down with earnest, love-filled eyes on the stooping figure of this young girl, who held all his earthly happiness in her keeping; "you knew what I meant, Elsa, did you not, when I came back to you the moment that I could, after all these years? It was only my own poverty which kept me from your side all this long while. But you did not think that I had forgotten you, did you, Elsa?—you could not think that. How could a man forget you who has once held you in his arms and kissed those sweet lips of yours? Why, there has not been a day or night that I did not think of you. ... Night and day while I worked in that land which seemed so far away from home. Homesick I was—very often—and though we all earned good money out there, the work was hard and heavy; but I didn't mind that, for I was making money, and every florin which I put by was like a step which brought me nearer to you."

"Andor!"

The poor girl was almost moaning now, for every word which he spoke was like a knife-thrust straight into her heart.

"Being so far away from home," he continued, speaking slowly and very earnestly now, in a voice that quivered and shook with the depth of the sentiment within him, "being so far away from home would have been like hell to me at times. I don't know what there is, Elsa, about this land of Hungary! how it holds and enchains us! but at times I felt that I must lie down and die if I did not see our maize-fields bordered with the tall sunflowers, our distant, low-lying horizon on which the rising and the setting sun paints such glowing colours. This land of Australia was beautiful too: there were fine fields of corn and vast lands stretching out as far as the eye could reach; but it was not Hungary. There were no white oxen with long, slender horns toiling patiently up the dusty high roads, the storks

71

did not build their nests in the tall acacia trees, nor did the arms of distant wells stretch up toward the sky. It was not Hungary, Elsa! and it would have been hell but for thinking of you. The life of an exile takes all the life out of one. I have heard of some of our Hungarian lads out in America who get so ill with homesickness that they either die or become vicious. But then," he added, with a quick, characteristic return to his habitual light-hearted gaiety, "it isn't everyone who is far from home who has such a bright star as I had to gaze at in my mind ... when it came night time and the lights were put out ..."

"Andor!" she pleaded.

But he would not let her speak just then. He had not yet told her all that there was to say, and perhaps the innate good-heartedness in him suggested that she was discomposed, that she would prefer to sit quietly and listen whilst she collected her thoughts and got over the surprise of his sudden arrival.

"Do you know, Elsa," he now said gaily, "I chalked up the days—made marks, I mean, in a book which I bought in Fiume the day before we sailed. Seven hundred and thirty days—for I never meant to stay away more than two years; and every evening in my bunk on board ship and afterwards in the farm where I lodged, I scratched out one of the marks and seemed to feel myself getting a little bit nearer and then nearer to you. By the Saints, my dove," he added, with a merry laugh, "but you should have seen me the time I got cheated out of one of those scratches. I had forgotten that accursed twenty-ninth of February last year. I don't think that I have ever sworn so wickedly in my life before. I had to go to Melbourne pretty soon, I tell you, and make confession of it to the kind Pater there. And then ..."

He paused abruptly. The laughter died upon his lips and the look of gaiety out of his eyes, for Elsa sat more huddled up in herself than before. He could no longer see her face, for that was hidden in her hands, he only saw her bowed shoulders, and that they were shaking as if the girl had yielded at last to a paroxysm of weeping.

"Elsa!" he said quietly, as a puzzled frown appeared between his brows, "Elsa! ... you don't say anything ... you ... you ..."

He passed his rough hand across his forehead, on which rose heavy beads of perspiration. For the first time in the midst of his joy and of his happiness a hideous doubt had begun to assail him.

A hideous, horrible, poison-giving doubt!

"Elsa!" he pleaded, and his voice grew more intense, as if behind it there was an undercurrent of broken sobs, "Elsa, what is the matter? You are not going to turn your back on me, are you? Look at me, Elsa! look at me! You wouldn't do it, would you ... you wouldn't do it? ... The Lord forgive me, but I love you, Elsa ... I love you fit to kill."

He was babbling like a child, and now he fell on his knees beside that low stool on which she sat hunched up, a miserable bundle of suffering womanhood. He hid his face in her petticoats—those beautiful, starched petticoats that were not to be crumpled—and all at once his manliness broke down in the face of this awful, awful doubt, and he sobbed as if his heart would break.

"Andor! Andor!" she cried, overwhelmed with pity for him, pity for herself, with the misery and the hopelessness of it all. "Andor, I beg of you, pull yourself together. Someone might come ... they must not see you like this."

She put her hand upon his head and passed her cool, white fingers through his hair. The gentle, motherly gesture soothed him: her words brought him back to his senses. Gradually his sobs were stilled; he made a great effort to become quite calm, and with a handkerchief wiped the tears and perspiration from his face.

Then he rose and went back to the table, and sat down on the corner of it as he always liked to do. The workings of his face showed the effort which he made to keep his excitement and those awful fears in check.

"You are quite right, Elsa," he said calmly. "Someone might come, and it would not be a very fine home-coming for Lakatos Andor, would it? to be found crying like an infant into a woman's petticoats. Why, what would they think? That we had quarrelled, perhaps, on this my first day at home. God forgive me, I quite lost myself that time, didn't I? It was foolish," he added, with heartbroken anxiety, "wasn't it, Elsa?"

"Yes, Andor," she said simply.

"It was foolish," he reiterated, still speaking calmly, even though his voice was half-choked with sobs, "it was foolish to think that you would turn your back on a fellow who had just lived these past five years for you."

"It isn't that, Andor," she murmured.

"It isn't that?" he repeated dully, and once more the frown of awful puzzlement appeared between his dark, inquiring eyes. "Then what is it? No, no, Elsa!" he added quickly, seeing that she threw a quick look of pathetic anxiety upon him, "don't be afraid, my dove. I am not going to make a fool of myself again. You ... you are not prepared to marry me just now, perhaps ... not just yet?—is that it? ... You have been angry with me. ... I am not surprised at that ... you never got my letter ... you thought that I had forgotten you ... and you want to get more used to me now that I am back ... before we are properly tokened. ... Is that it, Elsa? ... I'll have to wait, eh?—till

73

the spring, perhaps ... till we have known one another better again ... then ... perhaps ..."

He was speaking jerkily, and always with that burning anxiety lurking in the tone of his voice. But now he suddenly cried out like a poor creature in pain, vehemently, appealingly, longing for one word of comfort, one brief respite from this intolerable misery.

"But you don't speak, Elsa! ... you don't speak. ... My God, why don't you speak?"

And she replied slowly, monotonously, for now she seemed to have lost even the power of suffering pain. It was all so hopeless, so dreary, so desolate.

"I can never marry you, Andor."

He stared at her almost like one demented, or as if he thought that she, perhaps, had lost her reason.

"I can never marry you," she repeated firmly, "for I am tokened to Erös Béla. My farewell banquet is to-day; to-morrow is my wedding day; the day after I go to my new home. I can never marry you, Andor. It is too late."

She watched him while she spoke, vaguely wondering within her poor, broken heart when that cry of agony would escape his lips. His face had become ghastly in hue, his mouth was wide open as if ready for that cry; his twitching fingers clutched at the neckband of his shirt.

But the cry never came: the wound was too deep and too deadly for outward expression. He said nothing, and gradually his mouth closed and his fingers ceased to twitch. Presently he rose, went to the door, and pulled it open; he stood for a moment under the lintel, his arm leaning against the frame of the door, and the soft September breeze blew against his face and through his hair.

From far away down the village street came the sound of laughter and of singing. The people of Marosfalva were very merry to-day, for it was Kapus Elsa's wedding time and Erös Béla was being lavish with food and wine and music. Nobody guessed that in this one cottage sorrow, deep and lasting, had made a solemn entry and never meant to quit these two loving hearts again.

# CHAPTER XIII

## "He must make you happy"

Andor shut the door once more. He did not want the people of the village to see him just now.

He turned back quietly into the room, and went to sit at his usual place, across the corner of the table. Elsa, mechanically, absently, as one whose mind and soul and heart are elsewhere, was smoothing out the creases in her gown made wet by Andor's tears.

"How did it all come about, Elsa?" he asked.

"Well, you know," she replied listlessly, "since Klara Goldstein told you—that everyone here believed that you were dead. I did not believe it myself for a long time, though I did think that if you had lived you would have written to me. Then, as I had no news from you ... no news ... and mother always wished me to marry Béla ... why! I thought that since you were dead nothing really mattered, and I might as well do what my mother wished."

"My God!" he muttered under his breath.

"We were so poor at home," she continued, in that same listless, apathetic voice, for indeed she seemed to have lost all capacity even for suffering, "and father was so ill ... he wanted comfort and good food, and mother and I could earn so very little ... Béla promised mother that nice house in the Kender Road, he promised to give her cows and pigs and chickens. ... What could I do? It is sinful not to obey your parents ... and it seemed so selfish of me to nurse thoughts of one whom I thought dead, when I could give my own mother and father all the comforts they wanted just by doing what they wished. ... I had to think of father and mother, Andor. ... What could I do?"

"That is so, Elsa," he assented, speaking very slowly and deliberately. ... "That is so, of course ... I understand ... I ought to have known ... to have guessed something of the kind at any rate. ... My God!" he added, with renewed vehemence, "but I do seem to have been an accursed fool!—thinking that everything would go on just the same while I was weaving my dreams out there on the other side of the globe. ... I ought to have guessed, I suppose, that they wouldn't leave you alone ... you the prettiest girl in the county. ..."

"I held out as long as I could. ... But I felt that if you were dead nothing really mattered."

"My poor little dove," he whispered gently.

Gradually he felt a great calmness descending over him. It was

75

her helplessness that appealed to him, the pathos of her quiet resignation: he felt how mean and unmanly it would be to give way to that rebellious rage which was burning in his veins. Three years under the orders of ofttimes brutal petty officers had taught him a measure of self-restraint; the two further years of hard, unceasing toil under foreign climes, the patient amassing of florin upon florin to enable him to come back and claim the girl whom he loved, had completed the work of changing an irresponsible, untrammelled child of these Hungarian plains into a strong, well-balanced, well-controlled man of a wider world. His first instinct, when the terrible blow had been struck to all his hopes and all his happiness, had been the wild, unreasoning desire to strike back, and to kill. Had he been left to himself just then and then found himself face to face with the man who had robbed him of Elsa, the semi-civilization of the past five years would have fallen away from him, he would once more have relapsed into the primeval, unfettered state of his earlier manhood. The crude passions of these sons of the soil are only feebly held in check by the laws of their land: at times they break through their fetters, and then they are a law unto themselves.

But Andor loved Elsa with a gentler and purer love than usually dwells in the heart of a man of his stamp. He had proved this during the past five years spent in daily, hourly thoughts of her. Now that he found her in trouble, he would not add to her burden by parading his own before her.

Manlike, his first thought had been to kill, his second to seize his love with both arms and to carry her away with him, away from this village, from this land, if need be. After all, she was not yet a wife, and the promise of marriage is not so sacred nor yet so binding as a marriage vow.

He could carry her away, leaving the scandal-mongers to work their way with her and him: he could carry her to that far-off land which he knew already, where work was hard and money plentiful, and no one would have the right to look down on her for what she had done. But seeing her there, looking so helpless and so pathetic, he knew, by that unerring intuition which only comes to a man at such times as this, that such a dream could never be fulfilled. The future was as it was, as no doubt it had been pre-ordained by God and by Fate: nothing that he could do or say now would have the power to alter it. Tradition, filial duty and perhaps a certain amount of womanly weakness too, were all ranged up against him; but filial duty would fight harder than anything else and would remain the conqueror in the end.

The relentless hand of the Inevitable was already upon him, and because of it, because of that vein of Oriental fatalism which survives in every Hungarian peasant, the tumult in his soul had already subsided, and he was able to speak to Elsa now with absolute gentleness.

"So to-day is your maiden's farewell, is it?" he asked after awhile.

"Yes! It must be getting late," she said, as she rose from the low stool and shook out her many starched skirts, "mother will be back directly to fetch me for the feast."

"It will be in the schoolroom, I suppose," he said indifferently.

"Yes. And some of the lads are coming over presently to fetch father. They have arranged to carry him all the way. Isn't it good of them?"

"To carry him all the way?" he asked, puzzled.

"Father has not moved for two years," she said simply; "he was stricken with paralysis, you know."

"Ah, yes! Klara told me something about that."

"So in order to give me the pleasure of having father near me at my farewell feast, Móritz and Jenö and Imre and Jankó are going to fasten long poles to his chair and carry him to the schoolroom and back. Isn't it good of them? And I think they mean to do the same thing to-morrow and carry him to church. We are going to put his bunda round his shoulders. He has not worn his bunda for two years. ... It was yesterday, when I took it out in order to mend it, that I found the letter which you wrote me from Fiume. It had slipped between the pocket and the lining and ..."

"And are you happy, Elsa?" he broke in abruptly.

She hesitated almost imperceptibly for a moment, then she said quietly:

"Yes, Andor. I am fairly happy."

"Béla?" he asked again. "Is he fond of you?"

"I think so."

"You are not sure?"

"Oh, yes!" she said more firmly, "I am quite sure."

"He hasn't taken to drinking, has he? ... He was a little inclined that way at one time."

"Oh!" she said, with a shrug of her shoulders, "I don't think that he drinks more than other fellows of his age."

She went over to the window and somewhat ostentatiously, he thought, began turning over the contents of her work-box. There was something in her attitude now which worried him, and she seemed more determined than ever not to look him straight in the face.

"Elsa! I shall think the worst if you tell me nothing," he said firmly.

"There is nothing to tell, Andor."

"Yes, there is," he persisted; "there is something about Béla which makes you unhappy and which you won't tell me. ... Now, listen to me, Elsa, for I mean every word which I am going to say ... I can bring myself to the point of seeing you married to another man and happy in your new home, even though my own heart will break in the process ... but what I could never stand would be to see you married to another man and made unhappy by him. ... So if you won't tell me what is on your mind with regard to Béla, I will pick a quarrel with him this afternoon, and kill him if I can."

"Don't talk so wildly, Andor," she said, as she turned and faced him, for she was a little frightened at his earnestness and knew that he had it in him to act just as he said he would. "The whole thing is only foolishness on my part, I know."

"Then there is something?" he persisted obstinately.

"Well!" she said, after a little more hesitation, "it's only that he will go hanging about at the Goldsteins' all the time."

"Oh! it's Klara, is it?"

"I can't bear that girl," said Elsa, with sudden vehemence.

He looked at her keenly.

"You are jealous, Elsa," he said. "Is it because you love Béla?"

"I don't like his hanging round Klara," she replied evasively.

He rose from the table, drawing in his breath as he did so, with a curious hissing sound; perhaps the pain which he felt now was harder to bear even than that caused by the first crushing blow. The Inevitable had indeed placed its cruel hand upon his happiness; not all the boundless wealth of his love, of his will and of his daring could ever give Elsa back to him again.

"I had better go now, I suppose," he said.

"Mother will be here directly," she replied, "won't you see her?"

"Not just yet, I think. I thought of asking Pater Bonifácius if he could give me a bed for a night. Pali bácsi might not be ready for me yet."

"But you will come to my farewell feast?" asked Elsa, with that unconscious cruelty of which good women are so often capable.

"If you wish it, Elsa," he replied.

"I do wish it," she said, "and everyone will be so happy to see you. They would think it strange if you did not come, for everyone will know by then that you have returned."

"Then I will come," he concluded.

He went up to her and held out his hand; she put her own upon it. Of course he did not ask for a kiss; he had no longer a right to that. Somehow, in the last few moments a barrier seemed to have sprung up between him and her which had obliterated all the past.

78

He was a stranger now to her and she to him; that day five years ago was as if it had never been. Béla and her plighted troth to him stood now between Andor and that past which he must forget.

But as he stood now holding her hand, he looked at her earnestly, and her blue eyes, dimmed but serene, met his own gaze without flinching.

"The past, Elsa," he said, "is done with. Henceforth we shall be nothing to one another. You will forget me easily enough. ... I wish that I had never come back to disturb the peace which I see is rapidly spreading over your life. My only wish now is that with you it should be peace. My heart has already given you up to Béla—but not unconditionally, mind. ... He must make you happy ... I tell you that he must," he reiterated, almost fiercely. "If he does not, he will have to reckon with me. Heaven help him, I say, if he is ever unkind to you. ... I shall see it, I shall know it. ... I shall not leave this village till I am assured that he means to be kind—that he is kind to you, even though my heart should break in remaining a witness to your happiness."

He stooped, and with the innate chivalry peculiar to the Hungarian peasantry, he kissed the small, cold hand which trembled in his grasp: he kissed it as a noble lord would kiss the hand of a princess. Then, without looking on her again, he walked quietly out of the house, and Elsa was alone with yet another bitter-sweet memory to add to her store of regrets.

# CHAPTER XIV

## "It is true"

By the time that Andor turned the corner of the house into the street, he found that the news of his arrival had already spread through the village like wildfire. Klara Goldstein's ready tongue had been at work this past hour; she had quickly disseminated the news that the wanderer had come home. She did not say that the malice and love of mischief in her had caused her to say nothing to Andor about Elsa's coming wedding. She merely told the first neighbour whom she came across that Lakatos Andor had come back, just as she, for one, had always declared that he would.

Andor's friends had assembled in the street in a trice; here was too glorious an opportunity to shout and to sing and to make merry, to be lightly missed. And Andor had always been popular before. He was doubly so now that he had come back from America or wherever he may have been, and had made a fortune there; he shook one hundred and fifty hands before he could walk as far as the presbytery. The gypsies who had just arrived by train from Arad were not allowed to proceed straight to the schoolroom. They were made to pause in the great open place before the church, made to unpack their instruments then and there, and to strike up the Rákóczy March without more ado, in honour of the finest son of Marosfalva, who had been thought dead by some, and had returned safe and sound to his native corner of the earth.

It was with much difficulty that at last Andor succeeded in effecting his escape and running away from the series of ovations which greeted him when and wherever he was recognized. The women embraced him without further ado, the men worried him to tell them some of his adventures then and there. Above all, everyone wanted to hear how very much more wretched, uncomfortable and God-forsaken the rest of the wide, wide world was in comparison with Hungary in general and the village of Marosfalva in particular.

The heartfelt, if noisy, greetings of his old friends had the effect of soothing Andor's aching heart. The sight of his native village, the scent of the air, the dust of the road acted as a slight compensation for the heavy load of sorrow which otherwise would hopelessly have weighed him down.

With a final wave of his hat he disappeared from the enraptured gaze of his friends into the cool quietude of the presbytery garden. He stood still for a moment behind a huge clump of tall sunflowers and gaudy dahlias to recover his breath and rearrange his coat, which had been mishandled quite a good deal by his friends in the excess of their joy.

From the other side of the low gate came the buzz of animated talk, his own name oft-repeated, cries of surprise and of pleasure, when the news reached some late-comers, and through it all the soft, pathetic murmur of the gipsies' fiddles; they had lapsed from the inspiriting strains of the Rákóczy March to one of the dreamy Magyar love-songs which suited their own languid Oriental temperament far better than the martial music.

But here, in the small presbytery garden, the world seemed to have slipped back an hundred years or more. Perfect peace! the drowsing of flies and wasps, the call of thrushes, the crackling of tiny twigs in the branches of the old acacia tree in the corner! Only the flies and the birds and the flowers seemed to live, and the air was heavy with the pungent odour of the sunflowers.

Andor drew a long breath. He seemed suddenly to wake from a long, long dream. It was just over five years ago that he had stood one morning just like this in this little garden; the late roses had not then ceased to bloom. It was the day before he had to leave Marosfalva in order to become a soldier, and he had come after Mass to say a private good-bye to the kind priest.

Now it seemed as if those five years were just one long dream—the soldiering, the voyage across the sea, the two years in a strange, strange land, all culminating in that awful cataclysm which had for ever robbed him of happiness.

It seemed as if it could not all be true, as if Elsa was even now waiting for him to go out for a walk under the acacia trees as she had done on that morning five years ago. Even now he pulled the bell as he had done then, and now—as then—Pater Bonifácius himself came to the door.

His old housekeeper had already brought the news to the presbytery of Andor's home-coming, and the old Pater was overjoyed at seeing the lad—now become so strong and so manly. He took Andor to his heart, chiefly because he would not have the lad see the tears which had so quickly come to his eyes.

"It is true then, Pater," said Andor, when he had followed the old man into the little parlour all littered with papers and books. "It is true, or you would not have cried when first you embraced me."

"What is true, my son?" asked the Pater.

"That Elsa is to marry Erös Béla to-morrow?"

"Yes, my son, that is true," said the priest simply.

And thus Andor knew that, at any rate, the hideous present was not a dream.

# CHAPTER XV

## "That is fair, I think"

An hour later, Andor was in the street with the rest of the village folk, watching Elsa as she walked up toward the schoolroom in the company of her mother. Her fair hair shone like the gold beads round her neck, and her starched petticoats swung out from her hips as she walked.

She held her head a little downcast; people thought this most becoming in a young bride; but Andor, who stood in the forefront of the spectators as she passed, saw that she held her head down because her cheeks were pale and her eyes swollen with tears.

Irma néni walked beside her daughter with the proud air of a queen, and on ahead Barna Móritz, the mayor's second son, Fehér Jenö, whose father worked the water-mill on the Maros, and two other sturdy fellows were carrying the bride's paralysed father shoulder high in his chair.

Just as the little procession halted for a moment before entering the white washed school-house, Erös Béla, the bridegroom and hero of the hour, appeared, coming from the opposite direction, and with Klara Goldstein, the Jewess, upon his arm.

Klara—arrayed in fashionable town garments, with a huge hat covered in feathers, a tight modern skirt that forced her to walk with mincing steps, high-heeled shoes, open-work stockings and gloves reaching to the elbow—was indeed a curious apparition in amongst these peasant girls, with their bare heads and high red-leather boots and petticoats standing round them like balloons.

Andor frowned heavily when he caught sight of her; he had seen that Elsa's pale cheeks had become almost livid in hue and that her parted lips trembled as if she were ready to cry.

The looks that were cast by the village folk upon the Jewess were none too kindly, and there were audible mutterings of disapproval at Erös Béla's conduct; but neither looks nor mutterings disconcerted Klara Goldstein in the least. She knew well enough that envy of her fashionable attire bore a large share in the ill-will which was displayed against her, and the handsome Jewess, who so often had to bear the contempt and the sneers of these Magyar peasants whom she despised, was delighted that Erös Béla's admiration for her had induced him to give her an opportunity of queening it for once amongst them all.

She felt that she shone in her splendour in comparison with the pale-faced bride in all her village finery. She carried a sunshade and a reticule, her dark hair was arranged in frisettes under her broad-brimmed hat; she knew that the men were casting admiring glances on her, and in any case, for the moment, she was the centre of universal observation.

Whilst some of the young men were engaged in carrying old Kapus into the house, a proceeding which kept the festive throng waiting outside, she tripped up daintily to Elsa, and said in soft, cooing tones:

82

"It was kind of you, my dear Elsa, to include me among your personal friends on such an important occasion. As the young Count was saying to me only last night, 'You will give Irma néni and little Elsa vast pleasure by your presence at the child's maiden's farewell, and mind you wear that lovely hat which I admire so much.' So affable, the young Count, is he not? He told me that nothing would do but when I get married he must come himself to every feast in connection with my wedding."

But once she had delivered these several little pointed shafts, Klara Goldstein was far too clever to wait for a retort. Before Elsa, whose simple mind was not up to a stinging repartee, could think of something indifferent or not too ungracious to say, the handsome Jewess had already spied Andor's face among the crowd.

"There is the hero of the hour, Béla," she said, turning to the bridegroom, who had stood by surly and defiant; "these past five years have not changed him much, eh? ... Your future wife's old sweetheart," she added, with a malicious little laugh; "are you not pleased to see him?"

Then, as Béla somewhat clumsily, and with a pretence at cordiality which he was far from feeling, went up to Andor and held out his hand to him, Klara continued glibly:

"Poor old Andor! he is a trifle glum now. I never told him that his sweetheart was getting married to-morrow. Never mind, my little Andor," she added, turning her expressive dark eyes with a knowing look upon the young man; "there is more fish in the Maros than has come out of it. And I thought that you would prefer to get the truth direct from our pretty Elsa!"

"I think you did quite right, Klara," said Andor indifferently.

But in the meanwhile Béla had contrived to come up quite close to Elsa, and to whisper hurriedly in her ear:

"A bargain's a bargain, my dove!—you behave amiably to Klara Goldstein and I will keep a civil tongue in my head for your old sweetheart. ... That is fair, I think, eh, Irma néni?" he added, turning to the old woman.

"Don't be foolish, Béla," retorted Kapus Irma dryly. "Why you should be for ever teasing Elsa, I cannot think. You must know that all girls feel upset at these times, and as like as not you'll make her cry at her own feast. And that would be a fine disgrace for us all!"

"Don't be afraid, mother," said Elsa quietly; "I don't feel the least like crying."

"That's splendid," exclaimed Béla, with ostentatious gaiety. "Here's Irma néni trying to teach me something about girls. As if I didn't know about them all that there is to know. Eh, Andor, you agree with me, don't you?" he added, turning to the other man. "We men know more about women's moods and little tempers than their own mothers do. What? Now, Irma néni, take your daughter into the house. There is a clatter of dishes and bottles going on inside there which is very pleasant to the stomach. Miss Klara, will you honour me by accepting my arm? Friends, come in all, will you? All those, I mean, whom my wife that is to be has invited to her last girlhood's entertainment. Irma néni, do lead the way. Elsa looks quite pale for want of food—she had her breakfast very early, I suppose, and got tired dressing for this great occasion. Andor, you shall sit next to Elsa if you like. ... You must have lots to tell her. Your adventures among the cannibals and the lions and tigers. ... Eh? ... And Irma néni shall sit next to you on the other side, and don't let her have more wine than is good for her. Whew! but it is hot already! Come along, friends. By thunder, Klara, but that is a fine hat you have got on."

He talked on very volubly and at the top of his voice, making ostentatious efforts to appear jovial and amiable to everyone; but Erös Béla was no fool: he knew quite well that his attitude toward his bride and toward Klara the Jewess was causing many adverse comments to go round among his friends. But he was in a mood not to care. He was determined that everyone should know and see that he was the master here to-day, just as he meant to be master in his house throughout the years to come. Like every self-enriched peasant, he attached an enormous importance to wealth, and was inclined to have a contempt for the less fortunate folk who had not risen out of their humble sphere as he had done.

His wealth, he thought, had placed him above everyone else in Marosfalva, and above the unwritten laws of traditions and proprieties which are of more account in an Hungarian village than all the codes framed by the Parliament which sits in Budapesth. He was proud of his wealth, proud of his education, his book-learning and knowledge of the world, and reckoned that these gave him the right to be a law unto himself. His naturally domineering and masterful temperament completed his claim to be considered the head man of Marosfalva.

The Hungarian peasants are ready enough to give deference where deference is exacted, but, having given it, their cordial friendship dies away. They acknowledged a social barrier more readily, perhaps, than any other peasantry in Europe, but having once acknowledged it, they will not admit that either party can stand on both sides of it at one and the same time.

So now, though Erös Béla was flouting the local traditions and proprieties by his attentions to Klara Goldstein, no one thought of openly opposing him. Everyone was ready enough to accept his actions, as they would those of their social superiors—the gentlemen of Arad, the Pater, my lord the Count himself, but they were not ready to accept his cordiality nor to extend to him their simple-minded and open-hearted friendship.

The presence of the Jewess did not please them—she was a stranger and an alien—she looked like a creature from another world with her tight skirts, high-heeled shoes and huge, feathered hat. No one felt this more keenly than Andor, whose heart had warmed out—despite its pain—at sight of all his friends, their national costumes, their music, their traditions—all of which had been out of his life for so long.

He felt that Klara's presence on this occasion was in itself an outrage upon Elsa, even without Béla's conspicuously unworthy conduct. Elsa, with her tightly-plaited hair, her balloon skirts and bare neck and arms, looked ashamed beside this fashionable apparition all made up of billowy lace and clinging materials.

Andor cursed beneath his breath, and ground his heel into the dust in the impotency of his rage. He tried to remember all that the Pater had said to him half an hour ago about forbearance and about God's will.

Personally, Andor did not altogether believe that it was God's will that Elsa should be married to a man who would neither cherish her nor appreciate her as she deserved to be: and it was with a heart weighed down with foreboding as well as with sorrow that he followed the wedding party into the school-house.

# CHAPTER XVI

## "The waters of the Maros flow sluggishly"

But even the bridegroom's unconventional and reprehensible conduct had not the power to damp for long the spirits of the guests.

By the time the soup had been eaten and the glasses filled with wine, the noise in the schoolroom had already become deafening, and no person of moderate vocal calibre could have heard himself speak. The time had come for everyone to talk at the top of his or her voice, for no one to listen, and for laughter—irresponsible, immoderate laughter—to ring from end to end of the room.

The gipsies were scraping their fiddles, blowing their clarionets and banging their czimbalom with all the vigour of which they were capable. They, at any rate, were determined to be heard above the din. The leader, with his violin under his chin, had already begun his round of the two huge tables, pausing for awhile behind every chair—just long enough to play into the ear of every single guest his or her favourite song.

For thus custom demands it.

There are hundreds and hundreds of Hungarian folk-songs, and to a stranger's ear no doubt these have a great similarity among themselves, but to a Hungarian there is a world of difference in each: for to him it is the words that have a meaning. The songs are, for the most part, love-songs, and all are written in that quaint, symbolic style, full of poetic imagery, which is peculiar to the Magyar language.

When we remember that in the terrible revolution of '48, when these same Hungarian peasant lads who composed the bulk of Kossuth's followers fought against the Austrian army, and subsequently against the combined armies of Russia and of Austria, when we remember that throughout that terrible campaign they were always accompanied by their gipsy bands, we begin to realize how great a part national music plays in the national spirit of Hungary. The sweet, sad folk-songs rang in the fighting lads' ears when they fell in their hundreds before the superior arms and numbers of their powerful neighbours, they inspired them and urged them, they helped them to win while they could, and to yield only when overwhelming numbers finally crushed their powers of resistance. Gipsy musicians fell beside the young soldiers, playing to them until the last the songs that spoke to them of their village, their sweethearts and their home. And the sweet, sad strains rang in the ears of the lads when they closed their eyes in death.

And now when Andor—face to face with the first great sorrow of his life—felt as if his heart must break under it, he loved to hear the gipsy musician softly caressing the strings of his violin as he played close to his ear the sweetest, saddest melody among all the sweet, sad melodies in the Magyar tongue. It begins thus:

"A Maros vize folyik csendesen!"

"The waters of the Maros flow sluggishly—"

and it speaks of a broken-hearted lover whose sweetheart belongs to another. Andor had never cared for it before. He used to think it too sad, but now he understood it: it was attuned to his mood, and the soft sound of the instrument helped him to keep his ever-growing wrath in check, even while he was watching Elsa's pale, tearful face.

She had made pathetic efforts to remain cheerful and not to listen to Klara's strident voice and loud, continuous laughter. Béla had practically confined his attentions to the Jewess, and Elsa tried not to show how ashamed she was at being so openly neglected on this occasion. She should have been the queen of the feast, of course; the bridegroom's thoughts should have been only for her; everyone's eyes should have been turned on her. Instead of which she seemed of less consequence almost than anyone else here. If it had not been for Andor, who sat next to her and who saw to her having something to eat and drink—it was little enough, God knows!—she might have sat here like a wooden doll.

Something of the respect which Erös Béla demanded as his own right encompassed her, too, already: the cordiality of the past seemed to have vanished. She was already something of a lady: "ten's asszony" (honoured madam), she would be styled by and by. And this foreknowledge, which she was gradually imbibing while everybody round her made merry, caused her almost as much sadness as Béla's indifference towards her. It seemed as if all brightness was destined to go out of her life after to-day, and it was with tear-filled eyes that she looked up now and again from her plate and gazed round upon the festive scene before her.

The whitewashed schoolroom, where on ordinary working days brown and grimy little faces were wont to pore laboriously over slates and books, presented now a very lively appearance.

Two huge trestle tables ran down its length, and thirty guests were seated on benches each side of these. The girls in all their finery wanted a deal of sitting-room, with their starched petticoats standing out over their hips, and their bare arms and necks shone with the vigorous application of yellow soap: and the smooth hair, fair and dark, had an additional lustre after the stiff brushing which it had to endure. The matrons wore darker skirts and black silk handkerchiefs tied round their heads, ending in a bow under the chin: but everywhere ribbons fluttered and beads jingled, and the men had spurs to their high boots which gave a pleasing clinking when they clapped their heels together. Overhead, hung to the ceiling, were festoons of bright pink paper roses and still brighter green glazed calico leaves; the tables were spread with linen cloths, and literally threatened to break down under the weight of pewter dishes filled with delicacies of every sort and kind—home-killed meat and home-made sausages, home-made bread and home-grown wine. The Magyar peasant is an epicure. His rich soil and excellent climate give him the best of food, and though, when times are hard, he will live readily enough on maize bread and pumpkin, he knows how to enjoy a good spread when rich friends provide it for him.

And Erös Béla had done the feast in style. Nothing was stinted. You just had to sit down and eat your fill of roast veal or roast pork, of fattened capons from his farmyard or of fogas[4] from the river, or of the scores of dishes of all kinds of good things which stood temptingly about.

No wonder that spirits were now running high. The gipsy band was quite splendid, and presently Barna Móritz, the second son of the mayor—a smart young man who would go far—was on his feet proposing the health of the bride.

Well! Of course! One mugful was not enough to do honour to such a toast, they had to be refilled and then filled up again: wine was so plentiful and so good—not heady, but just a delicious white wine which tasted of nothing but the sweet-scented grape. Soon the bridegroom rose to respond, whereupon Fehér Jenö, whose father rented the mill from my lord the Count, loudly desired that everyone should drink the health of happy, lucky Erös Béla, and then, of course, the latter had to respond again.

Elsa felt more and more every moment a stranger among them all. Fortunately the innate kindliness of these children of the soil prevented any chaffing remarks being made about the silence of the bride. It is always an understood thing that brides are shy and nervous, and though there had been known cases in Marosfalva where a bride had been very lively and talkative at her "maiden's farewell" it was, on the whole, considered more seemly to preserve a semi-tearful attitude, seeing that a girl on the eve of her marriage is saying good-bye to her parents and to her home.

The bridegroom's disgraceful conduct was tacitly ignored: it could not be resented or even commented on without quarrelling with Erös Béla, and that no one was prepared to do. You could not eat a man's salt and drink his wine and then knock him on the head, which it seemed more than one lad—who had fancied himself in love with beautiful Kapus Elsa—was sorely inclined to do.

Kapus Benkó, in his invalid's chair, sat some distance away from his daughter, the other side of Klara Goldstein. Elsa could not even exchange glances with him or see whether he had everything he wanted. Thus she seemed cut off from everyone she cared for; only Andor was near her, and of Andor she must not even think. She tried not to meet his gaze, tried hard not to feel a thrill of pleasure every time that she became actively conscious of his presence beside her.

---

[4] A kind of pike peculiar to Hungarian rivers.

And yet it was good to feel that he was there, she had a sense that she was being protected, that things could not go very wrong while he was near.

# CHAPTER XVII

## "I am here to see that you be kind to her"

Pater Bonifácius came in at about four o'clock to remind all these children of their duty to God.

To-day was the vigil of St. Michael and All Angels, there would be vespers at half-past four, and the bride and bridegroom should certainly find the time to go to church for half an hour and thank the good God for all His gifts.

The company soon made ready to go after that. Everyone there intended to go to church, and in the meanwhile the gipsies would have the remnants of the feast, after which they would instal themselves in the big barn and dancing could begin by about six.

Bride and bridegroom stood side by side, close to the door, as the guests filed out both singly and in pairs, and as they did so they shook each one by the hand, wished them good health after the repast, and begged their company for the dancing presently and the wedding feast on the morrow. Once more the invalid father, hoisted up on the shoulders of the same sturdy lads, led the procession out of the schoolhouse, then followed all the guests, helter-skelter, young men and maids, old men and matrons.

The wide petticoats got in the way, the men were over bold in squeezing the girls' waists in the general scramble, there was a deal of laughing and plenty of shouting as hot, perspiring hands were held out one by one to Elsa and to Béla, and voices, hoarse with merriment, proffered the traditional "Egésségire!" (your very good health!), and then, like so many birds let out of a cage, streamed out of the narrow door into the sunlit street.

Andor had acquitted himself of the same duty, and Elsa's cool little hand had rested for a few seconds longer than was necessary in his own brown one. She had murmured the necessary words of invitation for the ceremonies on the morrow, and he was still standing in the doorway when Klara Goldstein was about to take her leave.

Klara had stayed very ostentatiously to the last, just as if she were the most intimate friend or an actual member of the family; she had stood beside Béla during the general exodus, her small, dark head, crowned with the gorgeous picture hat, held a little on one side, her two gloved hands resting upon the handle of her parasol, her foot in its dainty shoe impatiently tapping the ground.

As the crowd passed by, scrambling in their excitement, starched petticoats crumpled, many a white shirt stained with wine, hot, perspiring and panting, a contemptuous smile lingered round her thin lips, and from time to time she made a remark to Béla—always in German, so that the village folk could not understand. But Andor, who had learned more than his native Hungarian during his wanderings abroad, heard these sneering remarks, and hated the girl for speaking them, and Béla for the loud laugh with which he greeted each sally.

Now she held out her small, thin hand to Elsa.

"Your good health, my dear Elsa!" she said indifferently.

After an obvious moment of hesitation, Elsa put her toil-worn, shapely little hand into the gloved one for an instant and quickly withdrew it again. There was a second or two of silence. Klara did not move: she was obviously waiting for the invitation which had been extended to everyone else.

A little nervously she began toying with her parasol.

"The glass is going up; you will have fine weather for your wedding to-morrow," she said more pointedly.

"I hope so," said Elsa softly.

Another awkward pause. Andor, who stood in the doorway watching the little scene, saw that Béla was digging his teeth into his underlip, and that his one eye had a sinister gleam in it as it wandered from one girl to the other.

"May the devil! ..." began Klara roughly, whose temper quickly got the better of her airs and graces. "What kind of flea has bitten your bride, Béla, I should like to know?"

"Flea?" said Béla with an oath, which he did not even attempt to suppress. "Flea? No kind of a flea, I hope. ... Look here, my dove," he added, turning to Elsa suddenly, "you seem to be forgetting your duties—have you gone to sleep these last five minutes?—or can't you see that Klara is waiting."

"I can see that Klara is waiting," replied Elsa calmly, "but I don't know what she can be waiting for."

She was as white as the linen of her shift, and little beads of sweat stood out at the roots of her hair. Andor, whose love for her made him clear-sighted and keen, saw the look of obstinacy which had crept round her mouth—the sudden obstinacy of the meek, which nothing can move. He alone could see what this sudden obstinacy meant to her, whose natural instincts were those of duty and of obedience. She suffered terribly at this moment, both mentally and physically; the moisture of her forehead showed that she suffered.

But she had nerved herself up for this ordeal: the crushed worm was turning on the cruel foot that had trodden it for so long. She did not mean to give way, even though she had fully weighed in the balance all that she would have to pay in the future for this one moment of rebellion.

Parents first and husbands afterwards are masterful tyrants in this part of the world; the woman's place is to obey; the Oriental conception of man's supremacy still reigns paramount, especially in the country. Elsa knew all this, and was ready for the chastisement—either moral, mental or even physical—which would surely overtake her, if not to-day, then certainly after to-morrow.

"You don't know what Klara is waiting for?" asked Béla, with an evil sneer; "why, my dove, you must be dreaming. Klara won't come to our church, of course, but she would like to come to the ball presently, and to-morrow to our wedding feast."

A second or perhaps less went by while Elsa passed her tongue over her parched lips; then she said slowly:

"Since Klara does not go to our church, Béla, I don't think that she can possibly want to come to our wedding feast."

Béla swore a loud and angry oath, and Andor, who was closely watching each player in this moving little drama, saw that Klara's olive skin had taken on a greenish hue, and that her gloved hands fastened almost convulsively over the handle of her parasol.

"But I tell you ..." began Béla, who was now livid with rage, and turned with a menacing gesture upon his fiancée, "I tell you that ..."

Already Andor had interposed; he, too, was pale and menacing, but he did not raise his voice nor did he swear, he only asked very quietly:

"What will you tell your fiancée, man? Come! What is it that you want to tell her on the eve of her wedding day?"

"What's that to you?" retorted Béla.

In this land where tempers run high, and blood courses hotly through the veins, a quarrel swiftly begun like this more often than not ends in tragedy. On Andor's face, in his menacing eyes, was writ the determination to kill if need be; in that of Béla there was the vicious snarl of an infuriated dog. Klara Goldstein was far too shrewd and prudent to allow her name to be mixed up in this kind of quarrel. Her reputation in the village was not an altogether unblemished one; by a scandal such as would result from a fight between these two men and for such a cause she might hopelessly jeopardize her chances in life, even with her own people.

Her own common sense, too, of which she had a goodly share, told her at the same time that the game was not worth the candle: the satisfaction of being asked to the most important wedding in the village, and there queening it with her fashionable clothes and with the bridegroom's undivided attention over a lot of stupid village folk, would not really compensate her for the scandal that was evidently brewing in the minds of Andor and of Elsa.

So she preferred for the nonce to play the part of outraged innocence, a part which she further emphasized by the display of easy-going kindliness. She placed one of her daintily-gloved hands on Béla's arm, she threw him a look of understanding and of indulgence, she cast a provoking glance on Andor and one of good-humoured contempt on Elsa, then she said lightly:

"Never mind, Béla! I can see that our little Elsa is a trifle nervy to-day; she does me more honour than I deserve by resenting your great kindness to me. But bless you, my good Béla! I don't mind. I am used to jealousies: the petty ones of my own sex are quite endurable; it is when you men are jealous that we poor women often have to suffer. Leopold Hirsch, who is courting me, you know, is so madly jealous at times. He scarce can bear anyone to look at me. As if I could help not being plain, eh?"

Then she turned with a smile to Elsa.

"I don't think, my dear," she said dryly, "that you are treating Béla quite fairly. He won't let you suffer from his jealousies; why should you annoy him with yours?"

Another glance through her long, dark lashes on both the men, and Klara Goldstein turned to go. But before she could take a step toward the door, Béla's masterful hand was on her wrist.

"What are you doing?" he asked roughly.

"Going, my good Béla," she replied airily, "going. What else can I do? I am not wanted here now, or later at your feast; but there are plenty in this village and around it who will make me welcome, and their company will be more pleasing to me, I assure you, than that of your friends. We thought of having some tarok[5] this evening. Leopold will be with us, and the young Count is coming. He loves a gamble, and is most amusing when he is in the mood. So I am going where I shall be most welcome, you see."

---

[5] A game of cards—the source of much gambling in that part of Europe.

92

She tried to disengage her wrist, but he was holding her with a tight, nervous grip.

"You are not going to do anything of the sort," he muttered hoarsely; "she is daft, I tell you. Stay here, can't you?"

"Not I," she retorted, with a laugh. "Enough of your friends' company, my good Béla, is as good as a feast. Look at Elsa's face! And Andor's! He is ready to eat me, and she to freeze the marrow in my bones. So farewell, my dear man; if you want any more of my company," she added pointedly, "you know where to get it."

She had succeeded in freeing her wrist, and the next moment was standing under the lintel of the door, the afternoon sun shining full upon her clinging gown, her waving feathers and the gew-gaws which hung round her neck. For a moment she stood still, blinking in the glare, her hands, which trembled a little from the emotion of the past little scene, fumbled with her parasol.

Béla turned like a snarling beast upon his fiancée.

"Ask her to stop," he cried savagely. "Ask her to stop, I tell you!"

"Keep your temper, my good Béla," said Klara over her shoulder to him, with a laugh; "and don't trouble about me. I am used to tantrums at home. Leo is a terror when he has a jealous fit, but it's nothing to me, I assure you! His rage leaves me quite cold."

"But this sort of nonsense does not leave me cold," retorted Béla, who by now was in a passion of fury; "it makes my blood boil, I tell you. What I've said, I've said, and I'm not going to let any woman set her will up against mine, least of all the woman who is going to be my wife. Whether you go or stay, Klara, is your affair, but Elsa will damn well have to ask you to stay, as I told her to do; she'll have to do as I tell her, or ..."

"Or what, Béla?" interposed Andor quietly.

Béla threw him a dark and sullen look, like an infuriated bull that pauses just before it is ready to charge.

"What is it to you?" he muttered savagely.

"Only this, my friend," replied Andor, who seemed as calm as the other was heated with passion, "only this: that I courted and loved Elsa when she was younger and happier than she is now, and I am not going to stand by and see her bullied and brow-beaten by anyone. Understand?"

"Take care, Béla," laughed Klara maliciously; "your future wife's old sweetheart might win her from you yet."

"Take care of what?" shouted Béla in unbridled rage. He faced Andor, and his one sinister eye shot a glance of deadly hatred upon him. "Let me tell you this, my friend, Lakatos Andor. I don't know where you have sprung from to-day, or why you have chosen to-day

93

to do it ... and it's nothing to me. But understand that I don't like your presence here, and that I did not invite you to come, and that therefore you have no business to be here, seeing that I pay for the feast. And understand too that I'll trouble my future wife's sweetheart to relieve her of his presence in future, or there'll be trouble. And you may take that from me, as my last word, my friend. Understand?"

"What an ass you are, Béla!" came as a parting shot from Klara, who had succeeded in opening her parasol, and now stood out in the open, her face and shoulders in shadow, looking the picture of coolness and of good-temper.

"Andor," she added, with a pleasing smile to the young man, "you know your way to Ignácz Goldstein's. Father and I will be pleased to see you there at any time. The young Count will be there to-night, and we'll have some tarok. Farewell, Béla," she continued, laughing merrily. "Don't worry, my good man, it's not worth losing your temper about trifles on the eve of your wedding-day. And bless your eyes! I don't mind."

Then she swept a mock curtsy to Elsa.

"Farewell, my pretty one. Good luck to you in your new life."

She nodded and was gone. Her rippling laugh, with its harsh, ironical ring was heard echoing down the village street.

"Call her back!" shouted Béla savagely, turning on his fiancée.

She looked him straight in that one eye which was so full of menace, and said with meek but firm obstinacy:

"I will not."

"Call her back," he exclaimed, "you ..."

He was almost choking with rage, and now he raised his clenched fist and brandished it in her face.

"Call her back, or I'll ..."

But already Andor was upon him, had seized him by collar and wrist. He was as livid as the other man was crimson, but his eyes glowed with a fury at least as passionate.

"And I tell you," he said, speaking almost in a whisper, very slowly and very calmly, but with such compelling power of determination that Béla, taken unawares, half-choked with the grip on his throat, and in agonized pain with the rough turn on his wrist, was forced to cower before him, "I tell you that if you dare touch her ... Look here, my friend," he continued, more loudly, "just now you said that you didn't know where I'd sprung from to-day, or why I chose to-day in which to do it. Well! Let me tell you then. God in Heaven sent me, do you see? He sent me to be here so as to see that no harm come to Elsa through marrying a brute like you. You have shown me the door, and I don't want to eat your salt again and to

94

take your hospitality, for it would choke me, I know ... but let me tell you this much, that if you bully Elsa ... if you don't make her happy ... if you are not kind to her ... I'll make you regret it to your dying day."

He had gradually relaxed his hold on Béla's throat and wrist, and now the latter was able to free himself altogether, and to readjust his collar and the set of his coat. For a moment it almost seemed as if he felt ashamed and repentant. But his obstinate and domineering temper quickly got the better of this softened mood.

"You'll make me regret it, will you?" he retorted sullenly. "You think that you will be allowed to play the guardian angel here, eh? with all your fine talk of God in Heaven, which I am inclined to think even the Pater would call blasphemy. I know what's at the back of your mind, my friend, don't you make any mistake about that."

"You know what's at the back of my mind?" queried Andor, with a puzzled frown. "What do you mean?"

"I mean," said Béla, with a return to his former swagger, "that you have been saying to yourself this past half-hour: 'Oho! but Elsa is not married yet! The vows are not yet spoken, and until they are I still have my chance.' That's what you have been saying to yourself, eh, Mr. Guardian Angel?"

"You d——d liar!"

"Oh! insulting me won't help you, my friend. And I am not going to let you provoke me into a fight, and kill me perhaps, for no doubt that is what you would like to do. I am not going to give Elsa up to you, you need not think it; and you can't take her from me, you can't make her break her solemn promise to me, without covering her with a disgrace from which she would never recover. You know what happened when Bakó Mariska broke off her marriage on the eve of her wedding-day, just because Lajos had got drunk once or twice? Though her mother whipped her for her obstinacy, and her father broke his stick across her shoulders, the whole countryside turned against her. They all had to leave the village, for no one would speak to Mariska. A scandal such as that the ignorant peasants round about here will never forgive. Mariska ultimately drowned herself in the Maros: when she no longer could stand the disgrace that pursued her everywhere. When you thought that to make a girl break off her engagement the day before her wedding was such an easy matter, you had not thought of all that, had you, my friend?"

"And when you thought of frightening me by all that nonsensical talk," retorted Andor quietly, "you had not thought perhaps that there are other lands in the world besides Hungary,

95

and that I am not quite such an ignorant peasant as those whom you choose to despise. But you have been wasting your breath and your temper. I am not here to try and persuade Elsa into doing what she would think wrong; but I am here to see that at least you be kind to her."

"Pshaw!" ejaculated Béla, with a contemptuous snap of his fingers.

"Oh! you need not imagine that I wouldn't know how you treated her. I would know soon enough. I tell you," he continued, with slow and deliberate emphasis, "that what you do to her I shall know. I shall know if you bully her, I shall know if you make her unhappy. I shall know—and God help you in that case!—if you are not kind to her. Just think in future when you speak a rough word to her that Lakatos Andor will hear you and make you pay for every syllable. Think when you browbeat her that Lakatos Andor can see you! For I will see you, I tell you, in spite of your turning me out of your house, in spite of your fences and your walls. So just you ask her pardon now for your roughness, kiss her little hand and take her to vespers. But take this from me, my friend, that if you ever dare raise your hand against your wife I'll pay you out for it, so help me God!"

He had sworn the last oath with solemn earnestness. Now he turned to Elsa and took her cold little hand in his and kissed her trembling finger-tips, then, without another look on the man whom he hated with such an overwhelming and deadly hatred, he turned on his heel and fled precipitately from the room.

Béla stood sullen and silent for a moment after he had gone. Wrath was still heating his blood so that the veins in his forehead stood up like cords. But he was not only wrathful, he also felt humiliated and ashamed. He had been cowed and overmastered in the presence of Elsa. His swagger and domineering ways had availed him nothing. Andor had threatened him and he had not had the pluck or the presence of mind to stand up to that meddling, interfering peasant.

Now it was too late to do anything; the thoughts of retaliation which would come to his mind later on had not yet had the time to mature. All that he knew was that he hated Andor and would get even with him some day; for Elsa he felt no hatred, only a great wrath that she should have witnessed his humiliation and that her obstinacy should have triumphed against his will. The same pride in her and the same loveless desire was still in him. He did not hate her, but he meant to make her suffer for what he had just gone through. To him matrimony meant the complete subjection of the woman to the will of her lord; for every rebellion, for every struggle

96

against that subjection she must be punished in accordance with the gravity of her fault.

Elsa had caused him to be humiliated, and it was his firm resolve to humiliate her before many hours had gone by. Already a plan was forming in his brain; the quietude of vespers would, he thought, help him to complete it.

Outside, the lads and maids were loudly demanding the appearance of the bride and bridegroom: the vesper bell had long ago ceased its compelling call. Erös Béla offered his silent fiancée his arm. She took it without hesitation, and together they walked across the square to the church.

# CHAPTER XVIII

## "I must punish her"

The little village inn kept by Ignácz Goldstein was not more squalid, not more dark and stuffy, than are the village inns of most countries in Europe. Klara did her best to keep the place bright and clean, which was no easy matter when the roads were muddy and men brought in most of the mud of those roads on their boots, and deposited it on the freshly-washed floors.

The tap-room was low and narrow and dark. Round the once whitewashed walls there were rows of wooden benches with narrow trestle tables in front of them. Opposite the front door, on a larger table, were the bottles of wine and silvorium,[6] the jars of tobacco and black cigars, which a beneficent government licensed Ignácz Goldstein the Jew to sell to the peasantry.

The little room obtained its daylight mainly from the street-door when it was open, for the one tiny window—on the right as you entered—was not constructed to open, and its dulled glass masked more of daylight than it allowed to filtrate through.

Opposite the window a narrow door led into a couple of living rooms, the first of which also had direct access to the street.

---

[6] A highly alcoholic, very raw gin-like spirit distilled from a special kind of plum.

The tap-room itself was always crowded and always busy, the benches round the walls were always occupied, and Klara and her father were never allowed to remain idle for long. She dispensed the wine and the silvorium, and made herself agreeable to the guests. Ignácz saw to the tobacco and the cigars. Village women in Hungary never frequent the public inn: when they do, it is because they have sunk to the lowest depths of degradation: a woman in drink is practically an unknown sight in the land.

Klara herself, though her ways with the men were as free and easy as those of her type and class usually are, would never have dreamed of drinking with any of them.

This evening she was unusually busy. While the wedding feast was going on lower down in the village, a certain number of men who liked stronger fare than what is usually provided at a "maiden's farewell" dance, as well as those who had had no claim to be invited, strolled into the tap-room for a draught of silvorium, a gossip with the Jewess, or a game of tarok if any were going.

Ignácz Goldstein himself was fond of a game. Like most of his race, his habits were strictly sober. As he kept a cool head, he usually won; and his winnings at tarok made a substantial addition to the income which he made by selling spirits and tobacco. Leopold Hirsch, who kept the village grocery store, was also an inveterate player, and, like Goldstein, a very steady winner. But it was not the chance of a successful gamble which brought him so often to the tap-room. For years now he had dangled round Klara's fashionable skirts, and it seemed as if at last his constancy was to be rewarded. While she was younger—and was still of surpassing beauty—she had had wilder flights of ambition than those which would lead her to rule over a village grocery store: during those times she had allowed Leopold Hirsch to court her, without giving him more than very cursory encouragement.

As the years went on, however, and her various admirers from Arad proved undesirous to go to the length of matrimony, she felt more kindly disposed toward Leo, who periodically offered her his heart and hand, and the joint ownership of the village grocery store. She had looked into her little piece of mirror rather more closely of late than she had done hitherto, and had discovered two or three ominous lines round her fine, almond-shaped eyes, and noted that her nose showed of late a more marked tendency to make close acquaintance with her chin.

Then she began to ponder, and to give the future more serious consideration than she had ever done before. She ticked off on her long, pointed fingers the last bevy of her admirers on whom she might reasonably count: the son of the chemist over in Arad, the tenant of the Kender Road farm, the proprietor of the station cabs, and there were two or three others; but they were certainly falling away, and she had added no new ones to her list these past six months.

Erös Béla's formally declared engagement to Kapus Elsa had been a very severe blow. She had really reckoned on Béla. He was educated and unconventional, and though he professed the usual anti-Semitic views peculiar to his kind, Klara did not believe that these were very genuine. At any rate, she had reckoned that her fine eyes and provocative ways would tilt successfully against the man's racial prejudices.

Erös Béla was rich and certainly, up to a point, in love with her. Klara was congratulating herself on the way she was playing her matrimonial cards, when all her hopes were so suddenly dashed to the ground.

Béla was going to marry that silly, ignorant peasant girl, and she, Klara, would be left to marry Leopold after all.

Her anger and humiliation had been very great, and she had battled very persistently and very ably to regain the prize which she had lost. She knew quite well that, but for the fact that she belonged to the alien and despised race, Erös Béla would have been only too happy to marry her. His vanity alone had made him choose Kapus Elsa. He wanted the noted beauty for himself, because the noted beauty had been courted by so many people, and where so many people had failed he was proud to succeed.

Nor would he have cared to have it said that he had married a Jewess. There is always a certain thought of disgrace attached to such a marriage, whether it has been contracted by peer or peasant, and Erös Béla's one dominating idea in life was to keep the respect and deference of his native village.

But he had continued his attentions to Klara, and Klara had kept a wonderful hold over his imagination and over his will. She was the one woman who had ever had her will with him—only partially, of course, and not to the extent of forcing him into matrimony—but sufficiently to keep him also dangling round her skirts even though his whole allegiance should have belonged to Elsa.

The banquet this afternoon had been a veritable triumph. Whatever she had suffered through Béla's final disloyalty to herself, she knew that Kapus Elsa must have suffered all through the banquet. The humiliation of seeing one's bridegroom openly flaunting his admiration for another woman must have been indeed very bitter to bear.

Not for a moment did Klara Goldstein doubt that the subsequent scene was an act of vengeance against herself on Elsa's part. She judged other women by her own standard, discounted other women's emotions, thoughts, feelings, by her own. She thought it quite natural that Elsa should wish to be revenged, just as she was quite sure that Béla was already meditating some kind of retaliation for the shame which Andor had put upon him and for Elsa's obstinacy and share in the matter.

She had not spoken to anyone of the little scene which had occurred between the four walls of the little' schoolroom: on the contrary she had spoken loudly of both the bridegroom's and the bride's cordiality to her during the banquet.

"Elsa wanted me to go to the dancing this evening," she said casually, "but I thought you would all miss me. I didn't want this place to be dull just because half the village is enjoying itself somewhere else."

It had been market day at Arad, and at about five o'clock Klara and her father became very busy. Cattle-dealers and pig-merchants, travellers and pedlars, dropped in for a glass of silvorium and a chat with the good-looking Jewess. More than one bargain, discussed on the marketplace of Arad, was concluded in the stuffy tap-room of Marosfalva.

"Shall we be honoured by the young Count's presence later on?" someone asked, with a significant nod to Klara.

Everyone laughed in sympathy; the admiration of the noble young Count for Klara Goldstein was well-known. There was nothing in it, of course; even Klara, vain and ambitious as she was, knew that the bridge which divided the aristocrat from one of her kind and of her race was an impassable one. But she liked the young Count's attentions—she liked the presents he brought her from time to time, and relished the notoriety which this flirtation gave her.

She also loved to tease poor Leopold Hirsch. Leo had been passionately in love with her for years; what he must have endured in moral and mental torture during that time through his jealousy and often groundless suspicions no one who did not know him intimately could ever have guessed. These tortures which Klara wantonly inflicted upon the wretched young man had been a constant source of amusement to her. Even now she was delighted because, as luck would have it, he entered the tap-room at the very moment when everyone was chaffing her about the young Count.

Leopold Hirsch cast a quick, suspicious glance upon the girl, and his dull olive skin assumed an almost greenish hue. He was not of prepossessing appearance; this he knew himself, and the knowledge helped to keep his jealousy and his suspicion aflame.

He was short and lean of stature and his head, with its large, bony features, seemed too big for his narrow shoulders to carry. His ginger-coloured hair was lank and scanty; he wore it—after the manner of those of his race in that part of the world—in corkscrew ringlets down each side of his narrow, cadaverous-looking face.

His eyes were pale and shifty, but every now and then there shot into them a curious gleam of unbridled passion—love, hate or revenge; and then the whole face would light up and compel attention by the revelation of latent power.

This had happened now when a fellow who sat in the corner by the window made some rough jest about the young Count. Leopold made his way to Klara's side; his thin lips were tightly pressed together, and he had buried his hands in the pockets of his ill-fitting trousers.

"If that accursed aristocrat comes hanging round here much more, Klara," he muttered between set teeth, "I'll kill him one of these days."

"What a fool you are, Leopold!" she said. "Why, yesterday it was Erös Béla you objected to."

"And I do still," he retorted. "I heard of your conduct at the banquet to-day. It is the talk of the village. One by one these loutish peasants have come into my shop and told me the tale—curse them!—of how the bridegroom had eyes and ears only for you. You seem to forget, Klara," he added, while a thought of menace crept into his voice, "that you are tokened to me now. So don't try and make a fool of me, or ..."

"The Lord bless you, my good man," she retorted, with a laugh, "I won't try, I promise you. I wouldn't like to compete with the Almighty, who has done that for you already."

"Klara ..." he exclaimed.

"Oh! be quiet now, Leo," she said impatiently. "Can't you see that my hands are as full as I can manage, without my having to bother about you and your jealous tempers?"

She elbowed him aside and went to the counter to serve a customer who had just arrived, and more than a quarter of an hour went by before Leopold had the chance of another word with her.

"You might have a kind word for me to-night, Klara," he said ruefully, as soon as a brief lull in business enabled him to approach the girl.

"Why specially to-night?" she asked indifferently.

"Your father must go by the night train to Kecskemét," he said, with seeming irrelevance. "There is that business about the plums."

101

"The plums?" she asked, with a frown of puzzlement, "what plums?"

"The fruit he bought near Kecskemét. They start gathering at sunrise to-morrow. He must be there the first hour, else he'd get shamefully robbed. He must travel by night."

"I knew nothing about it," rejoined Klara, with an indifferent shrug of the shoulders. "Father never tells me when he is going to be away from home."

"No!" retorted Leopold, with a sneer, "he knows better than to give all your gallants such a brilliant opportunity."

"Don't be a fool, Leo!" she reiterated with a laugh.

"I don't give any of them an opportunity, either," resumed the young man, while a curious look of almost animal ferocity crept into his pale face. "Whenever your father has to be away from home during the night, I take up my position outside this house and watch over you until daylight comes and people begin to come and go."

"Very thoughtful of you, my good Leo," she rejoined dryly, "but you need not give yourself the trouble. I am well able to look after myself."

"If any man molested you," continued Leopold, speaking very calmly, "I would kill him."

"Who should molest me, you silly fool? And anyhow, I won't have you spying upon me like that."

"You must not call it spying, Klara. I love to stand outside this house in the peace and darkness of the night, and to think of you quietly sleeping whilst I am keeping watch over you. You wouldn't call a watchdog a spy, would you?"

"I know that to-night I shan't sleep a wink," she retorted crossly, "once father has gone. I shall always be thinking of you out there in the dark, watching this house. It will make me nervous."

"To-night ..." he began, and then abruptly checked himself. Once more that quick flash of passion shot through his pale, deep-set eyes. It seemed as if he meant to tell her something, which on second thoughts he decided to keep to himself. Her keen, dark eyes searched his face for a moment or two; she wondered what it was that lurked behind that high, smooth forehead of his and within the depths of that curiously perverted brain.

Before she had time, however, to question him, Erös Béla made noisy irruption into the room.

He was greeted with a storm of cheers.

"Hello, Béla!"

"Not the bridegroom, surely?"

"Who would have thought of seeing you here?"

While Leopold Hirsch muttered audibly:

102

"What devil's mischief has brought this fellow here to-day, I wonder?"

Béla seemed in boisterous good-humour—with somewhat ostentatious hilarity he greeted all his friends, and then ordered some of Ignácz Goldstein's best wine for everybody all round.

"Bravo, Béla!" came from every side, together with loud applause at this unexpected liberality.

"It is nice of you not to forget old friends," Klara whispered in his ear, as soon as he succeeded in reaching her side.

"Whew!" he ejaculated with a sneer, "you have no idea, my good Klara, how I've been boring myself these past two hours. Those loutish peasants have no idea of enjoyment save their eternal gipsy music and their interminable csárdás."

"For a man of your education, Béla," said Klara, with an insinuating smile, "it must be odiously dull. You would far rather have had a game of cards, wouldn't you now?"

"I would far rather have had you at that infernal dance, so as to have had somebody to talk to," he retorted savagely.

"Oh!" she said demurely, "that would never have done. Elsa must have such a lot to say to you herself. It would not be seemly for me to stand in the way."

"Elsa, as you know, has that silly csárdás on the brain. She has been dancing ever since six o'clock and has only given me about ten minutes of her company. She seems to belong to-night to every young fool that can dance, rather than to me."

"Ah well! When you are married you can stop all that, my good Béla. You can forbid your wife to dance the csárdás, you know. I know many men who do it. Then Elsa will learn to appreciate the pleasure of your conversation. Though she is no longer very young, she is still very ignorant. You will have to educate her ... bring her up to your own level of intelligence and of learning. In the meanwhile, do sit down and drink with those who, like yourself, have come here for an hour or two to break the monotony of perpetual czigány music and dancing."

She busied herself with drawing the corks of a number of bottles, which she then transferred from the end of the room where she stood to the tables at which sat her customers; she also brought out some fresh glasses. Béla watched her for a moment or two in silence, unconscious of the fact that he, too, was being watched by a pair of pale eyes in which lurked a gleam of jealousy and of hate. Suddenly, as Klara brushed past him carrying bottles and glasses, he took hold of her by the elbow and drew her close to him.

"These louts won't stay late to-night, will they?" he whispered in her ear.

103

"No, not late," she replied; "they will go on to the barn in time for the supper, you may be sure of that. Why do you ask?"

"I will have the supper served at ten o'clock," he continued to whisper, "but I'll not sit down to it. Not without you."

"Don't be foolish, Béla," she retorted. But even as he spoke, a little gleam of satisfaction, of gratified vanity, of anticipatory revenge, shot through her velvety dark eyes.

"I warned Elsa," he continued sullenly; "I told her that if you were not at the feast, I should not be there either. She has disobeyed me. I must punish her."

"So?" she rejoined, with an acid smile. "It is only in order to punish Elsa that you want to sup with me?"

"Don't be stupid, Klara," he retorted. "I'll come at ten o'clock. Will you have some supper ready for me then? I have two or three bottles of French champagne over at my house—I'll bring them along. Will you be ready for me?"

"Be silent, Béla," she broke in hurriedly. "Can't you see that that fool Leo is watching us all the time?"

"Curse, him! What have I got to do with him?" muttered Béla savagely. "You will be ready for me, Klara?"

"No!" she said decisively. "Better make your peace with Elsa. I'll have none of her leavings. I've had all I wanted out of you to-day—the banquet first and now your coming here. ... It'll be all over the village presently—and that's all I care about. Have a drink now," she added good-humouredly, "and then go and make your peace with Elsa ... if you can."

She turned abruptly away from him, leaving him to murmur curses under his breath, and went on attending to her customers; nor did he get for the moment another opportunity of speaking with her, for Leopold Hirsch hovered round her for some considerable time after that, and presently, with much noise and pomp and circumstance, no less a personage than the noble young Count himself graced the premises of Ignácz Goldstein the Jew with his august presence.

# CHAPTER XIX

## "Now go and fetch the key"

He belonged to the ancient family of Rákosy, who had owned property on both banks of the Maros for the past eight centuries, and Feri Rákosy, the twentieth-century representative of his mediæval forbears, was a good-looking young fellow of the type so often met with among the upper classes in Hungary: quite something English in appearance—well set-up, well-dressed, well-groomed from the top of his smooth brown hair to the tips of his immaculately-shod feet—in the eyes an expression of habitual boredom, further accentuated by the slight, affected stoop of the shoulders and a few premature lines round the nose and mouth; and about his whole personality that air of high-breeding and of good, pure blood which is one of the chief characteristics of the true Hungarian aristocracy.

He did little more than acknowledge the respectful salutations which greeted him from every corner of the little room as he entered, but he nodded to Erös Béla and smiled all over his good-looking face at Klara, who, in her turn, welcomed him with a profusion of smiles which brought a volley of muttered curses to Leopold Hirsch's lips.

While he held her one hand rather longer than was necessary she, with the other, took his hat from him, and then, laughing coquettishly, she pointed to a parcel which was causing the pocket of his well-cut Norfolk jacket to bulge immoderately.

"Is that something for me?" she asked.

"Of course it is," he replied lightly; "I bought it at the fair in Arad for you to-day."

"How thoughtful of you!" she said, with a little sigh of pleasure.

"Thoughtful?" he retorted, laughing pleasantly. "My good Klara, if I hadn't thought of you I would have died of boredom this afternoon. Here, give me a glass of your father's best wine and I'll tell you."

He sat down with easy familiarity on the corner of the table which served as a counter. Klara, after this, had eyes and ears only for him. How could it be otherwise, seeing that it was not often a noble lord graced a village tap-room with his presence. Conversations round the room were now carried on in whispers; tarok cards were produced and here and there a game was in

105

progress. Those who had drunk overmuch made themselves as inconspicuous as they could, drawing themselves closely against the wall, or frankly reclining across the table with arms outstretched and heads buried between them out of sight.

An atmosphere of subdued animation and decorum reigned in the place; not a few men, oppressed by their sense of respect for my lord, had effected a quiet exit through the door, preferring the jovial atmosphere of the barn, from whence came, during certain hushed moments, the sounds of music and of laughter.

The young man—whose presence caused all this revulsion in the usually noisy atmosphere of the tap-room—took no heed whatever of anything that went on around him: he seemed unconscious alike of the deference of the peasants as of the dark, menacing scowl with which Leopold Hirsch regarded him. He certainly did not bestow a single glance on Erös Béla who, at my lord's appearance, had retreated into the very darkest corner of the room. Béla did not care to encounter the young Count's sneering remarks just now—and these would of a certainty have been levelled against the bridegroom who was sitting in a tap-room when he should have been in attendance on his bride. But indeed my lord never saw him.

To this young scion of a noble race, which had owned land and serfs for centuries past, these peasants here were of no more account than his oxen or his sheep—nor was the owner of a village shop of any more consequence in my lord's eyes.

He came here because there was a good-looking Jewess in the tap-room whose conversation amused him, and whose dark, velvety eyes, fringed with long lashes, and mouth with full, red lips, stirred his jaded senses in a more pleasant and more decided way than did the eyes and lips of the demure, well-bred young Countesses and Baronesses who formed his usual social circle.

Whether his flirtation with Klara, the Jewess, annoyed the girl's Jew lover or not, did not matter to him one jot; on the contrary the jealousy of that dirty lout Hirsch enhanced his amusement to a considerable extent.

Therefore he did not take the trouble to lower his voice now when he talked to Klara, and it was quite openly that he put his arm round her waist while he held his glass to her lips—"To sweeten your father's vinegar!" he said with a laugh.

"You know, my pretty Klara," he said gaily, "that I was half afraid I shouldn't see you to-day at all."

"No?" she asked coquettishly.

"No, by gad! My father was so soft-hearted to allow Erös a day off for his wedding or something, and so, if you please, I had to go to

Arad with him, as he had to see about a sale of clover. I thought we should never get back. The roads were abominable."

"I hardly expected your lordship," she said demurely.

To punish her for that little lie, he tweaked her small ear till it became a bright crimson.

"That is to punish you for telling such a lie," he said gaily. "You know that I meant to come and say good-bye."

"Your lordship goes to-morrow?" she asked with a sigh.

"To shoot bears, my pretty Klara," he replied. "I don't want to go. I would rather stay another week here for you to amuse me, you know."

"I am proud ..." she whispered.

"So much do you amuse me that I have brought you a present, just to show you that I thought of you to-day and because I want you not to forget me during the three months that I shall be gone."

He drew the parcel out of his pocket and, turning his back to the rest of the room, he cut the string and undid the paper that wrapped it. The contents of the parcel proved to be a morocco case, which flew open at a touch and displayed a gold curb chain bracelet—the dream of Klara Goldstein's desires.

"For me?" she said, with a gasp of delight.

"For your pretty arm, yes," he replied. "Shall I put it on?"

She cast a swift, apprehensive glance round the room over his shoulder.

"No, no, not now," she said quickly.

"Why not?"

"Father mightn't like it. I'd have to ask him."

"D——n your father!"

"And that fool, Leopold, is so insanely jealous."

"D——n him too," said the young man quietly.

Whereupon he took the morocco case out of Klara's hand, shut it with a snap and put it back into his pocket.

"What are you doing?" cried Klara in a fright.

"As you see, pretty one, I am putting the bracelet away for future use."

"But ..." she stammered.

"If I can't put the bracelet on your arm myself," he said decisively, "you shan't have it at all."

"But ..."

"That is my last word. Let us talk of something else."

"No, no! We won't talk of something else. You said the bracelet was for me."

She cast a languishing look on him through her long upper lashes; she bared her wrist and held it out to him. Leopold and his jealousy might go hang for aught she cared, for she meant to have the bracelet.

The young man, with a fatuous little laugh, brought out the case once more. With his own hands he now fastened the bracelet round Klara Goldstein's wrist. Then—as a matter of course—he kissed her round, brown arm just above the bracelet, and also the red lips through which the words of thanks came quickly tumbling.

Klara did not dare to look across the room. She felt, though she did not see, Leopold's pale eyes watching this little scene with a glow in them of ferocious hate and of almost animal rage.

"I won't stay now, Klara," said the young Count, dropping his voice suddenly to a whisper; "too many of these louts about. When will you be free?"

"Oh, not to-day," she whispered in reply. "After the fair there are sure to be late-comers. And you know Erös Béla has a ball on at the barn and supper afterwards. ..."

"The very thing," he broke in, in an eager whisper. "While they are all at supper, I'll come in for a drink and a chat. ... Ten o'clock, eh?"

"Oh, no, no!" she protested feebly. "My father wouldn't like it, he ..."

"D——n your father, my dear, as I remarked before. And, as a matter of fact, your father is not going to be in the way at all. He goes to Kecskemét by the night train."

"How do you know that?"

"My father told me quite casually that Goldstein was seeing to some business for him at Kecskemét to-morrow. So it was not very difficult to guess that if your father was to be in Kecskemét to-morrow in time to transact business, he would have to travel up by the nine o'clock train this evening in order to get there."

Then, as she made no reply, and a blush of pleasure gradually suffused her dark skin, lending it additional charm and giving to her eyes added brilliancy, he continued, more peremptorily this time:

"At ten o'clock, then—I'll come back. Get rid of as many of these louts by then as you can."

She was only too ready to yield. Not only was she hugely flattered by my lord's attentions, but she found him excessively attractive. He could make himself very agreeable to a woman if he chose, and evidently he chose to do so now. Moreover Klara had found by previous experience that to yield to the young man's varied and varying caprices was always remunerative, and there was that gold watch which he had once vaguely promised her, and which she knew she could get out of him if she had the time and opportunity, as she certainly would have to-night if he came.

108

Count Feri, seeing that she had all but yielded, was preparing to go. Her hand was still in his, and he was pressing her slender fingers in token of a pledge for this evening.

"At ten o'clock," he whispered again.

"No, no," she protested once more, but this time he must have known that she only did it for form's sake and really meant to let him have his way. "The neighbours would see you enter, and there might be a whole lot of people in the tap-room at that hour: one never knows. They would know by then that my father had gone away and they would talk such scandal about me. My reputation ..."

No doubt he felt inclined to ejaculate in his usual manner: "D——n your reputation!" but he thought better of it, and merely said casually:

"I need not come in by the front door, need I?"

"The back door is always locked," she remarked ingenuously. "My father invariably locks it himself the last thing at night."

"But since he is going to Kecskemét ..." he suggested.

"When he has to be away from home for the night he locks the door from the inside and takes the key away with him."

"Surely there is a duplicate key somewhere? ..."

"I don't know," she murmured.

"If you don't know, who should?" he remarked, with affected indifference. "Well! I shall have to make myself heard at the back door—that's all!"

"How?"

"Wouldn't you hear me if I knocked?"

"Not if I were in the tap-room and a lot of customers to attend to."

"Well, then, I should hammer away until you did hear me."

"For that old gossip Rézi to hear you," she protested. "Her cottage is not fifty paces away from our back door."

"Then it will have to be the front door, after all," he rejoined philosophically.

"No, no!—the neighbours—and perhaps the tap-room full of people."

"But d——n it, Klara," he exclaimed impatiently, "I have made up my mind to come and spend my last evening with you—and when I have made up my mind to a thing, I am not likely to change it because of a lot of gossiping peasants, because of old Rézi, or the whole lot of them. So if you don't want me to come in by the front door, which is open, or to knock at the back door, which is locked, how am I going to get in?"

"I don't know."

"Well, then, you'll have to find out, my pretty one," he said

109

decisively, "for it has got to be done somehow, or that gold watch we spoke of the other day will have to go to somebody else. And you know when I say a thing I mean it. Eh?"

"There is a duplicate key," she whispered shyly, ". . . to the back door, I mean."

"I thought there was," he remarked dryly. "Where is it?"

"In the next room. ... It hangs on a nail by father's bedside."

"Go and get it, then," he said more impatiently.

"Not now," she urged. "Leopold is looking straight at you and me."

He shrugged his aristocratic shoulders.

"You are not afraid of that monkey?" he said with a laugh.

"Well, no! not exactly afraid. But he is so insanely jealous; one never knows what kind of mischief he'll get into. He told me just now that whenever father is away from home he takes his stand outside this house from nightfall till morning—watching!"

"A modern Argus—eh?"

"A modern lunatic!" she retorted.

"Well!" resumed the young man lightly, "lunatic or not, he won't be able to keep an eye on you to-night, even though your father will be away."

"How do you mean?"

"Hirsch is off to Fiume in half an hour."

"To Fiume?"

"Yes. You know he has a brother coming home from America."

"I know that."

"His ship is due in at Fiume the day after to-morrow. Leopold must start by the same train as your father to-night, in order to catch the express for Fiume at Budapesth to-morrow."

"Did he tell you all that?"

"I have known all along that he meant to meet his brother at Fiume, and yesterday he said something about it again. So you see, my pretty one, that we can have a comfortable little supper this evening without fear of interruption. We'll have it at ten o'clock, when the supper-party is going on at the barn, eh? We shan't be interrupted then. So give me that duplicate key, will you, and I can slip in quietly through the back door without raising a bit of gossip or scandal. Hurry up now! I shall have to be going."

"I can't now," she protested. "Leopold hasn't taken his eyes off me all this time."

"Oh! if that is all that is troubling you, my dear," said the young man coolly, "I can easily settle our friend Leopold. Hirsch!" he called loudly.

"My lord?" queried the other, with the quick obsequiousness habitual to the down-trodden race.

"My horse is kicking up such a row outside. I wish you'd just go and see if the boy is looking after him properly."

Of course it was impossible to do anything but obey. My lord had commanded; in the ordinary way the poor Jew shopkeeper would have felt honoured to have been selected for individual recognition. Nor did he do more now than throw one of those swift looks of his—so full of hatred and of menace—upon Klara and the young man; but the latter, having given his orders, no longer condescended to take notice of the Jew and had once more engaged the girl in animated conversation.

Had Klara thought of looking up when Leopold finally obeyed my lord's commands and went to look after the horse, she could not have failed to realize the danger which lurked in the young man's pale eyes then. His face, always pale and olive-tinted, was now the colour of ashes, grey and livid and blotched with purple, his lips looked white and quivering, and his eyebrows—of a reddish tinge—met above his nose in a deep, dark scowl.

But my lord had thrown out a casual hint about a gold watch, and Klara had no further thought for her jealous admirer.

"Now go and fetch the key," said Count Feri, as soon as the door had closed on Leopold.

The hint of the gold watch had stirred Klara's pulses. A tête-à-tête with my lord was, moreover, greatly to her liking. He could be very amusing when he chose, and was always generous; and Klara's life was often dull and colourless. A pleasant evening spent in his company would compensate her in a measure for her disappointment at not being asked to Elsa's ball, and there was the gold watch to look forward to, above all.

Taking an opportunity when her father was absorbed in his game of tarok, she went into the next room and presently returned with a key in her hand, which she surreptitiously gave to my lord.

"Splendid!" exclaimed the young man gaily. "Klara, you are a gem, and after supper you shall just ask me for anything you have a fancy for, and I'll give it to you. Now I'd better go. Good-bye, little one. Ten o'clock sharp, eh?"

"Ten o'clock," she repeated, under her breath.

He strode to the door, outside which he found Leopold waiting for him.

"The horse was quite quiet, my lord," said the Jew sullenly; "the boy had never left it for a moment."

"Oh! that's all right, Hirsch," rejoined my lord indifferently. "I only wanted to know."

111

Of course he never thought of saying a word of thanks or of excuse to the other man. What would you? A Jew! Bah! not even worth a nod of the head.

Count Feri Rákosy had quickly mounted his pretty, half-bred Arab mare—a click of the tongue and she was off with him, kicking up a cloud of dust in her wake.

But Leopold Hirsch had remained for a moment standing on the doorstep of Ignácz Goldstein's house. He watched horse and rider through that cloud of dust, and along the straight and broad highway, until both had become a mere speck upon the low-lying horizon.

"May you break your accursed neck!" he muttered fervently.

Then he went back to the tap-room.

# CHAPTER XX

### "You happen to be of my race and of my blood"

He strode at once to Klara, who greeted him with an ironical little smile and a coquettish look out of her dark eyes.

"You never told me that you were going away to-night, my dear Leopold," she said suavely.

"Who told you that I was?" he retorted savagely.

"It seems to be pretty well known about the place. You seemed to have been talking about it pretty freely that you were going to Fiume to meet your brother when the ship he is on comes in."

"I meant to tell you just now, only his lordship's arrival interrupted me," he said more quietly.

"And since then you have been busy making a fool of yourself before my lord, eh?" she asked.

"Bah!"

"And compromising me into the bargain, what? But let me tell you this, my good Leopold, before we go any further, that I am not married to you yet, and that I don't like your airs of proprietorship, sabe?"

He could not say anything more just then, for customers were departing, and she had to attend to them; he did not try to approach

112

her while she was thus engaged, but presently, when her back was turned, he contrived to work his way across to the door which gave on the inner room, and to push it slightly open with his hand, until he could peep through the aperture and take a quick survey of the room beyond.

Klara had not seen this manœuvre of his, although she had cast more than one rapid and furtive glance upon him while she attended to her customers. She was thankful that he was going away for a few days; in his present mood he was positively dangerous.

She had lighted the oil lamp which hung from the centre of the low, raftered ceiling, the hour was getting late, customers were all leaving now one by one.

Erös Béla was one of the last to go.

He had drunk rather more silvorium than was good for him. He knew quite well that by absenting himself from the pre-nuptial festivals he had behaved in a disgraceful and unjustifiable manner which would surely be resented throughout the village, and though he was quite sure that he did not care one brass fillér what all those ignorant peasants thought of him, yet he felt it incumbent upon him to brace up his courage now, before meeting the hostile fusillade of eyes which would be sure to greet him on his return to the barn.

He meant to put in a short appearance there, and then to finish his evening here in Klara's company. He felt that his dignity demanded that he should absent himself at any rate from the supper, seeing that Elsa had so grossly defied him.

"At ten o'clock I'll be back, Klara," he whispered, in the girl's ear, as he was about to take his departure along with some of his friends, who also intended to go on to the dance in the barn.

"Indeed you won't," she retorted decisively, "I have no use for you, my good Béla. You are almost a married man now, remember!" she added with a laugh.

"I'll bring those bottles of champagne," he urged; "don't be hard on me, Klara. I'll give you a good time to-night, and a nice present into the bargain."

"And ruin my reputation for ever, eh? By walking into the tap-room when it's full of people and carrying two bottles of champagne under your arm—or staying on ostentatiously after everyone has gone and for everyone to gossip. No, thank you; I've already told you that I am not going to lend myself to your little games of vengeance. It isn't me you want, it's petty revenge upon Elsa. To that I say no, thank you, my good man."

"Klara!" he pleaded.

"No!" she said, and unceremoniously turned her back on him.

113

He went off, sullen and morose, and not a little chaffed for his moroseness by his friends.

The tap-room was almost deserted for the moment. In one or two corners only a few stragglers lingered; they were sprawling across the tables with arms outstretched. Ignácz Goldstein's silvorium had proved too potent and too plentiful. They lay there in a drunken sleep—logs that were of no account. Presently they would have to be thrown out, but there was no hurry for that—they were not in the way.

Ignácz Goldstein had gone into the next room. Klara was busy tidying up the place; Leopold approached her with well-feigned contrition and humility.

"I am sorry, Klara," he said. "I seemed to have had the knack to-night of constantly annoying you. So I'd best begone now, perhaps."

"I bear no malice, Leo," she said quietly.

"I thought I'd come back at about nine o'clock," he continued. "It is nearly eight now."

She, thinking that he had his own journey in mind, remarked casually:

"You'd best be here well before nine. The train leaves at nine-twenty, and father walks very slowly."

"I won't be late," he said. "Best give me the key of the back door. I'll let myself in that way."

"No occasion to do that," she retorted. "The front door will be open. You can come in that way like everybody else."

"It's just a fancy," he said quietly; "there might be a lot of people about just then. I don't want to come through here. I thought I'd just slip in the back way as I often do. So give me the key, Klara, will you?"

"How can I give you the key of the back door?" she said, equally quietly; "you know father always carries it in his coat pocket."

"But there is a second key," he remarked, "which hangs on a nail by your father's bedside in the next room. Give me that one, Klara."

"I shan't," she retorted. "I never heard such nonsense! As if I could allow you to use the private door of this house just as it suits your fancy. If you want to come in to-night and say good-bye, you must come in by the front door."

"It's just a whim of mine, Klara," urged Leopold, now still speaking quietly—almost under his breath—but there was an ominous tremor in his voice and sudden sharp gleams in his eyes

114

which the girl had already noted and which caused the blood to rush back to her heart, leaving her cheeks pale and her lips trembling.

"Nonsense!" she contrived to say, with an indifferent shrug of the shoulders.

"Just a whim," he reiterated. "So I'll take the key, by your leave."

He turned to the door of the inner room and pushed it open, just as he had done awhile ago, and now—as then—he cast a rapid glance round the room.

Klara, through half-closed lids, watched his every movement.

"Why!" he exclaimed, turning back to her, and with a look of well-feigned surprise, "the key is not in its place."

"I know it isn't," she retorted curtly.

"Then where is it?"

"I have put it away."

"When? It was hanging on its usual nail when I first came here this afternoon. I remember the door being open, and my glancing into the room casually. I am sure it was there then."

"It may have been: but I put it away after that."

"Why should you have done that?"

"I don't know, and, anyhow, it's no business of yours, is it?"

"Give me that back-door key, Klara," insisted the young man, in a tone of savage command.

"No!" she replied, slowly and decisively.

There was silence in the little, low raftered room after that, a silence only broken by the buzzing of flies against the white globe of the lamp, and by the snores of the sleepers who sprawled across the tables.

Leopold Hirsch had drawn in his breath with a low, hissing sound; his face, by the yellow light of the lamp, looked ghastly in colour, and his hands were twitching convulsively as the trembling fingers clenched and opened with a monotonous, jerky movement of attempted self-control.

Klara had not failed to notice these symptoms of an agony of mind which the young man was so vainly trying to hide from her. For the moment she almost felt sorry for him—sorry and slightly remorseful.

After all, Leo's frame of mind, the agony which he endured, came from the strength of his love for her. Neither Erös Béla, nor the young Count, nor the many admirers who had hung round her in the past until such time as their fancy found more permanent anchorage elsewhere, would have suffered tortures of soul and of heart because she had indulged in a mild flirtation with a rival. Erös Béla would have stormed and cursed, the young Count would have

115

laid his riding-whip across the shoulders of his successful rival and there would have been an end of the matter. Leopold Hirsch would go down to hell and endure the torments of the damned, then return to heaven at a smile from her, and go back to hell again and glory in his misery.

But just now she was frightened of him; he looked almost like a living corpse; the skin on his face was drawn so tightly over the bones that it gave him the appearance of a skull with hollow eyes and wide, grinning mouth.

Outside an owl hooted dismally. Klara gave a slight shiver of fear and looked furtively round her to see if any of the drunkards were awake. Then she recollected that her father was in the next room, and presently, from afar, came shouts of laughter and the sound of music.

She woke as from a nightmare, gave her fine shoulders a little shake, and looked boldly into her jealous lover's face.

"By the Lord, Leo!" she said, with a little forced laugh, "you have given me the creeps, looking as you do. How dare you frighten me like that? With your clenched hands, too, as if you wanted to murder me. There, now, don't be such a silly fool. You have got a long journey before you; it's no use making yourself sick with jealousy just before you go."

"I am not going on a journey," he said, in a toneless, even voice, which seemed to come from a grave.

"Not going?" she said, with a frown of puzzlement. "You were going to Fiume to meet your brother, don't you remember? The ship he is on is due in the day after to-morrow. If you don't start to-night you won't be able to catch the express at Budapesth to-morrow."

"I know all that," he said, in the same dull, monotonous tone; "I am not going, that's all."

"But ..."

"I have changed my mind. Your father is going away. I must watch over you to see that no one molests you. Thieves might want to break in ... one never knows ... anyhow, my brother can look after himself ... I stay to look after you."

For a moment or two she stood quite still, her senses strained to grasp the meaning, the purport of the present situation—this madman on the watch outside—the young Count, key in hand, swaggering up to the back door at ten o'clock, when most folk would be at supper in the barn, her father gone, the village street wrapped in darkness!

Leopold, by a violent and sudden effort, had regained mastery over the muscles of his face and hands, these no longer twitched now, and he answered her look of mute inquiry with one of well-feigned quietude. Only his breath he could not control, it passed through his throat with a stertorous sound, and every now and then he had to pass his tongue over his dry, cracked lips.

Thus they stood for a moment eye to eye; and what she read in his glance caused a nameless fear to strike at her heart and to paralyse her will. But the next instant she had recovered her presence of mind. With quick, febrile movements she had already taken off her apron and with her hands smoothed her unruly dark hair. Then she made for the door.

Less than a second and already he had guessed her purpose: before she could reach the door he had his back against it and his nervy fingers had grasped her wrist.

"Where are you going?"

"Out," she said curtly.

"What for?"

"That's none of your business."

"What for?" he reiterated hoarsely.

"Let go my wrist," she exclaimed, "you are hurting me."

"I'll hurt you worse," he cried, in a broken voice, "if you cross this threshold to-night."

But he released her wrist, and she, wrathful, indignant, terrified, retreated to the other end of the room.

"Go out by the back door," he sneered, "if you want to go out. You have the key, haven't you?"

"My father ..." she began.

"Yes!" he said. "Go and tell your father that I, Leopold Hirsch, your affianced husband, am browbeating you—making a scene, what?—because you have made an assignation with my lord the young Count, here—at night—under your father's roof—under the roof of a child of Israel! You! An assignation with a dirty Christian! ... Bah! Go and tell your father that! And he will thrash you to within an inch of your life! We are Jews, he and I, and hold the honour of our women sacred—more sacred than their life!"

"Don't be a fool, Leopold," she cried, feeling that indeed, between her father and this madman, her life had ceased to be safe. She looked round her helplessly. Three or four besotted fools lying helpless across the tables, and all the village dancing and making merry some two hundred mètres away, her father—implacable, as she well knew, where her conduct was concerned—and this madman ready to kill to satisfy his lust of vengeance and of hate— she felt that indeed, unless Heaven performed a miracle, here was the beginning of an awful, an irredeemable tragedy.

"Leopold, don't be a fool," she reiterated, trying with all her might not to appear frightened or scared or confused. "I have

117

promised Kapus Elsa to go to her dance for half an hour. I had forgotten all about it. I must go now."

"Go and change your dress, then," he retorted with a sneer, "then you can go out by the back way. You have put the key away somewhere, haven't you? You know where it is."

"You are mad about doors to-night. I tell you I am going out now, by that front door—at once."

"And I tell you," he said, slowly and deliberately, "that if you cross the front door step I will call your father and tell him that you go and meet your lover—a Christian lover—the young Count—who would as soon think of marrying you as he would a nigger or a kitchen slut. Before you will have reached the high road your father and I will be on your heels, and either he or I will strangle you ere you come within sight of my lord's castle."

"You are mad!" she cried. "Or else an idiot."

"Better look for that back-door key," he retorted.

"What has the back-door key to do with it?" she asked sullenly.

"Only this," he replied, "that while that monkey-faced dog of a Christian was whispering to you just now, I know that the key was hanging on its usual peg, but I heard something about 'supper' and about 'ten o'clock.' May he break his neck, I say, and save me the job. Then he ordered me out of the room. Oh! I guessed! I am no fool, you know! When I came back I looked into your father's room—the key was gone, and I knew. And what I say is, why can't he come in by the front door like a man, if he has nothing to hide? Why must you let him come in like a thief by a back-door, if you have nothing to be ashamed of? The tap-room is open to anybody. Anybody can walk in and get a drink if they want to. Then why this whispering and this sneaking?"

He was working himself up to a greater and ever greater passion of fury. He kept his voice low because he didn't want Ignácz Goldstein to hear—not just yet, at any rate—for Ignácz was a hard man and a stern father, and God only knew what he might not do if he was roused. Leopold did not want Klara hurt—not yet, at any rate—not until he was quite sure that she meant to play him altogether false. She was vain and frivolous, over-fond of dress and of queening it over the peasant girls of the village, but there was no real harm in her. She was immensely flattered by the young Count's attentions and over-ready to accept his presents in exchange for kisses and whisperings behind closed doors, but there was no real harm in her—so at least Leopold Hirsch kept repeating to himself time and again, whenever jealousy gnawed at his heart more roughly than he could endure.

118

Just now that torment was almost unbearable, and the passion of fury into which he had worked himself blinded him momentarily to the dull, aching pain. Klara, as he spoke thus hoarsely, and brought his contorted face closer and closer to hers, had gradually shrunk more and more into the corner of the room, and there she remained now, flattened against the wall, her wide-open, terror-filled eyes fixed staringly upon this raving madman.

"You asked just now," he continued, in the same hoarse, guttural whisper, which seemed literally to be racking and tearing his throat as it came, "what the back-door key had to do with my not going to meet my brother at Fiume. Well! It has this much to do with it, that you happen to be my tokened wife, that you happen to be of my race and of my blood, a sober, clean-living Jewess, please God, and not one of those frivolous, empty-headed Christian girls— you are that now, I know; if you were not I would kill you first and myself afterwards: therefore, if to-night I catch a thief—any thief, I don't care who he is—sneaking into this house by a back door when you happen to be here alone and seemingly unprotected, if I catch any kind of thief or malefactor, I say ..."

He paused, and she, through teeth that chattered, contrived to murmur:

"Well? What do you say? Why don't you go on?"

"Because you understand," he said, with calm as sudden and as terrible as his rage had been awhile ago. "I am not a Christian, you know, nor yet a gentleman. I cannot walk up either to my lord's castle or to one of these Christian Magyar peasants and strike him in the face for trying to rob me of that which is more precious to me than life. I am a Jew ... a low-born, miserable Jew, whose whole race, origin and upbringing are despicable in the sight of the noble lords as well as of the Hungarian peasantry. Just a wretched creature whom one orders to hold one's horse, to brush one's boots, to stand out of one's way, anyhow; but not to meet as man to man, not to fight openly and frankly for the woman whom one loves. Well! You happen to be a Jewess too, and tokened to a Jew, and if either my lord or one of these d——d Magyar peasants chooses to come sneaking round you like a thief in the night, well ..."

He paused, and from the pocket of his shabby trousers he half drew out a long, sheathed hunting-knife, and then quickly hid it again from her sight.

Klara smothered a desperate cry of terror. Leopold now turned his back on her; he went up to the table and seizing a carafe of water, he poured himself out a huge mugful and drank it down at a draught. The edge of the mug rattled against his teeth, his hand was trembling so that half the contents were poured down on his

119

clothes. He did not look again on Klara, but having put the mug down, he passed his hand once or twice across his forehead as if to chase away some of those horrible thoughts which were still lurking in his brain.

Then he took his cigarette-case out of his pocket, selected a cigarette, struck a match and lit it, still avoiding Klara's fixed and staring gaze.

"I'll go and smoke this outside," he said quietly. "I can see both doors from the corner. When you have found that back-door key you may go to Elsa Kapus' wedding feast, but not before."

He took a final look round the room, and his eyes, which had once more become dull and pale, rested with an infinite look of contempt upon the two or three besotted drunkards who, throughout this scene, had done no more than open and blink a sleepy eye.

"Shall I turn these louts out for you now?" he asked.

"No, no," she replied mechanically, "let them have their sleep. When they wake they'll go away all right."

Just then the outer door was opened and Lakatos Andor's broad figure appeared upon the threshold. Leopold Hirsch gave him a nod, and without another look on Klara, he strode out into the night.

# CHAPTER XXI

## "Jealous, like a madman"

"I came to see if Béla was still here," said Andor, as soon as the door had closed on Leopold Hirsch. "One or two chaps whom I met awhile ago told me that he had not been seen in the barn this hour past, and that there was a lot of talk about it. I thought that if he were here, I could persuade you ..."

He paused, and looked more keenly at the girl.

"What is it, Klara?" he asked; "you seem ill or upset ..."

She closed her eyes once or twice like someone just waking out of a dream, then she passed her hands over her forehead and over her hair. She felt completely dazed and stupid, as if she had received a stunning blow on the head, and while Andor talked she looked at him with staring eyes, not understanding a word that he said.

"Yes—yes, Andor?" she said vaguely. "What can I do for you?"

"Nothing much, my good Klara," he replied; "it was only about Béla ..."

"Yes—about Béla," she stammered; "won't ... won't you sit down?"

"Thank you, I will for a moment."

She moved forward in order to get him a chair, but she found that she could not stand. The moment that she relinquished the prop of the wall, her knees gave way under her and she lurched forward against the table. She would have fallen had not Andor caught her and guided her to a chair, whereon she sank half fainting, with eyes closed and cheeks and lips the colour of ashes.

Just for the moment the wild thought flew through his mind that she had been induced to drink by one of the men, but a closer look on her wan, pale face and into those dilated eyes of hers convinced him that the girl was in real and acute mental distress.

He went up to the table and poured out a mug of wine, which he held to her lips. She drank eagerly, looking up at him the while with a strangely pathetic, eagerly appealing gaze.

When he had taken the mug from her and replaced it on the table, he drew a chair close to her and said as kindly as he could, for he did not feel very well-disposed toward the girl who was the cause of much unhappiness to Elsa:

"Now, Klara, you are going to tell me what is the matter with you."

But already she had recovered herself a little, and Lakatos Andor's somewhat dictatorial tone grated upon her sensitive ear.

"There's nothing the matter with me," she retorted, with a return of her habitual flippancy. "What should be the matter?"

"I don't know," he said dryly; "and, of course, if you tell me that it's a private affair of your own and none of my business, why I'll be quite satisfied, and not ask any more questions. But if it's anything to do with Béla ..."

"No, of course not," she broke in impatiently. "What should Béla have to do with my affairs? Béla has been gone from here this hour past."

"And he is not coming back?" asked Andor searchingly.

"I trust not," she replied fervently, and the young man noticed that the staring, terror-filled look once more crept into her eyes.

"Very well, then," he said, rising, "that is all I wanted to know. I am sorry to have disturbed you. Good-night, Klara."

"Good-night," she murmured.

121

He turned to go, and already his hand was on the latch of the door when an involuntary cry, like a desperate appeal, escaped her lips.

"Andor!"

"What is it?" he said, speaking over his shoulder.

He didn't like the girl: she had been offensive and insolent to Elsa, the cause of Elsa's tears; but just now, when he turned back in answer to that piteous call from her, she looked so forlorn, so pathetic, so terrified that all the kindliness and chivalry which are inherent in the true Magyar peasant rose up in his heart to plead on her behalf.

"You were quite right just now, Andor," she murmured. "I am in trouble—in grave, terrible trouble. ..."

"Is there anything I can do to help you?" he asked. "No, no, don't get up," he added hurriedly, for she had tried to rise and obviously was still unable to stand, "just stay where you are, and I'll come and sit near you. Is there anything I can do to help you?"

"Yes!" she whispered under her breath.

"What is it?"

"I don't know what you'll think of me."

"Never mind what I think," he said, a little impatiently; "if there's anything I can do to help you in your trouble I'll do it, but of course I can do nothing unless you tell me all about it."

She was trying to make up her mind to tell him, but it was desperately difficult.

She had always been so careful of her reputation—so careful that not a breath of real scandal should fall on her. She, of the downtrodden race, the Jewess whom even the meanest of the peasant girls thought it her right to despise, had been doubly careful not to give any loophole for gossip. She flirted with all the men, of course—openly and sometimes injudiciously, as in the case of Erős Béla on the eve of his wedding-day; but up to now she had never given any cause for scandal, nor anyone the right to look down on her for any other reason but that of her race and blood, which she could not help.

It was hard, therefore, to have to own to something that distinctly savoured of intrigue, and this to a man who she felt had no cause to be her friend. But the situation was desperate; there was that madman outside! God only knew of what he would be capable if he found that his jealous suspicions had some measure of foundation! And the young Count—ready to walk presently, without thought of coming danger, into the very clutches of that lunatic.

That of course was unthinkable. There had been murder in Leo's pale eyes when he fingered that awful-looking knife. The girl felt that such a risk could not be run: even the good opinion of the entire village became as nothing in her mind.

And of course there was the hope and chance that Andor would be chivalrous enough to hold his tongue. The young man's keen eyes had watched every phase of the conflict which was so distinctly reflected in the Jewess's mobile face. He waited patiently until he saw determination gradually asserting its sway over her hesitation. The girl interested him, and she was evidently in great trouble. Though he had no liking for her, he was anxious to know what had disturbed her so terribly and genuinely intended to be of use to her. He had no doubt that the trouble had something to do with Leopold Hirsch. Everyone knew the latter's jealous disposition, and Andor had not been home half a day before he had heard plenty of gossip on the subject.

"Well, Klara?" he asked quietly after awhile, when he saw that she appeared to be more calm and more able to speak coherently. "You don't deny that you are in trouble. ... You have half made up your mind to tell me. ... Well, then, out with it. ... What is it?"

"Only that Leopold is a swine," she blurted out roughly.

"Why? What has he done?"

"Jealous," she said; "like a madman."

"Oh?"

"And I'm at my wits' end, Andor," she moaned appealingly. "I don't know what to do."

"Hadn't you better tell me, then?"

She threw back her head and looked him squarely in the face with a sudden determination to end the present agonizing suspense at all costs.

"It is about young Count Feri."

"My lord?" he exclaimed—for, indeed, up to this last moment he had been quite sure in his mind that her trouble had to do with Erös Béla and with her impudent flirtation of this afternoon.

"Yes," she said sullenly, "he's a little sweet on me, you know— he admires me and thinks me amusing—he likes to come here sometimes, when he gets tired of starchy Countesses and Baronesses over at his castle. He means no harm," she added fiercely, "and if Leo wasn't such a beast ..."

"He has found you out, has he?" commented Andor dryly.

"Not exactly. There was nothing to find out. But Count Feri wanted to come and see me this evening to say 'good-bye,' as he is off to-morrow for some weeks to shoot bears. He couldn't come till about ten o'clock, and didn't want to be seen walking into the tap-room at that hour of the night. There is the back door, you know," she continued, talking a little excitedly and volubly, "which my

123

father always keeps locked and the key in his pocket, and Count Feri wanted me to give him the duplicate key, so that he could slip in that way unobserved."

"Hm!" mused Andor. "What would your father have said to that?"

"Father is going to Kecskemét presently by the nine o'clock train."

"And Leopold?"

"Leopold was going with him. He was to have gone to Fiume with the express to-morrow to meet his brother, who is coming home from America."

"Well—and ... ?"

"Well! He has changed his mind. He is not going to Fiume. He was watching me all the afternoon like a regular spy. People had told him that at the banquet to-day Erös Béla had been very attentive, so one of his jealous fits was on him."

"Not without cause, I imagine," said Andor, with a sarcastic laugh.

"Of course you would stick up for him," she retorted; "men always band themselves together against an unfortunate girl. But Leo has behaved like a brute. He watched me while my lord was talking to me, and caught snatches of our conversation. Then my lord sent him out of the room to look after his horse whilst he pressed me to give him the key of the back door."

"I understand."

"How could I guess that Leopold would be such a swine! It seems that when he came back he peeped into father's room and noticed at once that the key was gone. He guessed, of course—now he has threatened to tell father if I attempt to go out of this house. He won't let me out of his sight, and yet I must go and give Count Feri a warning and get that key back from him. If Leo tells father, father will half kill me, and already Leo has threatened to strangle me if he finds me on the high road on my way to the castle. My lord suspects nothing, of course ..." she added, while tears of impotence and of terror choked the words in her throat. "He'll come here presently, and as like as not Leopold will do for him."

She burst into a passionate fit of weeping. Andor waited quietly until the first paroxysm of sobs had subsided, and she could hear what he said, then he remarked quite quietly:

"As like as not, as you say."

"But I won't have him hurt," she murmured through her tears. "Leo would kill him for sure. You don't know, Andor, what Leopold is like when the jealous rage is in him. He is outside this house now, watching. And there he will stand and wait and watch; and he will

124

waylay Count Feri when he comes, and stab him with a hideous knife which he always carries in his pocket. Oh! It's horrible!" she moaned, "horrible! I don't know what to do. What can I do? Andor, tell me, what can I do?"

"What would you like to do?" he asked more gently, for indeed the girl's grief and terror were pitiable to behold.

"Run over to the castle," she replied, "and get the key back from Count Feri, and tell him on no account to come to-night. It is only a step; I could be back here in half an hour, and father is asleep in the next room. I should be back before he need start for the station. But Leopold is watching outside. He declared that he would strangle me or else tell father if I set foot outside this house. He is a brute, isn't he?"

"Well, you see, my dear Klara, I understand that you are tokened to Leopold now, and a man has a way of thinking that his affianced wife is his own, and not for other men to hang round her and make a fool of him!"

"Curse him!" she muttered savagely; "I'll never marry him after this."

"Oh, yes, you will," he retorted, with a light laugh; "you'll like him all the better presently for these outbursts of jealousy. A woman often gets fondest of the man she fears the most. But in the meanwhile you are at your wits' ends, eh, my pretty Klara? You can't think of any way out of your present difficulty, what? And to-night at ten o'clock there will be an awful scandal and worse—murder, perhaps!—and where will you be after that, eh, my pretty Klara? Even if your father does not break his stick over your shoulders, you'll have anyhow to leave this village, for the village will be too hot to hold you. And as your father does mighty good business at Marosfalva, he will not look too kindly on the daughter who, by her scandalous conduct, has driven him to seek a precarious fortune elsewhere. The situation certainly is a desperate one for you, my pretty one, what?"

"You need not tell me all that, Andor," she said sullenly. "Don't I know it?"

"It seems to me," he continued, slowly and deliberately, "that there never was a woman before quite so desperately in need of a friend as you are, eh, Klara?"

"I have no friend," she murmured.

"A friend, I mean, who would go and do your errand for you over at the castle, what?—and warn his young and noble lordship not to show his aristocratic face in Marosfalva to-night."

"I haven't such a friend, Andor, unless you ..."

125

"Well! You don't want me to go out and kill Leopold Hirsch, do you?" he said dryly.

"Of course not."

"Or engage him in a brawl while you run round to the castle?"

"It would be no good. He'd only tell father," she said, while a shiver ran through her body; "and they would kill me on my return."

"Exactly. What you want is, to stay here quite quietly, just as if nothing had happened, whilst the friend of whom I spoke just now went and got back that key which is causing so much trouble."

"Yes, yes, that's what I want, Andor," she cried eagerly; "and if you ..."

"Stop a bit," he broke in quietly; "I didn't say that I was that friend, did I?"

"Then you are only tormenting me. It isn't kind when I'm in such trouble."

"I didn't mean to torment you, Klara," he said more softly. "I will even go so far as to say that I might be that useful friend. You understand?"

"Yes! You'll make conditions for doing that friendly act for me. I understand well enough," she said, still speaking with fierce sullenness. "What are your conditions?" she asked.

"Look here, Klara," he replied earnestly, "a bargain is a bargain, isn't it? I will get you out of this trouble, and what's more, I'll hold my tongue about it. But you leave Erös Béla alone ... understand?"

"What do you mean?"

"Oh! You know well enough what I mean," he said, almost roughly now, for the name of Erös Béla, which he himself had brought into this matter, had at once conjured up in his mind the painful visions of this afternoon—Elsa's tears, her humiliation and unhappiness—and had once more hardened his heart against the woman who had been the cause of it all. "You know well enough what I mean. Erös Béla is full of vanity, your attentions to-day pleased him, and he neglected Elsa as he had no right to do. Now I don't say for a moment that you meant any harm. It was only your vanity that was pleasantly tickled too, but you made Elsa unhappy, and that is what I mean when I say that a bargain is a bargain. If I get you out of your trouble to-night, you must leave Erös Béla severely alone in the future."

"You are a fine one to preach," she retorted, with a harsh laugh. "As if you weren't in love with Elsa, though Elsa will be Béla's wife to-morrow."

"My being in love with Elsa has nothing to do with the matter.

Nor am I preaching to you. You want me to do you a service and I've told you my price. You can accept it or not as you please."

"I can't help Erös Béla running after me," came as a final sullen protest from the girl.

"Then you will have to try and help it, that's all," he said emphatically, "if you want me to help you."

She said nothing for a moment, whilst her dark eyes searched his own, trying to see how much determination lay behind that stern-looking face of his, then she murmured gently:

"And if I promise ... what you want me to promise, Andor ... will you go and see Count Feri at once?"

"A promise isn't enough," he said.

"An oath, then?"

"Yes. An oath."

"And you will bring me back that abominable key, and tell Count Feri just what has happened."

"If you will swear," he insisted.

"Yes, yes, I will swear," she cried eagerly now, for indeed a heavy load had been lifted off her heart, and her natural buoyancy of temperament was already reasserting its sway over her terrors and agony of mind. "What do you want me to say?"

"Swear by Almighty God," he said earnestly, "to leave Erös Béla alone, never to flirt with him or do anything to cause Elsa the slightest unhappiness."

"I swear it by Almighty God," she said solemnly, "and you need not be afraid," she added slowly; "I will not break my oath."

"No! I am not afraid that you will, for if you do ... Well! we won't talk about that," he continued more lightly. "I suppose there isn't much time to be lost."

"No, no, there isn't," she urged, "and don't make straight for the main road; go up the village first and then back through the fields; Leopold might suspect something—one never knows."

"All right, Klara, I'll do my best. We can but pray that I shall find my lord at home, in which case I can be back in twenty minutes. I'll pick up a friend or even two when I return, as then we can all walk into the tap-room together. It won't be so conspicuous as if I came in alone. What is the time now?" he asked.

She went to the partition door, opened it and peeped into her father's room.

"Just ten minutes to nine," she said; "father will have gone by the time you come back."

"That'll be as well, won't it?" he concluded, as he finally turned to go. "If you are not in the tap-room when I come back, what shall I do with the key?"

127

She pointed to a small brass tray which stood on the table in among the litter of bottles, glasses, mugs and tobacco-jars.

"Just on there," she said, "then if I come into the room later, I can see it there at a glance; and oh! what a relief it will be!"

The colour had come back to her cheeks. Indeed, she felt marvellously cheerful now and reassured. She knew that Andor would fulfil his share of the bargain, and the heavy cloud of trouble and of terror would be permanently lifted from her within the next half-hour.

In her usual, light-hearted, frivolous way she blew a kiss to Andor. But the young man, without looking again on her, had already opened the door, and the next moment he had gone out into the dark night on his errand of friendship.

# CHAPTER XXII

### "I go where I shall be more welcome"

In the meanwhile, in the barn time had been flying along on the wings of enjoyment. Ever since six o'clock, when vespers were well over and the gipsies had struck up the first csárdás, merry feet had been tripping it almost incessantly.

It is amazing what a capacity the young Hungarian peasant—man or woman—has for footing the national dance. With intervals of singing and of gossiping these young folk in the barn had been going on for over three hours.

And they were not even beginning to get tired. To the Hungarian peasants, be it remembered, the csárdás is not merely a dance, though they enjoy the movement, of course, the exhilaration and the excitement of the music, just as all healthy young animals would enjoy gambolling on a meadow; there is a deeper meaning to these children of the plains in the sweet, sad strains of their songs and in the mazes and intricacies of their dance.

They put their whole life, their entire sentiment for country and sweetheart, in the music and in the dance, and the music and the dance give outward expression to their feelings, speak in the language of poetry which they feel well enough, but which their untutored tongue cannot frame.

128

A Hungarian peasant in sorrow or distress will probably, like his Western prototype, seek to drown his grief in drink; far be it from his chronicler's mind to suggest that his sentiments are more elevated than those of the peasantry of other nations, or his morality more sound. He will get drunk, too, like men of other nations, but he will do it to the accompaniment of music. The gipsy band must be there, when he is in trouble or in joy—one or two fiddles, perhaps a clarionet, always a czimbalom—just these few instruments to play his favourite songs. They don't ease his sorrow, but they help to soothe it by bringing tears to his eyes and softening the bitterness of his grief.

And in joy he will invariably dance; when he is in love he will dance, for the csárdás helps him to explain to the girl whom he loves exactly what he feels for her. And she understands. One csárdás will reveal to a Hungarian village maid the state of her lover's heart far more clearly than do all the whisperings behind hedges in more civilized lands.

It was in the csárdás five years ago that Elsa had learned from Andor how much he loved her; it was during the mazes of the dance that she was able to overcome her shyness and tell him mutely that she loved him in return.

And now it was in the csárdás that she was bidding farewell to-day to her girlhood and to the companions of her youth; to Jenö and Móritz, who had loved her ardently and hopelessly these past two years, and who must henceforth become to her mere friends. It was in the turns and the twirls, with the wild music marking step, that she conveyed all that there was in her simple heart of regret for the past and cheerful anticipation for the future.

Elsa was a perfect dancer; it was a joy to have her for a partner, and she was indefatigable this afternoon. It seemed as if living fire was in her blood, her cheeks glowed, her eyes shone like dark-blue stars; she gave herself neither rest nor respite. Determined to enjoy every minute of the day, she had forcibly put behind her the sorrowful incidents of the afternoon. She would not remember and she would not think.

Andor was not here, and as the spirit of music and of dancing crept more and more into her brain, she almost got to the stage of believing that his appearance to-day had only been a dream. Nor would she look to see if Erös Béla were here.

She knew that he had gone off soon after dancing began. He had slipped away quietly, and at first no one had noticed his absence. He had always professed a lofty contempt for gipsy music and for the csárdás, a contempt which has of late come into fashion in Hungary among the upper classes, and has unfortunately been

129

aped by those whose so-called education has only succeeded in obliterating the fine national spirit of the past without having the power to graft more modern Western culture into this Oriental race.

Erös Béla belonged to this same supercilious set, and had made many enemies by his sarcastic denunciations of things that were almost thought sacred in Marosfalva. It was therefore quite an understood thing that the moment a csárdás was struck up, Erös Béla at once went to seek amusement elsewhere.

Of course to-day was a very different occasion to the more usual village entertainments. To-day he should have thought of nothing but his fiancée's pleasure. She was over-fond of dancing, and looked a picture when she danced. It was clearly a bridegroom's duty, under these circumstances, to stand by and watch his fiancée with all the admiration that should be filling his heart.

After the wedding, if he disapproved of the csárdás, why of course he could forbid his wife to dance it, and there would be an end of the matter. To-day he was still the groom, the servant of his fiancée—to-morrow only would he become her master.

But everyone was so intent upon enjoyment that a long time went by before gossip occupied itself exclusively with Erös Béla's absence from his pre-nuptial feast. When once it began it raged with unusual bitterness. The scandal during the banquet was being repeated now. Béla was obviously sitting in the tap-room of the inn, flirting with the Jewess, when he should have been in attendance on his bride.

Elsa could not help but hear the comments that were being made by all the mothers and fathers and older people who were not dancing, and who, therefore, had plenty of leisure for talk. All the proprieties were being outraged—so it was declared—and Elsa, who might have married so well at one time, was indeed now an object of pity.

She hated to hear all this talk, and felt hideously ashamed that people should be pitying her. Vainly did she try to get some measure of comfort from her mother. Kapus Irma, irritated by the looks of commiseration which were being levelled at her daughter, dubbed the latter a fool for not having the sense to know how to keep her bridegroom by her side.

It was past eight o'clock before Béla put in an appearance at all.

A csárdás was in full swing. The compact group of dancers was crowded round the musicians' platform, for the csárdás can only be properly danced under the very bow—as it were—of the gipsy leader. The barn looked gaily lighted up with oil-lamps swinging down from the rafters above, and it had been most splendidly decorated for the occasion with festoons of paper flowers and tri-colour flags. Petticoats and ribbons were flying, little feet in red leather boots were kicking up clouds of dust.

There was no moon to-night, the sky was heavy with clouds, so the village street had been very dark. Erös Béla blinked as he entered the barn, so dazzling did the picture present itself to his gaze.

And there was such an atmosphere of merriment and of animation about the place that instinctively Béla's thoughts flew back to the dismal and dingy little tap-room whence he had just come, with a few drunken fellows sprawling in corners and Leopold Hirsch's ugly face leering out of the shadows.

Here everyone was gay and good-tempered. The gipsies scraped their fiddles till one would have thought their arms would break, the young people danced, the men shouted and sang. It was a pandemonium of giddiness and music and laughter.

And Béla, as he blinked and looked upon the scene, remembered that he had paid for it all. He had paid for the hire of the barn, the music and the lighting; he had paid for the lavish supper which would be served presently. And as he had had more silvorium to drink in the tap-room than was altogether good for the clearness of his brain, he fell to thinking that he ought now to be received and welcomed with all the deference which his lavishness deserved. He thought that the young people should have left off dancing when he appeared, and should have greeted him, as they would undoubtedly have greeted my lord the Count, had the latter deigned to come.

And what, after all, was my lord on such an occasion in comparison with the donor of the feast?

Even Elsa—though she must, of course, have seen him—did not stop in her senseless gyrations. She was dancing with Barna Móritz—the mayor's youngest son and a splendid dancer—and the two young people went on twirling and twisting and flirting and laughing just as if he—the real host—had not been there.

Enraged at all this indifference, this want of recognition of his dignity, he elbowed his way through the dense group of spectators which formed a phalanx round the dancers. The wide and voluminous petticoats of the women formed a veritable hedge through which he had to scramble and to push. As the people recognized him they gave him pleasant greetings, for the Hungarian peasant is by nature kindly and something of an opportunist; there was no occasion to quarrel openly with Erös Béla, who was rich and influential.

But he paid no heed either to the greetings or to the whispered comments that followed in their wake. He just felt that he was the master of this place, and he meant everyone else to know and acknowledge this fact. So he strode up to the czigány and ordered them peremptorily to draw this interminable csárdás to an end; it had lasted quite long enough, he said, and the girls looked a sight with their crimson, perspiring faces; he was not going to have such vulgar goings-on at any of his wedding feasts.

The gipsy leader never thought of disobeying, of course; it was the tekintetes úr (honoured gentleman) who was paying them for their work, and they had to do as they were told.

Despite loud protests from the dancers, the csárdás was brought to a lovely and whirling close. Panting, hot and beaming, the dancers now mingled with the rest of the throng, and a pandemonium of laughter and chatter soon filled the barn from end to end.

Elsa, in accordance with the custom which holds sway even at village dances, was even now turning to walk away with her partner, whose duty it was to conduct her to her mother's side. She felt wrathful with Béla—as wrathful, at least, as so gentle a creature could be. She was ashamed of his behaviour, ashamed for herself as well as for him, and she didn't want to speak with him just now.

But he, still feeling dictatorial and despotic, had not yet finished asserting his authority. He called to her loudly and peremptorily:

"Elsa! I want a word with you."

"I'll come directly, Béla," she replied, speaking over her shoulder. "I want to speak to mother for a minute."

"You can speak to her later," he rejoined roughly. "I want a word with you now."

And without more ado he pushed his way up close to Elsa's side, elbowing Barna Móritz with scant ceremony. An angry word rose to the younger man's lips, and a sudden quarrel was only averted by a pleading look from Elsa's blue eyes. It would have been very unseemly, of course, to quarrel with one's host on such an occasion. Móritz, swallowing his wrath, withdrew without a word, even though he cursed Béla for a brute under his breath.

Béla took Elsa's arm and led her aside out of the crowd.

"You know," he said roughly, "how I hate you to mix with that rowdy lot like you do; and you know that I look on the csárdás as indecent and vulgar. Why do you do it?"

"The rowdy lot, as you call them, Béla," she replied firmly, "are my friends, and the csárdás is a dance which all true Magyars dance from childhood."

"I don't choose to allow my wife to dance it," he retorted.

132

"And after to-morrow I will obey you, Béla. To-day I asked my mother if I might dance. And she said yes."

"Your mother's a fool," he muttered.

"And remember that to-night I take leave of my girlhood," she said gently, determined not to quarrel. "My friends like to monopolize me ... it's only natural."

"Well! They are not my friends, anyway, and I'd rather you did not dance another csárdás to-night."

"I am sorry, Béla," she said quietly, "but I have promised Fehér Károly and also Jenö. They would be disappointed if I broke my promise."

"Then they'll have to be disappointed, that's all."

She made no reply, but looking at her face, which he saw in profile, he could not fail to note that her lips were tightly set and that there was an unwonted look of determination round her mouth. He drew in his breath, for he was quite ready for a second conflict of will to-day, nor, this time, was the issue for a moment in doubt in his mind. Women were made to obey—their parents first and then their husbands. In this case Béla knew well enough that his authority was fully backed by that of Elsa's mother—the invalid father, of course, didn't count, but Kapus Irma wanted that house on the Kender Road, she wanted the servant and the oxen, the chickens and the pigs, she wanted all the ease and the luxury which her rich son-in-law would give her.

No! There was no fear that Elsa would break her tokened word. In this semi-Oriental land, where semi-Oriental thought prevails, girls do not do that sort of thing—if they do, it is to their own hurt, and Elsa was not of the stuff of which rebellious or perjured women are made.

Therefore Béla now had neither fear nor compunction in asserting that authority which would be his to the full to-morrow. He felt that there was a vein of rebellion in Elsa's character, and this he meant to drain and to staunch till it had withered to nothingness. It would never do for him—of all men—to have a rebellious or argumentative wife.

"Well, then, that's settled," he said, with absolute finality, "you can go and talk to your precious friends as much as you like, so long as you behave yourself as a tokened bride should, but I will not have you dance that abominable csárdás again to-night."

"And have you behaved to-day, Béla," she retorted quite gently, "as a tokened bridegroom should?"

"That's nothing to do with it," he replied, with a harsh laugh. "I am a man, and you are a girl, and even the most ignorant Hungarian peasant will tell you that there is a vast difference there.

But I am not going to argue about it with you, my dear. I merely forbid you to dance a dance which I consider indecent. That's all."

"And I am sorry, Béla," she said, speaking at least as firmly as he did, "but I have given my promise, and even you would not wish me to break my word."

"You mean to disobey me, then?" he asked.

"Certainly not after to-morrow. To-day I have my mother's permission, and I am going to dance one csárdás now with Fehér Károly and one after supper again with Jenö."

They had both unconsciously raised their voices during these last few words, and thus aroused the attention of some of the folk, who had stood by to listen. Of course, everyone knew of Béla's aversion to the csárdás, and curiosity prompted gaffers and gossips to try and hear what would be the end of this argument between the pretty bride—who certainly looked rather wilful and obstinate now—and her future lord and master.

"Well said, little Elsa!" came now in ringing accents from the foremost group in the little crowd; "we must see you dance the csárdás once or twice more before that ogre has the authority to shut you up in his castle."

"Moreover, your promise has been made to me," asserted Fehér Károly lustily, "and I certainly shall not release you from it."

"Nor I," added Jenö.

"Don't you listen to Béla, my little Elsa," said one of the older women; "you are still a free girl to-day. You just do as you like—to-morrow will be time enough to do as he tells you."

But this opinion the married men present were not prepared to endorse, and one or two minor arguments and lectures ensued anent a woman's duty of obedience.

Béla had said nothing while these chaffing remarks were being passed over his head; and now that public attention was momentarily diverted from him, he took Elsa's hand and passed it under his arm.

"You had better go to your mother now, hadn't you?" he said, with what seemed like perfect calm. "You said just now that you wished to speak to her."

Elsa allowed him to lead her away. She tried vainly to guess what was going on in his mind. She knew, of course, that he must be very angry. Erös Béla beaten in an argument was at no time a very pleasant customer, and now he surely was raging inwardly, for he had set his heart on exerting his authority over this matter of the csárdás and had signally failed.

But she could not see how he felt, for he kept his face averted from her inquiring gaze.

Kapus Irma greeted her future son-in-law with obvious acerbity.

"I hear you have been teasing Elsa again," she said crossly. "Why can't you let her enjoy herself just for to-night, without interfering with her?"

"Oh! I am not going to interfere with her," he replied, with a sneer. "You have given her such perfect lessons of disobedience and obstinacy that it will take me all my time in the future to drill her into proper wifely shape. But to-night I am not going to interfere with her. She has told me plainly that she means to do just as she likes and that you have given her leave to defy me. Public opinion, it seems, is all in her favour too. So I have just brought your dutiful daughter back to you, and now I am free to make myself scarce."

"To make yourself scarce?" exclaimed Irma. "What do you mean?"

"Just what I say. I am not going to stay here, where I am jeered at by a lot of loutish, common peasants, who seem to have forgotten that I am paying for their enjoyment and for all the food and drink which they will consume presently. However, that's neither here nor there. Everyone seems to look upon this entertainment as Elsa's feast, and upon Elsa as the hostess and the queen. I am so obviously in the way and of no consequence. I go where I shall be more welcome."

He had dropped Elsa's arm and was turning to go, but Irma had caught hold of his coat.

"Where are you going?" she gasped.

"That's nothing to do with you, is it, Irma néni?" he replied dryly.

"Indeed it is," she retorted; "why, you can't go away like that— not before supper—you can't for Elsa's sake—what would everybody say?"

"I don't care one brass fillér what anybody says, Irma néni, and you know it. As for Elsa, why should I consider her? She has plenty of friends to stand by her, it seems, in her disobedience to my wishes. She has openly defied me, and made me look a fool. I am not going to stand that, so I go elsewhere—or I might do or say something which I might be sorry for later on—see?"

He tried to speak quietly and not to raise his voice, but it was also obvious that self-control was costing him a mightily vigorous effort, for the veins in his temples were standing up like cords, and his one eye literally shone with a sinister and almost cruel glow.

Kapus Irma turned to her daughter.

"Elsa," she said fretfully, "don't be such a goose. I won't have you quarrelling with Béla like this, just before your wedding. Just

135

you kiss him now, and tell him you didn't mean to vex him. We can't have everybody gossiping about this affair! My goodness! As if a csárdás or two mattered." ...

But here Béla's harsh laugh broke in on her mutterings.

"Don't waste your breath, Irma néni," he said roughly. "Even if Elsa were to come and beg my pardon now I would not remain here. I don't care for such tardy, perfunctory obedience, and this she will learn by and by. For to-night, if you and she feel ashamed and uncomfortable, well! so much the better. Village gossip doesn't affect me in the least. I do as I like, and let all the chattering women go to h——l. Good-night, Irma néni—good-night, Elsa! I hope you will be in a better frame of mind to-morrow."

And before Kapus Irma could detain him or utter another protest, he was gone, and she turned savagely on her daughter.

"Elsa!" she said, "you are never going to let us all be shamed like this? Run after him at once, and bring him back!"

"He wouldn't come back, mother, if I begged him ever so ..." said Elsa drearily; "and besides—where should I find him?"

"On his way to Ignácz Goldstein's, of course. If you run you can easily overtake him."

"I can't, mother," protested Elsa; "how can I?"

"You'll just do as I tell you, my girl!" said Irma firmly, and with a snap of her lean jaws. "By the Holy Virgin, child! Are you going to disobey your mother now? God will punish you, you know, if you go on like that. Go at once as I tell you. Run out by this door here. No one will see you, you will overtake Béla before he is half-way down the street, and then you must just bring him back. That's all."

Long habits of obedience were so ingrained in the girl that at this moment—though she felt quite sure that all her attempts would be in vain, and though she felt bitterly humiliated at having to make such attempts—she never thought of openly defying her mother. Indeed, she quite believed that God would punish her if she rebelled so constantly, for this had been drilled into her since her earliest childhood's days.

Fortunately for the moment everyone's attention was concentrated on a table of liquid refreshments in a remote corner of the barn, and Elsa and her mother were practically isolated here, and the last little scene had gone by unobserved.

Irma picked a shawl from off her own shoulders and put it round her daughter; then she gave her a final significant push. Elsa, with her tear-dimmed eyes, could scarcely find the little side door which was fashioned in the wooden wall itself, and gave direct access into the street.

God would punish her if she defied her mother; well! God's wrath must be harder to bear than the bitter humiliation to which her mother had so airily condemned her. To beg Béla's forgiveness, to assure him of her obedience, to stand shamed before him and before all her friends, surely God couldn't want her to do all that?

But already she had crossed the threshold and was out in the dark, silent street. She ran on mechanically in the direction of the inn; her mother's commands seemed to be moving her along, for certainly her own will had nothing to do with it. Her cheeks were aflame, and her eyes burned with all the tears which she would not shed, but she herself felt cold and numb, as she ran on blindly, stupidly, to where she had just seen a tiny speck of light.

The night was dark but exquisitely calm—perfectly still, yet full of those mysterious whisperings which come from the bosom of the plain, the flutter of birds' wings, snug in their night's lodgings amongst the drooping branches of pollarded willows, the quiver of the plumed heads of maize, touched by some fairy garment as it brushed by, the call of the cricket from among the tall sunflowers and the quiver of the glow-worm on the huge pumpkin leaves.

Elsa knew all these soft whisperings; she was a child of this immense and majestic plain, and all the furtive little beasts that dwelt within its maze were bosom friends of hers.

At other times, when her mind and heart had been at peace, she loved these dark, calm nights, when heavy clouds hid the light of the moon and sounds grew louder and more distinct as the darkness grew more tense; neither fluttering of unseen wings nor quiver of stealthy footsteps had the power to startle her; they were all her friends, these tiny dwellers of the plain, these midnight marauders of whom townsfolk are always so afraid.

At first, when she perceived the tiny speck of light on ahead, she thought that it must be a glow-worm settled on the leaves of the dahlias outside the school-house, for glow-worms had been over-abundant this late summer, but soon she saw that the burning speck was moving along, on ahead in the same direction as she herself was going—on the way to Ignácz Goldstein's.

Béla had lighted a cigar when he left the barn; nursing his resentment, he had walked along rapidly toward the inn, his head whirling with thoughts of the many things which he meant to do in order to be revenged on Elsa this night.

Of course a long visit to Klara fully entered into those schemes, and now he paused just at the foot of the verandah steps breathing in the soft evening air with fully dilated nostrils and lungs, so that his nerves might regain some semblance of that outward calm which his dignity demanded.

And thus, standing still, he heard through the silence the patter of small, high-heeled boots upon the hard road. He guessed at once that Elsa had been sent along by her mother to bring him back, and a comforting glow of inward satisfaction went right through his veins as, after a slight moment of hesitation, he made up his mind to await Elsa's coming here, to listen to her apologies, to read her the lecture which she fully deserved, but nevertheless to continue the plan of conduct which he had mapped out for himself.

# CHAPTER XXIII

## "On the eve of one's wedding day too"

He could not see Elsa till she was quite close to him, and even then he could only vaguely distinguish the quaint contour of her wide-sleeved shift and of her voluminous petticoats.

But his cigar had gone out, and when Elsa stood quite close to him, and softly murmured his name, he struck a match very deliberately, and held it to the cigar so that it lighted up his face for a few seconds. He wanted her to see how indifferent was the expression in his eye, and that there was not the slightest trace of a welcoming smile lurking round his lips.

Therefore he held the lighted match close to his face much longer than was necessary; he only dropped it when it began to scorch his fingers. Then he blew a big cloud of smoke out of his cigar straight into her face, and only after that did he say, speaking very roughly:

"What do you want?"

"Mother sent me, Béla," she said timidly, as she placed a trembling little hand on his coat-sleeve. "I wouldn't have come, only she ordered me, and I couldn't disobey her, so I ..."

"Couldn't disobey your mother, eh?" he sneered; "you couldn't defy her as you did me, what?"

"I didn't mean to defy you, Béla," she said, striving with all her might to keep back the rebellious words which surged out of her overburdened heart to her quivering lips. "I couldn't be unkind to Jenö and Károly, and all my old friends, just this last evening, when I am still a girl amongst them."

138

"You preferred being obstinate and wilful toward me, I suppose?"

"Don't let us quarrel, Béla," she pleaded.

"I am not quarrelling," he retorted. "I came to the barn just now looking forward to the pleasure of having you to myself for a little bit. There was a lot I wanted to say to you—just quietly, in a corner by our two selves. And how did I find you? Hot and panting, after an hour's gyrations, hardly able to stand, and certainly not able to speak; and at my simple request that you should give up a dance of which I whole-heartedly disapprove, you turned on me with impudence and obstinacy. I suppose you felt yourself backed up by your former sweetheart, and thought you could just treat me like the dirt under your feet."

He certainly had proved himself a good advocate in his own cause. The case thus put succinctly and clearly before her appeared very black to Elsa against herself. Ever ready for self-deprecation, she began to think that indeed she had behaved in a very ugly, unwomanly and aggressive manner, and her meekness cost her no effort now when she said gently:

"I am sorry, Béla! I seem to have been all queer the whole of to-day. It is a very upsetting time for any girl, you must remember. But Pater Bonifácius said that if any sin lay on my conscience since my last confession, I could always find him in church at seven o'clock to-morrow morning, before our wedding Mass, so as to be quite clear of sin before Holy Communion."

"That's all right, then," he said, with a hard laugh. "You had better find him in church to-morrow morning, and tell him that you have been wilful and perverse and disobedient. He'll give you absolution, no doubt. So now you'd better go back to your dancing. Your many friends will be pining for you."

"Won't you ... won't you come back with me, Béla?" she pleaded.

"No. I won't. I have told your mother plainly enough that I wasn't coming back. So why she should have sent you snivelling after me, I can't think."

"I think that even if mother hadn't sent me I should have come ultimately. I am not quite sure, but I think I should have come. I know that I have done wrong, but we are all of us obstinate and mistaken at times, aren't we, Béla? It is rather hard to be so severely punished," she added, with a wistful little sigh, "on the eve of one's wedding day too, which should be one of the happiest days in a girl's life."

"Severely punished?" he sneered. "Bah! As if you wanted me over there. You've got all your precious friends."

139

"But I do want you, Béla. All the time that you were not in the barn this afternoon I ... I felt lonesome."

"Then why didn't you send for your old sweetheart? He would have cheered you up."

"Don't say that, Béla," she said earnestly, and once more her little hand grasped his coat-sleeve; "you don't know how it hurts. I don't want to think of Andor. I only want to think of you, and if you would try and be a little patient, I am sure that we would understand one another better very soon."

"I hope so, my dear," he rejoined dryly, "for your sake—as I am not a patient man; let me tell you that. Come, give me a kiss and run back to your mother. I can't bear to have a woman snivelling near me like that."

He drew her toward him with that rough, perfunctory gesture which betokened the master rather than the lover. Then with one hand he raised her chin up and brought her face quite close to his. Even then he could not see her clearly because of the heavy clouds in the sky. But the air seemed suddenly to have become absolutely still, not a breath of wind stirred the leaves of the acacia trees, and all those soft sighings and mysterious whisperings which make the plain always appear so full of life were for the moment hushed. Only from far away came the murmur of the sluggish waters of the Maros, and from its shores the call of a heron to its mate. Elsa made vigorous efforts to swallow her tears. The exquisite quietude of Nature, that call of the heron, the scent of dying flowers which lingered in the autumn air, made her feel more strongly than she had ever felt before how beautiful life might have been.

Pater Bonifácius' words rang in her ears: "You are going to be happy in God's way, my child, which may not be your way, but must be an infinitely better one."

Well! For the moment Elsa didn't see how this was going to be done; she did not see how she could ever be happy beside this tyrannical, arrogant man who would be, and meant to be, her master rather than her mate.

Even now the searching look wherewith his one eye, with its sinister expression, tried to read her very soul had in it more of pride of possession, more of the appraiser of goods than the ardour of a bridegroom. Béla cursed the darkness which prevented his reading now every line of that pure young face which was held up to his; he longed with all the passionate masterfulness of his temperament to know exactly how much awe, how much deference, how much regard she felt for him. Of love he did not think, nor did he care if it never came; but this beautiful prize which had been coveted by so many was his at last, and he meant to mould it and wield it in accordance with his pleasure.

But in spite of his callousness and his selfishness, the intense womanliness of the girl stirred the softer emotions of his heart; there was so much freshness in her, so much beauty and so much girlishness that just for one brief second a wave, almost of tenderness, swept over his senses.

He kissed the pure young lips and drank in greedily their exquisite sweetness, then he said somewhat less harshly:

"You are too pretty, my dove, to put on those modern airs of emancipated womanhood. If you only knew how much better you please me like this, than when you try to argue with me, you would always use your power over me, you little goose."

She made no reply, for, despite the warm woollen shawl round her shoulders, she had suddenly felt cold, and a curious shiver had gone right through her body, even whilst her future lord did kiss her. But no doubt it was because just then an owl had hooted in the poplar trees far away.

"You are coming back then, Béla?" she asked, after a few seconds of silence and with enforced cheerfulness.

"I'll think about it," he said condescendingly.

"But ..."

"There, now, don't begin again," he broke in impatiently. "Haven't I said that I'll think about it? You run back to your mother now. I may come later—or I may not. But if you bother me much more I certainly won't. If I come, I come of my own free will; there's no woman living who has ever persuaded me to do anything against my will."

And without vouchsafing her another word or look, without deigning to see her safely on her way back to the barn, he turned leisurely on his heel, and mounting the steps of the verandah before him, he presently pushed open the tap-room door and disappeared within.

141

# CHAPTER XXIV

## "If you loved me"

Elsa stood for a moment quite still there in the dark, with the silence of the night and all its sweet sounds encompassing her, and the scent of withered flowers and slowly-dying leaves mounting to her quivering nostrils.

What did it all mean? What did life mean? And what was the meaning of God? She, the ignorant, unsophisticated peasant girl, knew nothing save what Pater Bonifácius had taught her, and that was little enough—though the little was hard enough to learn.

Resignation to God's will; obedience to parents first and to husband afterwards; renunciation of all that made the days appear like a continual holiday and filled the nights with exquisite dreams!

But if life only meant that, only meant duty and obedience and resignation, then why had God made such a beautiful world, why had He made the sky and the birds and the flowers, the nodding plumes of maize and the tiny, fleecy clouds which people the firmament at sunset?

Was it worth while to deck this world in such array if the eyes of men were always to be filled with tears, and their backs bent to their ever-recurring tasks?

A heavy sigh escaped from the girl's overburdened heart: the riddle of the universe was too hard an one for her simple mind to solve. Perhaps it was best after all not to think of these things which she was too ignorant to understand. She looked at the door of the tavern through which Béla had gone. He had left it wide open, and she caught a glimpse of him now as he sat at one of the tables, and leaning his elbow on it, rested his chin in his hand.

Then, with another little sigh, she was just turning to go when the sound of her name spoken in a whisper and quite close to her sent her pulses quivering and made her heart beat furiously.

"Elsa! Wait a moment!"

"Is that you, Andor?" she whispered.

"Yes. I came up just now and heard your voice and Béla's. I waited on the off-chance of getting a word with you."

"I mustn't stop, Andor. Mother will be wondering."

"No, she won't," he retorted with undisguised bitterness. "The mother who sent you on this abominable and humiliating errand won't worry much after you."

"No one seems to worry much about me, do they, Andor?" she said, a little wistfully.

He drew a little closer to her, so close that he could feel her shoulder under the shawl quivering against his arm. Her many petticoats brushed about his shins, and he could hear her quick, warm breath as it came and went. He bent his head quite close to her, as he had done that day, five years ago, in the mazes of the csárdás, and now—as then—his lips almost touched her soft young neck.

"Then why should you worry about them, Elsa?" he whispered slowly in her ear. "Why shouldn't you let them all be?"

"Let them all be?" she said. "But everyone will be wondering if I don't go back—at least for supper."

"I don't mean about the dance and the supper, Elsa," he continued, still speaking in a whisper and striving to subdue the hoarseness in his voice which was engendered by the passion which burned in his veins, "I don't only mean to-night. I mean ... for good." ...

"For good?" she repeated slowly.

"Let me take you away, Elsa," he entreated, "away from here. Leave all these rough, indifferent and selfish folk. Come out with me to Australia, and let all these people be."

At first, of course, she didn't understand him; but gradually his meaning became clear and she gave one long, horrified gasp.

"Andor! How can you?"

"It has been borne upon me, Elsa, these hours past, that I am a coward and a villain to let you go on with this miserable life. Nay! it's worse than that, for your future life with that bully, that brute, will be far more wretched than you have any idea now. He doesn't care for you, Elsa—not really—not as I care for you, not as you—the sweetest, gentlest, purest woman in the world—should be cared for and cherished. He doesn't love you, Elsa, he doesn't even really want you—not as I want you—I, who would give my life, every drop of my blood, to have you for myself alone!"

Gradually, as he spoke, his arms had clasped round her, his passionate whispers came in short gasps to her ear. Gently now she disengaged herself.

"But I am tokened to Béla, Andor," she said gently. "To-morrow is my wedding day. I have made my confession. Pater Bonifácius has prepared me for Holy Communion. My word is pledged to Béla."

"He doesn't love you, Elsa, and he is not your husband yet. Your pledged word does not bind you before God. To-day you are still free. You are free until you have sworn before the altar of God.

143

Elsa! Béla doesn't want you, he doesn't love you. And I love you and want you with my whole heart and soul."

"Don't speak like that, Andor, don't," she almost pleaded. "You must know how wrong it is for you to speak and for me to listen."

"But I must speak, Elsa," he urged, "and you have got to listen. We could get away now, Elsa, to-night, by the nine-twenty train. Over at the barn no one would know that you had gone until it got too late to run after you. Never mind about your clothes. I have plenty of money in my pocket, and to-morrow when we get to Budapesth we can get what you want. By the next day we should be in Fiume, and then we would embark on the first ship that is outward bound. I know just how to manage, Elsa. You would have nothing to do, nothing to think of, but just give yourself over into my keeping. You are a free woman, Elsa, bound to no one, and the first opportunity we had we would get married. Out there in Australia I can get plenty of work and good pay: we shouldn't be rich, Elsa—not as rich as you would be if you married Erös Béla, but by God I swear that we would be happy, for every minute of my life would be devoted to your happiness."

All the while that he spoke she had made persistent efforts to disengage herself from his grasp. She felt that she must get away from him, away from his insinuating voice, from the ardour of those whispered words which seemed to burn into her very soul. The very night seemed to be in league with him, the darkness and the silence and all those soft sounds of gently-murmuring river and calls of birds and beasts, and the fragrance of dying flowers which numbed the senses and obliterated the thought of God, of duty and of parents.

"No, no, Andor," she murmured feebly, "you have no right to speak like that. I am tokened to Béla. I have sworn that I would be his wife. My hand was in his and the Pater blessed us; and it was after Holy Communion and when Christ Himself was in my heart! And there is mother too and father, the house which Béla promised them, the oxen and the pigs, a maid to look after father. Mother would curse me if I cheated her of all that now."

"When we are settled in Australia," he pleaded earnestly, "we will write to your parents and send them money to come out and join us."

"Father is paralysed. How could he come? And mother would curse me. And a mother's curse, Andor, is registered by God."

"Elsa, if you loved me you would leave father and mother and come with me."

"Then perhaps I do not love you, Andor," she said slowly, "for

144

I could not bear my mother's curse, I could not break the pledge which I swore after Holy Communion! I could not commit so great a sin, Andor, not even for your sake, for if I did remorse would break my heart, and all your love for me would not compensate me for the sin."

And before he could say another word, before his arms could once more close round her or his trembling hands clutch at her fluttering petticoats, she was gone—vanished out of his grasp and into the darkness, and only the patter of her little feet broke the silence of the night.

# CHAPTER XXV

### "In any case Elsa is not for you"

Andor with a sigh of heartbroken disappointment now turned to go into the inn. He had the key in his hand which my lord the young count had given him with a careless laugh and a condescending nod of acknowledgment for the service thus rendered to him and to Klara.

The door of the tap-room was still wide open, a narrow wedge-shaped light filtrated through on to the beams and floor of the verandah, making the surrounding blackness seem yet more impenetrable.

Andor entered the tap-room and walked straight up to the centre table, and he placed the key upon the small tray which Klara had pointed out to him. Then he turned and looked around him: Klara was not there, and the room was quite deserted. Apparently the sleepers of awhile ago had been roused from their slumbers and had departed one by one. For a moment Andor paused, wondering if he should tell Klara that he had been successful in his errand. He could hear the murmur of the girl's voice in the next room talking to her father.

No! On the whole he preferred not to meet her again: he didn't like the woman, and still felt very wrathful against her for the impudent part she had played at the feast this afternoon.

He had just made up his mind to go back to the presbytery where the kind Pater had willingly given him a bed, when Erös

Béla's broad, squat figure appeared in the open doorway. He had a lighted cigar between his teeth and his hands were buried in the pockets of his trousers; he held his head on one side and his single eye leered across the room at the other man.

When he encountered Andor's quick, savage glance he gave a loud, harsh laugh.

"She gave it you straight enough, didn't she?" he said as he swaggered into the room.

"You were listening?" asked Andor curtly.

"Yes. I was," replied Béla. "I was in here and I heard your voice, so I stole out on to the verandah. You were not ten paces away; I could hear every word you said."

"Well?"

"Well what?" sneered the other.

"What conclusion did you arrive at?"

"What conclusion?" retorted Béla, with a laugh. "Why, my good man, I came to the conclusion that in spite of all your fine talk about God and so on, and all your fine airs of a gentleman from Australia, you are nothing but a low-down cur who comes sneaking round trying to steal a fellow's sweetheart from him."

"I suppose you are right there, Béla," said Andor, with a quick, impatient sigh and with quite unwonted meekness. "I suppose I am, as you say, nothing but a low-down cur."

"Yes, my friend, that's just it," assented the other dryly; "but she's let you know pretty straight, hasn't she? that she wouldn't listen to your talk. Elsa will stick by me, and by her promise to me, you may bet your shirt on that. She is too shrewd to think of exchanging the security of to-day for any of your vague promises. She is afraid of her mother and of me and of God's curses and so on, and she does not care enough about you to offend the lot of us, and that's about how it stands."

"You are right there, Béla, that is about how it stands."

"And so, my fine gentleman," concluded Béla, with a sneer, "you cannot get rid of me unless you are ready to cut my throat and to hang for it afterwards. In any case, you see, Elsa is not for you."

Andor said nothing for the moment. It seemed as if vaguely in his mind some strong purpose had already taken birth and was struggling to subjugate his will. His bronzed face marked clearly the workings of his thoughts: at first there had been a dulled, sombre look in his dark, deep-set eyes; then gradually a flame seemed to flicker in them, feebly at first, then dying down for awhile, then rising again more triumphant, more glowing than before, even as the firm lines around the tightly-closed lips became more set and more expressive of a strong resolve.

146

Ignácz Goldstein's querulous voice was heard in the other room, giving fussy directions to his daughter about the collecting and packing up of his things. Anon, he opened the door and peered out into the tap-room: he had heard the confused murmur of footsteps and of voices, and possible customers must not be neglected even at an anxious moment of departure.

Seeing Béla and Andor there, he asked if anything was wanted.

"No, no," said Béla impatiently, "nothing more to-night. Andor and I are going directly."

The narrow hatchet-face once more disappeared behind the door. Klara's voice was heard to ask:

"Who is in the tap-room, father?"

"Andor and Béla," replied the old man, "but never you mind about the tap-room. Just see that you don't forget my red handkerchief, and my fur cap for the journey, and my bottle of ..."

His mumblings became inaudible, and after awhile Béla reiterated, with an airy laugh:

"No, my friend! Elsa is not for you."

Then it was that Andor's confused thoughts shaped themselves into a resolve.

"Not unless you will give her up, Béla," he said slowly: "you yourself, I mean—now—at this eleventh hour."

"I?" queried the other harshly—not understanding. "Give her up?"

"Yes. Tell her that you have thought the whole matter over; that you have realized that nothing but unhappiness can come from your union together. She would feel a little humiliated at first, perhaps, but she would come to me, if you would let her go. I can deal with Irma néni after that. If you will release Elsa yourself of her promise she would come to me, I know."

Béla looked for awhile in silence at the earnest face of the other man, then he burst into a loud, mocking laugh.

"You are mad," he said, "or else drunk."

"I am neither," rejoined the other calmly. "It is all perfectly feasible if only you will release Elsa. You have so often asserted that you don't care one brass fillér for the opinion of village folk."

"And I don't."

"Then it cannot matter to you if some blame is cast on you for breaking off with Elsa on the eve of your wedding. People must see how unsuited you are to each other and how unhappy your marriage must eventually turn out. You have no feeling about promises, you have no parents who might curse you if you break them. Break your promise to Elsa now, Béla, and you will be doing the finest action of your life. Break your promise to her, man, and let her come to me."

Béla was still staring at Andor as if indeed he thought the other mad, but now an evil leer gradually spread over his face and his one eye closed until it looked like a mere slit through which he now darted on Andor a look of triumph and of hate.

"Break my promise to Elsa?" he said slowly and deliberately. "I wouldn't do it, my good man, if you offered me all the gold in your precious America."

"But you don't love her, Béla," urged Andor, with ardent earnestness. "You don't really want her."

"No, I don't," said the other roughly, "but I don't want you to have her either."

"What can it matter to you? There are plenty of pretty girls this side of the Maros who would be only too glad to step into Elsa's shoes."

"I don't care about any pretty girls on this side of the Maros, nor on the other either for that matter. I won't give Elsa up to you, my friend, and she won't break her promise to me because she fears God and her mother's curse. See?"

"She's far too good for you," cried Andor, with sudden vehemence, for he had already realized that he must give up all hope now, and the other man's manner, his coarseness and callousness had irritated him beyond the bounds of endurance. He hated this cruel, selfish brute who held power over Elsa with all the hatred of which his hot Magyar blood was capable. A red mist seemed at times now to rise before his eyes, the kind of mist that obscures a man's brain and makes him do deeds which are recorded in hell.

"She's far too good for you," he reiterated hoarsely, even as his powerful fists clenched themselves in a violent effort to keep up some semblance of self-control. The thought of Elsa still floated across his mental vision, of Elsa whose pure white hand seemed to dissipate that ugly red mist with all the hideous thoughts which it brought in its trail. "You ought to treat her well, man," he cried in the agony of his soul, "you've got to treat her well."

The other looked him up and down like a man does an enemy whom he believes to be powerless to do him any harm. Then he said with a sneer through which, however, now there was apparent an undercurrent of boiling wrath:

"I'll treat her just as I choose, and you, my friend, had best in the future try to attend to your own business."

But Andor, obsessed by the one idea, feeling his own helplessness in the matter, would not let the matter drop.

"How you can look at another woman," he said sombrely, "while Elsa is near you I cannot imagine."

He looked round him vaguely, as if he wanted all the dumb, inanimate things around him to bear witness to this monstrous idea: Elsa flouted for another woman! Elsa! the most beautiful woman on God's earth, the purest, the best—flouted! And for whom? for what?—other girls—women—who were not worthy to walk in the same street as Elsa! The thought made Andor giddy, his glance became more wandering, less comprehending ... that awful red mist was once more blurring his vision.

And as he looked round him—ununderstanding and wretched—his glance fell upon the key which he himself had placed upon the brass tray a few moments ago; and the key brought back to his mind the recollection of Klara the Jewess, her domination over Béla, her triumph over Elsa, and also the terrible plight in which she had found herself when she had begged Andor for friendly help, and given him in exchange the solemn promise which he had exacted from her.

This recollection eased somewhat the heavy burden of his anxiety, and there was quite a look of triumph in his eyes when he once more turned to Béla.

"Well!" he said, "there's one thing certain, and that is that Elsa won't have to suffer again from the insolence of that Jewess. I have cut the ground from under your feet in that direction, my friend."

"Indeed!" retorted Béla airily. "How did you manage to do that?"

"I rendered her a service this afternoon—she was in serious trouble and asked me to help her."

"Oh?—and may I ask the nature of the trouble—and of the service?" sneered the other.

"Never mind about the nature of the service. I did help Klara in her trouble, and in return she has given me a solemn promise to have nothing whatever more to do with you."

"Oh! did she?" cried Béla, whose savage temper, held in check for awhile, had at last risen to its habitual stage of unbridled fury. All the hot blood had rushed to his head, making his face crimson and his eye glowing and unsteady, and his hand shook visibly as he leaned against the table so that the mugs and bottles rattled, as did the key upon the metal tray. He, too, felt that hideous red mist enveloping him and blurring his sight. He hated Andor with all his might, and would have strangled him if he had felt that he had the physical power to do it as well as the moral strength. His voice came hoarse and hissing through his throat as he murmured through tightly clenched teeth:

149

"She did, did she? And you made her give you that promise which is not going to bind her, let me tell you that. But let me also tell you in the meanwhile, my fine gentleman from America, that your d——d interference will do no good to your former sweetheart, who is already as good as my wife—and will be my wife to-morrow. Klara Goldstein is my friend, let me tell you that, and ..."

He paused a moment ... something had arrested the words in his throat. As so often occurs in the mysterious workings of Fate, a small, apparently wholly insignificant event suddenly caused the full tide of his destiny to turn—and not only of his own destiny but that of many others!

An event—a tiny fact—trivial enough for the moment: the touch of his hand against the key upon the brass tray.

Mechanically he picked up the key: his mind was not yet working quite clearly, but the shifty glance of his one eye rested upon the key, and contemplated it for awhile.

"Well!" he murmured vaguely at last, "how strange!"

"What is strange?" queried the other—not understanding.

"That this key should, so to speak, fall like this into my hand."

"That isn't strange at all," said Andor, with a shrug of the shoulders, for now he thought that Béla was drunk, so curious was the look in his eye, "considering that I put that key there myself half an hour ago—it is the key of the back door of this house."

"I know it is," rejoined Béla slowly, "I have had it in my possession before now ... when Ignácz Goldstein has been away from home, and it was not thought prudent for me to enter this house by the front door ... late at night—you understand."

Then, as Andor once more shrugged his shoulders in contempt, but vouchsafed no further comment, he continued still more slowly and deliberately:

"Isn't it strange that just as you were trying to interfere in my affairs, this key should, so to speak, fall into my hand. Fate plays some funny little pranks sometimes, eh, Mr. Guardian Angel?"

"What has Fate got to do with it?" queried Andor roughly.

"You don't see it?"

"No."

"Then perhaps you were not aware of the fact," said Béla blandly, as he toyed with the key, "that papa Goldstein is going off to Kecskemét to-night."

"Yes," replied Andor slowly, "I did know that, but ..."

"But you didn't know, perhaps, that pretty Klara likes a little jollification and a bit of fun sometimes, and that papa Goldstein is a very strict parent and mightily particular about the proprieties. It is a way those cursed Jews have, you know."

150

"Yes!" said Andor again, "I did know that too."

He was speaking in a curious, dazed kind of way now: he suddenly felt as if the whole world had ceased to be, and as if he was wandering quite alone in a land of dreams. Before him, far away, was that red misty veil, and on ahead he could dimly see Béla, with a hideous grin on his face, brandishing that key, whilst somehow or other the face of Leopold Hirsch, distorted with passion and with jealousy, appeared to beckon to him from behind that distant crimson veil.

"Well, you see," continued Béla, in the same suave and unctuous tones which he had suddenly assumed, "since pretty Klara is fond of jollification and a bit of fun, and her father is over-particular, why, that's where this nice little key comes in. For presently papa will be gone and the house worthily and properly shut up, and the keys in papa Goldstein's pocket, who will be speeding off to Kecskemét; but with the help of this little key, which is a duplicate one, I—who am a great friend of pretty Klara—can just slip into the house quietly for a comfortable little supper and just a bit of fun; and no one need be any the wiser, for I shall make no noise and the back door of this house is well screened from prying eyes. Have you any further suggestion to make, my fine gentleman from America?"

"Only this, man," said Andor sombrely, "that it is you who are mad—or drunk."

"Oh! not mad. What harm is there in it? You chose to interfere between Klara and me, and I only want to show you that I am the master of my own affairs."

"But it'll get known. Old Rézi's cottage is not far and she is a terrible gossip. Back door or no back door, someone will see you sneaking in or out."

"And if they do—have you any objection, my dear friend?"

"It'll be all over the village—Elsa will hear of it."

"And if she does?" retorted Béla, with a sudden return to his savage mood. "She will have to put up with it: that's all. She has already learned to-day that I do as I choose to do, and that she must do as I tell her. But a further confirmation of this excellent lesson will not come amiss—at the eleventh hour, my dear friend."

"You wouldn't do such a thing, Béla! You wouldn't put such an insult on Elsa! You wouldn't ..."

"I wouldn't what, my fine gentleman, who tried to sneak another fellow's sweetheart?" sneered Béla as he drew a step or two nearer to Andor. "I wouldn't what? Come here and have supper with Klara while Elsa's precious friends are eating the fare I've provided for them and abusing me behind my back? Yes, I would! and I'll stay

151

just as long as I like and let anyone see me who likes ... and Elsa may go to the devil with jealousy for aught I care."

He was quite close to Andor now, but being half a head shorter, he had to look up in order to see the other eye to eye. Thus for a moment the two men were silent, measuring one another like two primitive creatures of these plains who have been accustomed for generations past to satisfy all quarrels with the shedding of blood. And in truth, never had man so desperate a longing to kill as Andor had at this moment. The red mist enveloped him entirely now, he could see nothing round him but the hideous face of this coarse brute with its one leering eye and cruel, sensuous lips.

The vision of Elsa had quite faded from before his gaze, her snow-white hands no longer tried to dissipate that hideous blood-red veil. Only from behind Erös Béla's shoulder he saw peering at him through the mist the pale eyes of Leopold Hirsch. But on them he would not look, for he felt that that way lay madness.

What the next moment would have brought the Fates who weave the destinies of mankind could alone have told. Béla, unconscious or indifferent to the menace which was glowing in Lakatos Andor's eyes, never departed for a moment from his attitude of swaggering insolence, and even now with an ostentatious gesture he thrust the key into his waistcoat pocket.

Andor gave a hoarse and quickly-smothered cry like that of a beast about to spring:

"You cur!" he muttered through his teeth, "you d——d cur!"

His hands were raised, ready to fasten themselves on the other man's throat, when the door of the inner room was suddenly thrown open and Ignácz Goldstein's querulous voice broke the spell that hung over the two men.

"Now then, my friends, now then," he said fussily as he shuffled into the room, "it is time that this respectable house should be shut up for the night. I am just off to catch the slow train to Kecskemét—after you, my friends, after you, please."

He made a gesture toward the open door and then went up to the table and poured himself out a final stirrup-cup. He was wrapped from head to foot in a threadbare cloth coat, lined with shaggy fur, a fur-edged bonnet was on his head, and he carried a stout stick to which was attached a large bundle done up in a red cotton handkerchief. This now he slung over his shoulder.

"Klara, my girl," he called.

"Yes, father," came Klara's voice from the inner room.

"I didn't see the back-door key—the duplicate one I mean—hanging in its usual place."

152

"No, father, I know," she replied. "It's all right. I have it in my pocket. I'll hang it up on the peg in a minute."

"Right, girl," he said as he smacked his lips after the long draft of wine. "You are quite sure Leopold changed his mind about coming with me?"

"Quite sure, father."

"I wonder, then, he didn't wait to say good-bye to me."

"Perhaps he'll meet you at the station."

"Perhaps he will. Now then, gentlemen," added the old Jew as he once more turned to the two men.

Indeed Andor felt that the spell had been lifted from him. He was quite calm now, and that feeling of being in dreamland had descended still more forcibly upon his mind.

"You have nothing more to say to me, have you, my good Andor?" said Béla, with a final look of insolent swagger directed at his rival.

"No," replied Andor slowly and deliberately. "Nothing."

"Then good-night, my friend!" concluded the other, with a sarcastic laugh. "Why not go to the barn, and dance with Elsa, and sup at my expense like the others do? You'll be made royally welcome there, I assure you."

"Thank you. I am going home."

"Well! as you like! I shall just look in there myself now for half an hour—but I am engaged later on for supper elsewhere, you know."

"So I understand!"

"Gentlemen! My dear friends! I shall miss my train!" pleaded old Ignácz Goldstein querulously.

He manœuvred the two men toward the door and then prepared to follow them.

"Klara!" he called again.

"Coming, father," she replied.

She came running out of the room, and as she reached the door she called to Andor.

"Andor, you have not said good-night," she said significantly.

"Never mind about that now," said Ignácz Goldstein fretfully, "I shall miss my train."

He kissed his daughter perfunctorily, then said:

"There's no one in the tap-room now, is there? I didn't notice."

"No," she replied, "no one just now."

"Then I'd keep the door shut, if I were you. I'd rather those fellows back from Arad didn't come in to-night. The open door

153

would attract them—a closed one might have the effect of speeding them on their way."

"Very well, father," she said indifferently, "I'll keep the door closed."

"And mind you push all the bolts home to both the doors," he added sternly. "A girl alone in a house cannot be too careful."

"All right, father," she rejoined impatiently, "I'll see to everything. Haven't I been alone like this before?"

The other two men were going down the verandah steps. Goldstein went out too now and slammed the door behind him.

And Klara found herself alone in the house.

# CHAPTER XXVI

## "What had Andor done?"

She waited for a moment with her ear glued to the front door until the last echo of the men's footsteps had completely died away in the distance, then she ran to the table. The tray was there, but no key upon it. With feverish, jerky movements she began to hunt for it, pushing aside bottles and mugs, opening drawers, searching wildly with dilated eyes all round the room.

The key was here, somewhere ... surely, surely Andor had not played her false ... he would not play her false ... He was not that sort ... surely, surely he was not that sort. He had come back from his errand—of course she had seen him just now, and ... and he had said nothing certainly, but . . .

Well! He can't have gone far; and her father wouldn't hear if she called. She ran back to the door and fumbled at the latch, for her hands trembled so that she bruised them against the iron. There! At last it was done! She opened the door and peered out into the night. Everything was still, not a footstep echoed from down the street. She took one step out, on to the verandah ... then she heard a rustle from behind the pollarded acacia tree and a rustle amongst its leaves. Someone was there!—on the watch!—Leopold!

She smothered a scream of terror and in a moment had fled back into the room and slammed and bolted the door behind her. Now she stood with her back against it, arms outstretched, fingers twitching convulsively against the wood. She was shivering as with cold, though the heat in the room was close and heavy with fumes of wine and tobacco: her teeth were chattering, a cold perspiration had damped the roots of her hair.

She had wanted to call Andor back, just to ask him definitely if he had been successful in his errand and what he had done with the key. Perhaps he meant to tell her; perhaps he had merely forgotten to put the key on the tray, and still had it in his waistcoat pocket; she had been a fool not to come out and speak to him when she heard his voice in the tap-room awhile ago. She had wanted to, but her father monopolized her about his things for the journey. He had been exceptionally querulous to-night and was always ready to be suspicious; also Béla had been in the tap-room with Andor, and she wouldn't have liked to speak of the key before Béla. What she had been absolutely sure of, however, until now was that Andor would not have come back and then gone away like this, if he had not succeeded in his errand and got her the key from Count Feri.

But the key was not there: there was no getting away from that, and she had wanted to call Andor back and to ask him about it—and had found Leopold Hirsch standing out there in the dark ... watching.

She had not seen him—but she had felt his presence—and she was quite sure that she had heard the hissing sound of his indrawn breath and the movement which he had made to spring on her—and strangle her, as he had threatened to do—if she went out by the front door.

Mechanically she passed her hand across her throat. Terror—appalling, deadly terror of her life—had her in its grasp. She tottered across the room and sank into a chair. She wanted time to think.

What had Andor done? What a fool she had been not to ask him the straight question while she had the chance. She had been afraid of little things—her father's temper, Erös Béla's sneers—when now there was death and murder to fear.

What had Andor done?

Had he played her false? Played this dirty trick on her out of revenge? He certainly—now she came to think of it—had avoided meeting her glance when he went away just now.

Had he played her false?

The more she thought on it, the more the idea got root-hold in her brain. In order to be revenged for the humiliation which she had helped to put upon Elsa, Andor had chosen this means for bringing her to everlasting shame and sorrow—the young Count murdered outside her door, in the act of sneaking into the house by a back way, at dead of night, while Ignácz Goldstein was from home;

155

Leopold Hirsch—her tokened fiancé—a murderer, condemned to hang for a brutal crime; she disgraced for ever, cursed if not killed by her father, who did not trifle in the matter of his daughter's good name. ... All that was Andor's projected revenge for what she had done to Elsa.

The thought of it was too horrible. It beat into her brain until she felt that her head must burst as under the blows of a sledge-hammer or else that she must go mad.

She pushed back the matted hair from her temples, and looked round the tiny, dark, lonely room in abject terror. From far away came the shrill whistle of the engine which bore her father away to Kecskemét. It must be nearly half-past nine, then, and close on half an hour since she had been left here alone with her terrors. Yet another half-hour and . . .

No, no! This she felt that she could not endure—not another half-hour of this awful, death-dealing suspense. Anything would be better than that—death at Leopold's hands—a quick gasp, a final agony—yes! That would be briefer and better—and perhaps Leo's heart would misgive him—perhaps ... but in any case, anything must be better than this suspense.

She struggled to her feet; her knees shook under her: for the moment she could not have moved if her very life had depended on it. So she stood still, propped against the table, her hands clutching convulsively at its edge for support, and her eyes dilated and staring, still searching round the room wildly for the key.

At last she felt that she could walk; she tottered back across the room, back to the door, and her twitching fingers were once more fumbling with the bolts.

The house was so still and the air was so oppressive. When she paused in her fumbling—since her fingers refused her service—she could almost hear that movement again behind the acacia tree outside, and that rustling among the leaves.

She gave a wild gasp of terror and ran back to the chair—like a frightened feline creature, swift and silent—and sank into it, still gasping, her whole body shaken now as with fever, her teeth chattering, her limbs numb.

Death had been so near! She had felt an icy breath across her throat! She was frightened—hideously, abjectly, miserably frightened. Death lurked for her, there outside in the dark, from behind the acacia tree! Death in the guise of a jealous madman, whose hate had been whetted by an hour's lonely watch in the dark—lonely, but for his thoughts.

Tears of self-pity as well as of fear rose to the unfortunate girl's eyes; convulsive sobs shook her shoulders and tore at her heart till she felt that she must choke. She threw out her arms across the table and buried her face in them and lay there, sobbing and moaning in her terror and in her misery.

How long she remained thus, crying and half inert with mental anguish and pain, she could not afterwards have told. Nor did she know what it was that roused her from this torpor, and caused her suddenly to sit up in her chair, upright, wide-awake, her every sense on the alert.

Surely she could not have heard the fall of footsteps at the back of the house! There was the whole width of the inner room and two closed doors between her and the yard at the back, and the ground there was soft and muddy; no footstep, however firm, could raise echoes there.

And yet she had heard! Of that she felt quite sure, heard with that sixth sense of which she, in her ignorance, knew nothing, but which, nevertheless, now had roused her from that coma-like state into which terror had thrown her, and set every one of her nerves tingling once more and pulsating with life and the power to feel.

For the moment all her faculties seemed merged into that of hearing. With that same sixth sense she heard the stealthy footsteps coming nearer and nearer. They had not approached from the village, but from the fields at the back, and along the little path which led through the unfenced yard straight to the back door.

These footsteps—which seemed like the footsteps of ghosts, so intangible were they—were now so near that to Klara's supersensitive mind they appeared to be less than ten paces from the back door.

Then she heard another footstep—she heard it quite distinctly, even though walls and doors were between her and them—she heard the movement from behind the acacia tree—the one that stands at the corner of the house, in full view of both the doors—she heard the rustle among its low-hanging branches and that hissing sound as of an indrawn breath.

She shot up from her chair like an automaton—rigid and upright, her mouth opened as for a wild shriek, but all power of sound was choked in her throat. She ran into the inner room like one possessed, her mouth still wide open for the frantic shriek which would not come, for that agonizing call for help.

She fell up against the back door. Her hands tore at the lock, at the woodwork, at the plaster around; she bruised her hands and cut her fingers to the bone, but still that call would not come to her throat—not even now, when she heard on the other side of the door, less than five paces from where she lay, frantic with horror, a groan,

157

a smothered cry, a thud—then swiftly hurrying footsteps flying away in the night.

Then nothing more, for she was lying now in a huddled mass, half unconscious on the floor.

# CHAPTER XXVII

## "The shadow that fell from the tall sunflowers"

How Klara Goldstein spent that terrible night she never fully realized. After half an hour or so she dragged herself up from the floor. Full consciousness had returned to her, and with it the power to feel, to understand and to fear.

A hideous, awful terror was upon her which seemed to freeze her through and through; a cold sweat broke out all over her body, and she was trembling from head to foot. She crawled as far as the narrow little bed which was in a corner of the room, and just managed to throw herself upon it, on her back, and there to remain inert, perished with cold, racked with shivers, her eyes staring upwards into the darkness, her ears strained to listen to every sound that came from the other side of the door.

But gradually, as she lay, her senses became more alive; the power to think coherently, to reason with her fears, asserted itself more and more over those insane terrors which had paralysed her will and her heart. She did begin to think—not only of herself and of her miserable position, but of the man who lay outside—dying or dead.

Yes! That soon became the most insistent thought.

Leopold Hirsch, having done the awful deed, had fled, of course, but his victim might not be dead, he might be only wounded and dying for want of succour. Klara—closing her eyes—could almost picture him, groaning and perhaps trying to drag himself up in a vain endeavour to get help.

Then she rose—wretched, broken, terrified—but nevertheless resolved to put all selfish fears aside and to ascertain the full extent of the tragedy which had been enacted outside her door. She lit the storm-lantern, then, with it in her hand, she went through the tap-room and opened the front door.

158

She knew well the risks which she was running, going out like this into the night, and alone. Any passer-by might see her—ask questions, suspect her of connivance when she told what it was that she had come out to seek in the darkness behind her own back door. But to this knowledge and this small additional fear she resolutely closed her mind. Drawing the door to behind her, she stepped out on to the verandah and thence down the few steps into the road below.

A slight breeze had sprung up within the last half-hour, and had succeeded in chasing away the heavy banks of cloud which had hung over the sky earlier in the evening.

Even as Klara paused at the foot of the verandah steps in order to steady herself on her feet, the last filmy veil that hid the face of the moon glided ethereally by. The moon was on the wane, golden and mysterious, and now, as she appeared high in the heaven, surrounded by a halo of prismatic light, she threw a cold radiance on everything around, picking out every tree and cottage with unfailing sharpness and casting black, impenetrable shadows which made the light, by contrast, appear yet more vivid and more clear.

All around leaves and branches rustled with a soft, swishing sound, like the whisperings of ghosts, and from the plains beyond came that long-drawn-out murmur of myriads of plume-crowned maize as they bent in recurring unison to the caress of the wind.

Klara's eyes peered anxiously round. Quickly she extinguished her lantern, and then remained for a while clinging to the wooden balusters of the verandah, eyes and ears on the alert like a hunted beast. Two belated csikós[7] from a neighbouring village were passing down the main road, singing at the top of their voices, their spurred boots clinking as they walked. Klara did not move till the murmur of the voices and the clinking of metal had died away and no other sound of human creature moving or breathing close by broke the slumbering echoes of the village.

Only in the barn, far away, people were singing and laughing and making merry. Klara could hear the gipsy band, the scraping of the fiddles and banging of the czimbalom, followed now and then by one of those outbursts of jollity, of clapping of mugs on wooden tables, of banging of feet and shouts of laughter which characterize all festive gatherings in Hungary.

Cautiously now Klara began to creep along the low wall which supported the balustrade. Her feet made no noise in the soft, sandy earth, her skirts clung closely to her limbs; at every minute sound

---

[7] Herdsmen in charge of foals.

she started and paused, clinging yet closer to the shadow which enveloped her.

Now she came to the corner. There, just in front of her was the pollarded acacia, behind which the murderer had cowered for an hour—on the watch. The slowly withering leaves trembled in the breeze and their soughing sounded eerie in the night, like the sighs of a departing soul.

Further on, some twenty paces away, was old Rézi's cottage. All was dark and still in and around it. Klara had just a sufficient power of consciousness left to note this fact with an involuntary little sigh of relief. The murderer had done his work quickly and silently; his victim had uttered no cry that would rouse the old gossip from her sleep.

When Klara at last rounded the second corner of the house and came in full view of the unfenced yard in the rear, she saw that it was flooded with moonlight. For a moment she closed her eyes, for already she had perceived that a dark and compact mass lay on the ground within a few feet of the back door. She wanted strength of purpose and a mighty appeal to her will before she would dare to look again. When she reopened her eyes, she saw that the mass lay absolutely still. She crept forward with trembling limbs and knees that threatened to give way under her at every moment.

Now she no longer thought of herself; there was but little fear of anyone passing by this way and seeing her as she gradually crawled nearer and nearer to that inert mass which lay there on the ground so rigid and silent. Beyond the yard there were only maize-fields, and a tall row of sunflowers closed the place in as with a wall. And not a sound came from old Rézi's cottage.

Klara was quite close to that dark and inert thing at last; she put out her hand and touched it. The man was lying on his face; just as he had fallen, no doubt; with a superhuman effort she gathered up all her strength and lifted those hunched-up shoulders from the ground. Then she gave a smothered cry; the pallid face of Erös Béla was staring sightlessly up at the moon.

Indeed, for the moment the poor girl felt as if she must go mad, as if for ever and ever after this—waking or sleeping—she would see those glassy eyes, the drooping jaw, that horrible stain which darkened the throat and breast. For a few seconds, which to her seemed an eternity, she remained here, crouching beside the dead body of this unfortunate man, trying in vain in her confused mind to conjecture what had brought Béla here, instead of the young Count, within the reach of Leopold's maniacal jealousy and revenge.

But her brain was too numbed for reasoning and for coherent

160

thought. She had but to accept the facts as they were: that Erös Béla lay here—dead, that Leopold had murdered him, and that she must save herself at all costs from being implicated in this awful, awful crime!

At last she contrived to gather up a sufficiency of strength—both mental and physical—to turn her back upon this terrible scene. She had struggled up to her feet and was turning to go when her foot knocked against something hard, and as—quite mechanically—her eyes searched the ground to see what this something was, she saw that it was the key of the back door, which had evidently escaped from the dead man's hand as he fell.

To stoop for it and pick it up—to run for the back door, which was so close by—to unlock and open it and then to slip through it into the house was but the work of a few seconds—and now here she was once again in her room, like the hunted beast back in its lair—panting, quivering, ready to fall—but safe, at all events.

No one had seen her, of that she felt sure. And now she knew—or thought she knew—exactly what had happened. Lakatos Andor had been to the castle; he had seen my lord and got the key away from him. He wanted to ingratiate himself with my lord and to be able to boast in the future that he had saved my lord's life, but evidently he did mean to have his revenge not only on herself—Klara—but also on Erös Béla for the humiliation which they had put upon Elsa. It was a cruel and a dastardly trick of revenge, and in her heart Klara had vague hopes already of getting even with Andor one day. But that would come by and by—at some future time—when all this terrible tragedy would have been forgotten.

For the present she must once more think of herself. The key was now a precious possession. She went to hang it up on its accustomed peg. Even Leopold—if he stayed in the village to brazen the whole thing out—could not prove anything with regard to that key. Erös Béla might have been a casual passer-by, strolling about among the maize-fields, not necessarily intent on visiting Klara at dead of night. The key was now safely on its peg; who would dare swear that Erös Béla or anyone else ever had it in his possession?

In fact, the secret rested between five people, of which she—Klara—was one and the dead man another. Well, the latter could tell no tales, and she, of course, would say nothing. Already she had determined—even though her mind was still confused and her faculties still numb—that ignorance would be the safest stronghold behind which she could entrench herself.

There remained Leo himself, the young Count, and, of course, Andor. Which of these three would she have the greatest cause to fear?

There was Leo mad with jealousy, the young Count indifferent, and Andor with curious and tortuous motives in his heart which surely he would not wish to disclose.

She had a sufficiency of presence of mind to go out and fetch the storm-lantern from where she had left it at the foot of the verandah steps. A passer-by who saw her in the act wished her a merry good-night, to which she responded in a steady voice. Then she carefully locked the front door, and finally undressed and went to bed. There was no knowing whether some belated wayfarer might not presently come on the dead man lying there in the yard: and having roused the neighbours, the latter might think of calling on Ignácz Goldstein for spirit or what not. It was not generally known that Ignácz Goldstein was from home, and if people thumped loudly and long at her door, she must appear as if she had just been roused from peaceful sleep.

She felt much more calm and fully alive, above all, to her own danger. That kind of superstitious, unreasoning terror which had assailed her awhile ago had almost entirely left her. She seemed more composed, more sure of herself, now that she had been out in the yard and seen the whole mise en scène of the tragedy, which before that she had only vaguely imagined.

But what she felt that she could not do was to lie here alone in the dark, with only the silvery light of the moon creeping in weirdly through the dulled panes of the tiny window. So she picked up her black skirt, and stuffed it into the narrow window embrasure, until not a ray of light from within could be seen to peep through on the other side. She had placed the storm-lantern in the corner, and this she left alight. It threw a feeble, yellowish glimmer round the room; after a few moments, when her eyes were accustomed to this semi-gloom, she found that she could see every familiar object quite distinctly; even the shadows did not seem impenetrable, nor could ghosts lurk in the unseen portions of the tiny room.

Of course there was no hope of sleep—Klara knew well the moment that she looked on the dead man's face, that she would always see it before her—to the end of her days. She saw it now, quite distinctly—especially when she closed her eyes; the moonlit yard, the shadow that fell from the tall sunflowers, and the huddled, dark mass on the ground, with the turned-up face and the sightless eyes. But she was not afraid; she only felt bitterly resentful against Andor, who, she firmly believed, had played her an odious trick.

She almost felt sorry for Leopold, who had only sinned because of his great love for her.

# CHAPTER XXVIII

## "We shall hear of another tragedy by and by"

And so in Marosfalva there was no wedding on the festival day of S. Michael and All Angels; instead of that, on the day following, there was a solemn Mass for the dead in the small village church, which was full to overflowing on that great occasion.

Erös Béla had been found—out in the open—murdered by an unknown hand. Fehér Károly and his brother, who lived down the Fekete Road, had taken a cut across the last maize-field—the one situated immediately behind the inn kept by Ignácz Goldstein, and they had come across Béla's body, lying in the yard, with face upturned and eyes staring up sightlessly at the brilliant blue sky overhead.

It was then close on eight o'clock in the morning. The dancing in the barn had been kept up till then, even though the two most important personages of the festive gathering were not there to join in the fun.

The bridegroom had not been seen since his brief appearance an hour or two before supper, and Elsa had only just sat through the meal, trying to seem cheerful, but obviously hardly able to restrain her tears. After supper, when her partner sought her for the csárdás, she was nowhere to be found. Kapus Irma—appealed to—said that the girl was fussy and full of nerves—for all the world like a born lady. She certainly wasn't very well, had complained of headache, and been allowed by her mother to go home quietly and turn into bed.

"She has another two jolly days to look forward to," Irma néni had added complacently. "Perhaps it is as well that she should get some rest to-night."

Ah, well! it was a queer wedding, and no mistake! The queerest that had ever been in Marosfalva within memory of man. A bride more prone to tears than to laughter! A bridegroom surly, discontented, and paying marked attentions to the low-down Jewess over at the inn under his future wife's very nose!

It was quite one thing for a man to assert his own independence, and to show his bride at the outset on whose feet the highest-heeled boots would be, but quite another to flout the customs of the countryside and all its proprieties.

When, after supper, good and abundant wine had loosened all tongues, adverse comments on the absent bridegroom flowed pretty

163

freely. This should have been the merriest time of the evening—the merriest time, in fact, of all the three festive days—the time when one was allowed to chaff the bride and to make her blush, to slap the lucky bridegroom on the back and generally to allow full play to that exuberance of spirits which is always bubbling up to the surface out of a Magyar peasant's heart.

No doubt that Béla's conduct had upset Elsa and generally cast a gloom over the festive evening. But the young people were not on that account going to be done out of their dancing; the older ones might sit round and gossip and throw up their hands and sigh, but that was no reason why the gipsies should play a melancholy dirge.

A csárdás it must be, and of the liveliest! And after that another and yet another. Would it not be an awful pity to waste Erös Béla's money, even though he was not here to enjoy its fruits? So dancing was kept up till close on eight o'clock in the morning—till the sun was high up in the heavens and the bell of the village church tolled for early Mass. Until then the gipsies scraped their fiddles and banged their czimbalom almost uninterruptedly; hundreds of sad and gay folk-songs were sung in chorus in the intervals of dancing the national dance. Cotton petticoats of many hues fluttered, leather boots—both red and black—clinked and stamped until the morning.

Then it was that the merry company at last broke up, and that Fehér Károly and his brother took the short cut behind the inn, and found the bridegroom—at whose expense they had just danced and feasted—lying stark and stiff under the clear September sun.

They informed the mayor, who at once put himself in communication with the gendarmerie of Arad: but long before the police came, the news of the terrible discovery was all over the village, and there was no thought of sleep or rest after that.

Worried to death, perspiring and puzzled, the police officers hastily sent down from Arad had vainly tried to make head or tail of the mass of conflicting accounts which were poured into their ears in a continuous stream of loud-voiced chatter for hours at a stretch: and God only knows what judicial blunders might have been committed before the culprit was finally brought to punishment if the latter had not, once for all, himself delivered over the key of the mystery.

Leopold Hirsch had hanged himself to one of the beams in his own back shop. His assistant found him there—dead—later in the day.

As—by previous arrangement—the whole village was likely to be at Elsa Kapus' wedding, there would not have been much use in keeping the shop open. So the assistant had been given a holiday, but he came to the shop toward midday, when the whole village was full of the terrible news and half the population out in the street gossiping and commenting on it—marvelling why his employer had not yet been seen outside his doors.

The discovery—which the assistant at once communicated to the police—solved the riddle of Erös Béla's death. With a sigh of relief the police officers adjourned from the mayor's parlour, where they had been holding their preliminary inquiries, to the castle, where it was their duty to report the occurrence to my lord the Count.

At the castle of course everyone was greatly surprised: the noble Countess raised her aristocratic eyebrows and declared her abhorrence of hearing of these horrors. The Count took the opportunity of cursing the peasantry for a quarrelsome, worrying lot, and offered the police officers a snack and a glass of wine. He was hardly sorry for the loss of his bailiff, as Erös Béla had been rather tiresome of late—bumptious and none too sober—and his lordship anyhow had resolved to dispense with his services after he was married. So the death really caused him very little inconvenience.

Young Count Feri knew nothing, of course. He was not likely to allow himself or his name to be mixed up with a village scandal: he shuddered once or twice when the thought flashed through his mind how narrowly he had escaped Erös Béla's fate, and to his credit be it said he had every intention of showing Lakatos Andor—who undoubtedly had saved his life by giving him timely warning—a substantial meed of gratitude.

Of Klara Goldstein little or nothing was seen or heard. The police officers had certainly gone to the inn in the course of the morning and had stayed there close on half an hour: but as no one had been allowed to go into the tap-room during that time, the occurrences there remained a matter of conjecture. After the officers went away Klara locked the front door after them and remained practically shut up in the house, only going in the evening as far as the post, but refusing to speak to anyone and going past with head erect and a proud, careless air which deceived no one.

"She'll sing her tune in a minor key by and by, when Ignácz Goldstein comes home," said the gossips complacently.

"Those Jews are mighty hard on their daughters," commented the older folk, "if any scandal falls upon them. Ignácz is a hard man and over-ready with his stick."

"I shouldn't be surprised," was the universal conclusion, "if we should hear of another tragedy by and by."

"In any case, Klara can't stay in the village," decided the bevy of young girls who talked the matter over among themselves, and were none too sorry that the smart, handsome Jewess—who had such a way with the men—should be comfortably out of the way.

But everyone went to the Mass for the dead on the day following that which should have been such a merry wedding feast; and everyone joined in the Requiem and prayed fervently for the repose of the soul of the murdered man.

He lay in state in the centre of the aisle, with four tall candles at each corner of the draped catafalque; a few bunches of white and purple asters clumsily tied together by inexperienced hands were laid upon the coffin.

Pater Bonifácius preached a beautiful sermon about the swift and unexpected approach of Death when he is least expected. He also said some very nice things about the dead man, and there was hardly a dry eye in the church while he spoke.

In the remote corner of a pew, squeezed between a pillar and her mother, Elsa knelt and prayed. Those who watched her—and there were many—declared that not only did she never stop crying for a moment during Mass, but that her eyes were swollen and her cheeks puffy from having cried all the night and all the day before.

After Mass she must have slipped out by the little door which gave on the presbytery garden. It was quite close to the pillar against which she had been leaning, and no doubt the Pater had given her permission to go out that way. From the presbytery garden she could skirt the fields and round the top of the village, and thus get home and give all her friends the slip.

This, no doubt, she had done, for no one saw her the whole of that day, nor the next, which was the day of the funeral, and an occasion of wonderful pomp and ceremony. Béla's brother had arrived in the meanwhile from Arad, where he was the manager of an important grain store, and he it was who gave all directions and all the money necessary that his brother should have obsequies befitting his rank and wealth.

The church was beautifully decorated: there were huge bunches of white flowers upon the altar, and eight village lads carried the dead man to his last resting-place; and no less than thirty Masses were ordered to be said within the next year for the repose of the soul of one who in life had enjoyed so much prosperity and consideration.

And in the tiny graveyard situated among the maize-fields to the north of Marosfalva, and which is the local Jewish burial ground, the suicide was quietly laid to rest. There was no religious service, for there was no minister of his religion present; an undertaker came down from Arad and saw to it all; there was no concourse of people, no singing, no flowers. Ignácz Goldstein—

home the day before from Kecskemét—alone followed the plain deal coffin on its lonely journey from the village to the field.

It was the shop assistant who had seen to it all. He had gone up to Arad and seen a married sister of his late master's—Sara Rosen, whose husband kept a second-hand clothes shop there, and who gave full instructions to an undertaker whilst declaring herself unable—owing to delicate health—to attend the funeral herself.

The undertaker had provided a cart and a couple of oxen and two men to lift the coffin in and out. They came late on the Thursday evening, at about eight o'clock, and drew up at the back of the late Leopold Hirsch's shop. No one was about and the night was dark.

Slowly the cart, creaking on its wheels and axles, wound its way through some maize stubble, up a soft, sandy road to the enclosed little bit of ground which the local Jews have reserved for themselves.

And the mysterious veil which divides the present from the past fell quickly over this act of the village tragedy, as it had done with pomp and circumstance after the banquet which followed the laying to rest of the murdered man.

# CHAPTER XXIX

## "Some day"

A week went by after the funeral before Elsa saw Andor again. She had not purposely avoided him, any more than she had avoided everyone else: but unlike most girls of her class and of her nationality she had felt a great desire to be alone during the most acute period of this life's crisis through which she was passing just now.

At first on that never-to-be-forgotten morning when she woke to her wedding-day—her white veil and wreath of artificial white roses lying conspicuously on the top of the chest of drawers, so that her eyes were bound to alight on them the moment they opened— and saw her mother standing beside her bed, dishevelled, pale, and obviously labouring under some terrible excitement, she had been

167

conscious as of an awful blow on the head, a physical sensation of numbness and of pain.

Even before she had had time to formulate a question she knew that some terrible calamity had occurred. In jerky phrases, broken by moans and interjections, the mother had blurted out the news: Erös Béla was dead—he had been found just now—murdered outside Klara Goldstein's door—there would be no wedding—Elsa was a widow before she had been a bride. Half the village was inclined to believe that Ignácz Goldstein had done the deed in a moment of angry passion, finding Béla sneaking round his daughter's door when he himself was going away from home—others boldly accused Andor.

Elsa had said nothing at the time. That same imagined blow on the head had also deprived her of the power of speech. Fortunately Irma talked so loudly and so long that she paid no attention to her daughter's silence, and presently ran out into the village to gather more news.

And Elsa remained alone in the house, save for the helpless invalid in the next room. She washed and dressed herself quickly and mechanically, then sat down on her favourite low chair, close beside her crippled father's knee, cowering there like some little field mouse, attentive, alert, rigidly still, for very fear of what was to come.

Irma did not come back for two or three hours: when she did it was to bring the exciting news that Leopold Hirsch had been found hanging to a beam in his back shop, with the knife wherewith he had killed Erös Béla lying conspicuously on a table close by.

Elsa felt as if the weight of the world had been lifted from off her brain. All through these hours the thought of Andor having committed such an abominable crime never once entered her mind, but nevertheless when her mother told the news about Leopold Hirsch, and that the police officers had already left the village, she was conscious of an overwhelming sense of relief.

Fortunately her mother was busy all day gossiping with her cronies and Elsa was allowed the luxury of sitting alone most of the day, silent and absorbed, doing the usual work of the house in the morning and in the afternoon busying herself with carefully putting away the wedding dress, the veil, the wreath which would not be wanted now.

Late in the evening, when there was a chance of finding the street deserted, she ran out as far as the presbytery. Fortunately the night was dark: a thin drizzle was falling, and it spread a misty veil all down the village street. Elsa had tied one of her mother's dark-coloured handkerchiefs over her head and put her darkest-coloured petticoat on the top of all the others. She had also wrapped her mother's dark shawl round her shoulders, and thus muffled up she was able to flit unperceived down the street, a swift little dark figure undistinguishable from the surrounding darkness of the night.

Fortunately the Pater was at home and ready to see her. She heaved a sigh of relief as she entered the bare narrow little hall which led on the right to the Pater's parlour.

She had been able to tell Pater Bonifácius exactly what was troubling her—that sense of peace, almost of relief, which had descended into her soul when she heard that she never, never need be Erös Béla's wife. Since this morning, when first she had heard the terrible news, she had not thought of his death—that awful fate which had so unexpectedly overtaken him—she had only thought of her own freedom, the peace which henceforth would be hers.

That was very wrong of course—a grievous sin no doubt the Pater would call it. She shed many tears of contrition, listened eagerly to a kind homily from the old priest on the subject of unnecessary and unprofitable searchings of conscience, and went away satisfied.

Strangely enough, after this confession she felt far more sorry for poor Béla than she had done before, and she cried her eyes out both before and after the funeral because, do what she would, she always saw him before her as he was that last day of his life—quarrelsome, dictatorial, tyrannical—and she remembered how she had almost hated him for his bullying ways and compared him in her mind with Andor's kindness and chivalry.

And now she cried with remorse because she had hated him during the last hours of his life; she cried because he had gone to his death unloved, and lay now in his coffin unregretted; she cried because her heart was full and heavy and because in the past week—before her wedding day—she had swallowed so many unshed tears.

And while she felt miserable and not a little forlorn she didn't want to see anybody, least of all Andor. Whenever she thought of Andor, the same remorse about Béla gnawed again at her heart, for when she thought of him she not only felt at peace, but it seemed as if a ray of happiness illumined the past darkness of her life.

Once or twice during the last day or two, when she had sat stitching, she caught herself singing softly to herself, and once she knew for certain that she had smiled.

Then the day came when Andor called at the house. Irma fortunately was out, having coffee and gossip with a friend. No doubt he had watched until he was sure that she was well out of the way. Then he knocked at the door and entered.

Elsa was sitting as usual on the low chair close by the sick

169

man. She looked up when he entered and all at once the blood rushed to her pale cheeks.

"May I come in?" he asked diffidently.

"If you like, Andor," she replied.

He threw down his hat and then came to sit on the corner of the table in his favorite attitude and as close to Elsa as he dared. The eyes of the paralytic had faintly lit up at his approach.

"Are you quite well, Elsa?" he asked after a long pause, during which the girl thought that she could hear the beating of her own heart.

"Yes. Quite well thank you, Andor," she replied softly.

"No one has seen you in the village this past week," he remarked.

"No," she said, "I am not very fond of gossip, and there was a deal too much of it in Marosfalva this past week to please me."

"You are right there, Elsa," he rejoined, "but there were others in the village, you know, those who did not gossip—but whose heart would have been gladdened by a sight of you."

"Yes, Andor," she murmured.

We may take it that the young man found these laconic answers distinctly encouraging, for presently he said abruptly:

"Perhaps, Elsa, it isn't right for me to begin talking to you ... about certain matters ..."

"What matters, Andor?" she asked ingenuously.

"Matters which have lain next to my heart, Elsa, for more years now than I would care to count."

"Perhaps it is a little too soon, Andor—yet—" she whispered under her breath.

Oh! She could have whipped herself for that warm blush which now covered not only her cheeks but her neck and bosom, and for that glow of happiness which had rushed straight at her heart at his words. But he had already seen the blush, and caught that expression of happiness in her blue eyes which suddenly made her look as she did of old—five years ago—before that wan, pathetic expression of resignation had altered her sweet face so completely.

"I don't want to worry you, Elsa," he said simply.

"You couldn't worry me, Andor," she said, "you have always been the best friend I had in the world."

"That is because I have loved you more dearly than anyone ever loved you on this earth," he said earnestly.

"God bless you for that, Andor."

He leaned forward, nearer to her now: his gaze had become more fixed, more compelling. Since he had seen that look on her face and that blush he was sure of his ground; he knew that, given time and peace, the wheel of fate, which had already taken an upward turn for him, would soon carry him to the summit of his desires—the woman whom he loved was no longer unattainable and she had remained faithful throughout all this time.

"Do you think, Elsa," he asked more insistently now, and sinking his voice to that whisper which reaches a woman's ear far more truly than the loudest beating of drum, "do you think that, now that you are free, you could bring yourself to ... to care ... to ... ? You were very fond of me once, Elsa," he pleaded.

"I am fond of you now, Andor," she whispered in response. "No, no," she added hurriedly, for already he had made a movement towards her and the next moment would have been down on his knees with his arms around her, but for the gently-restraining touch of her hand, "it is too soon to talk about that."

"Yes—too soon," he assented with enforced calm, even though his heart was beating furiously; "it is too soon I know, and I won't worry you, Elsa—I said I wouldn't and I won't. ... I am not a cur to come and force myself on you when you are not ready to listen to me, and we won't talk about it all ... not just yet." . . .

His throat felt very dry, and his tongue felt several sizes too large for his mouth. It was mightily difficult to keep calm and to speak soberly when one's inclination was firstly to dance a war-dance of triumph and of joy and then to take that dear, sweet angel of a woman in one's arms and to kiss her till she was ready to faint.

"When do you think I might speak to you again, Elsa?" he said, with a certain pathetic hesitancy, "about ..."

"About what, Andor?" she asked.

"About our getting married—later on."

"Not just yet," she murmured, "but ..."

"No, no, of course I understand. There are the proprieties and all that ... you were tokened to that blackguard and ... Oh! All right, I am not going to say anything against him," he added quickly as he saw that words of protest and reproach were already hovering on her lips. "I won't say anything about him at all except that he is dead now and buried, thank the good God! ... And you ... you still care for me, Elsa," he continued, whilst a wave of tenderness seemed to sweep all other thoughts away. "No, no, don't say anything—not now—it is too soon, of course—and I've just got to wait till the time comes as best I can. But you mustn't mind my talking on at random like this ... for I tell you I am nearly crazy with joy—and I suppose that you would think it very wrong to rejoice like this over another man's death."

His talk was a little wild and rambling—it was obvious that he was half distracted with the prospect of happiness to come. She sat

171

quite still, listening silently, with eyes fixed to the ground. Only now and then she would look up—not at Andor, but at the paralytic who was gazing on her with the sad eyes of uncomprehension. Then she would nod and smile at him and coo in her own motherly way and he would close his eyes—satisfied.

And Andor, who had paused for that brief moment in his voluble talk, went rambling on.

"You know," he said, "that it's perfectly wonderful ... this room, I mean ... when I look round me I can hardly credit my eyes. ... Just a week ago ... you remember? ... I sat just there ... at the opposite corner of the table, and you had your low chair against the wall just here ... and ... and you told me that you were tokened to Erös Béla and that your wedding would be on the morrow ... well! That was little more than a week ago ... before your farewell feast ... and I thought then that never, never could I be happy again because you told me that never, never could we be anything to each other except a kind of friendly strangers. ... I remember then how a sort of veil seemed to come down in front of my eyes ... a dark red veil ... things didn't look black to me, you know, Elsa ... but red. ... So now I am quite content just to bide my time—I am quite content that you should say nothing to me—nothing good, I mean. ... It'll take some time before the thought of so much happiness has got proper root-hold of my brain."

"Poor Andor!" she sighed, and turned a gaze full of love upon the sick man. Her heart was brimming over with it, and so the paralytic got the expression of it in its fullest measure, since Andor was not entitled to it yet.

"But just tell me for certain, Elsa ... so that I shouldn't have to torment myself in the meanwhile ... just tell me for certain that one day ... in the far-distant future if you like, but one day ... say that you will marry me."

"Some day, Andor, I will marry you if God wills," she said simply.

"Oh! But of course He will!" he rejoined airily, "and we will be married in the spring—or the early summer when the maize is just beginning to ripen ... and we'll rent the mill from Pali bácsi—shall we, Elsa?"

"If you like, Andor."

"If I like!" he exclaimed. "If I like! The dear God love me, but I think that if I stay here much longer I shall go off my head. ... Elsa, you don't know how much I love you and what I would not do for your sake. ... I feel a different man even for the joy of sitting here and talking to you and no one having the right to interfere. ... And I would make you happy, Elsa, that I swear by the living God. I would

172

make you happy and I would work to keep you in comfort all the days of my life. You shall be just as fine as Erös Béla would have made you—and besides that, there would be a smile on your sweet face at every hour of the day ... your hands would be as white as those of my lady the Countess herself, for I would have a servant to wait on you. And your father would come and live with us and we would make him happy and comfortable too, and your mother ... well! your mother would be happy too, and therefore not quite so cantankerous as she sometimes is."

To Andor there was nothing ahead but a life full of sunshine. He never looked back on the past few days and on the burden of sin which they bore. Béla had been a brute of the most coarse and abominable type; by his monstrous conduct on the eve of his wedding day he had walked to his death—of his own accord. Andor had not sent him. Oh! he was quite, quite sure that he had not sent Béla to his death. He had merely forborn to warn him—and surely there could be no sin in that.

He might have told Béla that Leopold Hirsch—half mad with jealousy—was outside on the watch with a hunting-knife in his pocket and murder in his soul. Andor might have told Béla this and he had remained silent. Was that a sin? considering what a brute the man was, how his action that night was a deadly insult put upon Elsa, and how he would in the future have bullied and browbeaten Elsa and made her life a misery—a veritable hell upon earth.

Andor had thought the problem out; he had weighed it in his mind and he was satisfied that he had not really committed a sin. Of course he ought before now to have laid the whole case before Pater Bonifácius, and the Pater would have told him just what God's view would be of the whole affair.

The fact that Andor had not thought of going to confession showed that he was not quite sure what God—as represented by Pater Bonifácius—would think of it all; but he meant to go by and by and conclude a permanent and fulsome peace treaty with his conscience.

In the meanwhile, even though the burden of remorse should at times in the future weigh upon his soul and perhaps spoil a little of his happiness, well! he would have to put up with it, and that was all!—Elsa was happy—one sight of her radiant little face was enough for any fool to see that an infinite sense of relief had descended into her soul. Elsa was happy—freed from the brute who would have made her wretched for the rest of her life; and surely the good God, who could read the secret motives which lay in a fellow's heart, would not be hard on Andor for what he had done—or left undone— for Elsa's sake.

# CHAPTER XXX

## "Kyrie eleison"

But the daily routine of everyday life went on at Marosfalva just as it had done before the double tragedy of St. Michael's E'en had darkened the pages of its simple history.

The maize had all been gathered in—ploughing had begun—my lord and his guests were shooting in the stubble. The first torrential rain had fallen and the waters of the Maros had begun to swell.

Gossip about Erös Béla's terrible end and Leopold Hirsch's suicide had not by any means been exhausted, but it was supplemented now by talk of Lakatos Pál's wealth. The old man had been ailing for some time. His nephew Andor's return had certainly cheered him up for a while, but soon after that he seemed to collapse very suddenly in health, like old folk do in this part of the world—stricken down by one or other of the several diseases which are engendered by the violent extremes of heat and cold—diseases of the liver for the most part—the beginning of a slowly-oncoming end.

He had always been reputed to be a miser, and those who were in the know now averred that Andor had found several thousand florins tucked away in old bits of sacking and hidden under his uncle's straw paillasse. Pali bácsi was also possessed of considerable property—some land, a farm and the mill; there was no doubt now that Andor would be a very rich man one of these days.

Mothers with marriageable daughters sighed nevertheless in vain. Andor was not for any of them. Andor had eyes only for Elsa. He had become an important man in the village now that his uncle was so ill and he was left to administer the old man's property; and he took his duties very earnestly in the intervals of courting Kapus Elsa.

As to this no one had cause to make any objection. They had loved one another and been true to one another for five years; it was clearly the will of the good God that they should come together at last.

And now October was drawing to its close—to-day was the fourth Sunday in the month and one of the numerous feasts of our Blessed Lady, one on which solemn benediction is appointed to be sung in the early afternoon, and benediction is followed by a procession to the shrine of the Virgin which stands on the roadside on the way to Saborsó some two kilomètres distant from Marosfalva. It is a great festival and one to which the peasantry of the countryside look forward with great glee, for they love the procession and have a great faith in the efficacy of prayer said at the shrine.

Fortunately the day turned out to be one of the most glorious sunshiny days which mid-autumn can yield, and the little church in the afternoon was crowded in every corner. The older women—their heads covered with dark-coloured handkerchiefs, occupied the left side of the aisle, the men crowded in on the right and at the back under the organ loft. Round about the chancel rail and steps the bevy of girls in gayest Sunday dresses looked like a garden of giant animated flowers. When the sexton went the round with the collecting-bag tied to the end of a long pole, he had the greatest difficulty in making his way through the maze of many-hued petticoats which, as the girls knelt, stood all round them like huge bells, with their slim shoulders and small heads above looking for all the world like the handles.

The children were all placed in the chancel to right and left of the altar, solemn and well-behaved, with one eye on the schoolmistress and the other on the Pater.

After the service the order of procession was formed, inside the church: the children in the forefront with banner carried by the head of the school—a sturdy maiden on the fringe of her teens, very proud to carry the Blessed Virgin's banner. She squared her shoulders well, for the banner was heavy, and the line of her young hips—well accentuated by the numerous petticoats which a proud mother had tied round her waist—gave a certain dignity to her carriage and natural grace to her movements.

Behind the children came the young girls—those of a marriageable age whom a pious custom dedicates most specially to the service of Our Lady. Their banner was of blue silk, and most of them were dressed in blue, whilst blue ribbons fluttered round their heads as they walked.

Then came Pater Bonifácius under a velvet-covered dais which was carried by four village lads. He wore his vestments and carried a holy relic in his hands; the choir-boys swinging their metal censers were in front of him in well-worn red cassocks and surplices beautifully ironed and starched for the occasion.

In the rear the crowd rapidly closed in; the younger men had a banner to themselves, and there were the young matrons, the mothers, the fathers, the old and the lonely.

The sexton threw open the doors, and slowly the little

175

procession filed out. Outside a brilliant sunshine struck full on the whitewashed walls of the little schoolhouse opposite. It was so dazzling that it made everybody blink as they stepped out from the semi-dark church into this magnificent flood of light.

In the street round the church a pathetic group awaited the appearance of the procession, those that were too old to walk two kilomètres to the shrine, those who were lame and those who were sick. Simply and with uninquiring minds, they knelt or stood in the roadway, content to watch the banners as they swung gaily to the rhythmic movements of the bearers, content to see the holy relics in the Pater's hand, content to feel that subtle wave of religious sentiment pass over them which made them at peace with their little world and brought the existence of God nearer to their comprehension.

Slowly the procession wound its way down the village street. Pater Bonifácius had intoned the opening orisons of the Litany:

"Kyrie eleison!"

And men and women chanted the response in that quaintly harsh tone which the Magyar language assumes when it is sung. The brilliant sunlight played on the smooth hair of the girls, the golds, the browns and the blacks, and threw sharp glints on the fluttering ribbons of many colours which a light autumn breeze was causing to dance gaily and restlessly. The whole village was hushed save for the Litany, the clinking of the metal chains as the choir-boys swung the censers and the frou-frou of hundreds of starched petticoats— superposed, brushing one against the other with a ceaseless movement which produced a riot of brilliant colouring.

Soon the main road was reached, and now the vast immensity of the plain lay in front and all round—all the more vast and immense now it seemed, since not even the nodding plumes of maize or tall, stately sunflowers veiled the mystery of that low-lying horizon far away.

Nothing around now, save that group of willow trees by the bank of the turbulent Maros—nothing except the stubble—stumps of maize and pumpkin and hemp, and rigid lines of broken-down stems of sunflowers, with drooping, dead leaves, and brown life still oozing out of the torn stems.

And in the immensity, the sweet, many-toned sounds of summer—the call of birds, the quiver of growing things, the trembling of ripening corn—has yielded to the sad tune of autumn— a tune made up of the hushed sighs of dying nature, as she sinks slowly and peacefully into her coming winter's sleep. The swallows and the storks have gone away long ago. They know that in this land of excessive heat and winter rigours, frost and snow tread hard on

176

the heels of a warm, autumnal day. Only a flight of rooks breaks the even line of the sky; their cawing alone makes at times a weird accompaniment to the chanting of the Litany. And the Maros—no longer sluggish—now sends her swollen waters with a dull, rumbling sound westward to the arms of the mother stream.

Silence and emptiness!

Nothing except the sky, with its unending panorama of ever-varying clouds, and its infinite, boundless, mysterious horizon, which enfolds the world of the plains in a limitless embrace. Nothing except the stubble and the sky, and far, very far away, a lonely cottage, with its surrounding group of low, mop-head acacias, and the gaunt, straight arm of a well pointing upwards to the sun.

And through the silent, vast immensity the little procession of village folk, with banners flying and quaint, harsh voices singing the Litany, winds its way along the flat, sandy road, like a brightly-coloured ribbon thrown there by a giant hand, and made to flutter and to move by a giant's breath.

Presently the shrine came in sight: just a dark speck at first in the midst of the great loneliness, then more and more distinct—there on the roadside—all by itself without a tree near it—lonely in the bosom of the plain.

The procession came to a halt in front of it, and two hundred pairs of eyes, brimful with simple faith and simple trust, gazed in reverence on the naïve wax figure behind the grating, within its throne of rough stone and whitewash. It was dressed in blue calico spangled with tinsel, and had a crown on its head made of gilt paper and a veil of coarse tarlatan. Two china pots containing artificial flowers were placed on either side of the little image.

It was all very crude, very rough, very naïve, but a fervent, unsophisticated imagination had endowed it with a beauty all the more real, perhaps, because it only existed in the hearts of a handful of ignorant children of the soil. It made Something seem real to them which otherwise might have been difficult to grasp; and now when Pater Bonifácius in his gentle, cracked voice intoned the invocations of the Litany, the "Salus infirmorum" and "Refugium peccatorum" and, above all, the "Consolatrix afflictorum" the response "Ora pro nobis" came from two hundred trusting hearts—praying, if not for themselves, then for those who were dear to them: the infirm, the sinner, the afflicted.

And among those two hundred hearts none felt the need for prayer more than Andor and Elsa. They had left affliction behind them, they stood upon the threshold of a new life—where happiness alone beckoned to them, and sorrow and parting lay vanquished behind the gates of the past. But in spite, or perhaps because, of this

177

happiness which beckoned so near now, there was a tinge of sadness in their hearts, that sadness which always comes with joy once extreme youth has gone by ... the sadness which hovers over finite things, the sense of future which so quickly becomes the past.

From where Andor stood, holding the dais above Pater Bonifácius' head, he could see Elsa's smooth, fair head among the crowd of other girls. She had tied her hair in at the nape of the neck with a bit of blue ribbon, leaving it to fall lower down in two thick plaits well below her waist. She looked like a huge blue gentian kissed by the sun, for her top petticoat was of blue cotton, and her golden head seemed like the sweet-scented stamen.

Andor thought that he could hear her voice above that of everyone else, and when Pater Bonifácius intoned the "Regina angelorum" he thought that indeed the heavenly Queen had no fairer subject up there than Elsa.

When the little procession was once more ready to return to the village, the bearers of the dais were relieved by four other lads, and Andor found the means, during the slight hubbub which occurred while the procession was being formed, of working his way close to Elsa's side.

It was not an unusual thing for young men and girls who had much to say to one another to fall away from the procession on its way home, and to wander back arm in arm through the maize-fields or over the stubble, even as their shadows lengthened out upon the ground.

Andor's hand had caught hold of Elsa's elbow, and with insistent pressure he kept her out of the group of her companions. Gradually the procession was formed, and slowly it began to move, the banners fluttered once more in the breeze, once more the monotonous chant broke the silence of the plain.

But Elsa and Andor had remained behind close beside the shrine. She had yielded to his insistence, knowing what it was that he meant to say to her while they walked together toward the sunset. She knew what he wanted to say, and what he expected her to promise, and he knew that at last she was ready to listen, and that she would no longer hold her heart in check, but let it flow over with all the love which it contained, and that she was ready at last to hold up to him that cup of happiness for which he craved.

One or two couples had also remained behind, but they had already wandered off toward the bank of the Maros. Elsa had knelt down before the crude image of the "Consoler of the afflicted;" her rosary was wound round her fingers, she prayed in her simple soul, fervently, unquestioningly, for happiness and for peace.

Then, when the little procession in the distance became

wrapped in the golden haze which hung over the plain, and the chanting of the Litany came but as a murmur on the wings of the autumn breeze, she took Andor's arm, and together they walked slowly back toward home.

The peace which rests over the plain enveloped them both; from the sky above the last vestige of cloud had been driven away by the breeze, and far away on that distant horizon where lay the land of the unknown the sun was slowly sinking to rest.

Like a huge, drooping rose it seemed—its rays like petals falling away from it one by one. Mute yet quivering was the plain around, pulsating with life, yet silent in its autumnal agony. From far away came the sweet sound of the evening Angelus rung from the village church—distant and soft, like a sound from heaven or like an echo of some beautiful dream.

And these two were alone with the sunset and with the stubble—alone in this vastness which is so like the sea—alone—two tiny, moving black specks with a background of radiance and a golden haze to envelop them. In this immensity it seemed so much more easy to speak of love—for love could fill the plain and find room for its own immensity in this vastness which knows no trammels. To Andor and Elsa it seemed as if at last the plain had revealed its secret to them, had lifted for them that veil of mystery which wraps her up all round where earth and sky meet in the golden distance beyond.

They knew suddenly just what lay behind the veil, they knew if it were lifted what it was that they would see—the land of gold was the land of love, where men and women wandered hand in hand, where sorrow was a dwarf and grief a cripple, since love—the Almighty King of the unknown land—had wounded them and vanquished them both.

And they, too, now wandered toward that land, even though it still seemed very far away. To the accompaniment of the Angelus bell they wandered, with the distant echo of the chanted Litany still ringing in their ear. The plain encompassed her children with her all-embracing peace, and she gave them this one supreme moment of happiness to-day, while the setting sun clothed the horizon with gold.

# CHAPTER XXXI

## "What about me"

And time slipped by with murmurings of words that have no meaning save for one pair of ears. Andor talked fondly and foolishly, and Elsa mostly was silent. She had loved this walk over the stubble, and the plain had been in perfect peace save for the rumbling of the Maros, insistent and menacing, which had struck a chill to the girl's heart, like a presage of evil.

She tried to swallow her fears, chiding herself for feeling them, doing her best to close her ears to those rumbling, turbulent waters that seemed to threaten as they tumbled along on their way.

Gradually as they neared the village that curious feeling of impending evil became more strong: she could not help speaking of it to Andor, but he only laughed in that delightfully happy—almost defiantly happy—way of his, and for a moment or two she was satisfied.

But when at about half a kilomètre from home she caught sight of Klara Goldstein walking away from the village straight toward her and Andor, it seemed as if her fears had suddenly assumed a more tangible shape.

Klara looked old and thin, she thought, pathetic, too, in her plain black dress—she who used to be so fond of pretty clothes. Elsa gave her a hearty greeting as soon as she was near enough to her, and extended a cordial hand. She had no cause to feel well-disposed toward the Jewess, but there was something so forlorn-looking about the girl now, and such a look of sullen despair in her dark eyes, that Elsa's gentle nature was at once ready to forgive and to cheer.

"It is a long time since I have seen you, Klara," she said pleasantly.

"No wonder," said the other girl, with a shrug of her thin shoulders, "father won't let me out of his sight."

She had nodded to Andor, but by tacit consent they had not shaken hands. Klara now put her hands on her hips, and, like a young animal let free after days of captivity, she drew in deep breaths of sweet-scented air.

"Ah!" she said with a sigh, "it is good to be out again; being a prisoner doesn't suit me, I can tell you that."

"Your dear father seems to be very severe with you, Klara," said Elsa compassionately.

"Yes! curse him!" retorted the Jewess fiercely, as a savage, cruel look flashed through her sunken eyes. "He nearly killed me when he came home from Kecskemét that time—beat me like a dog—and now ..."

"Poor Klara!"

"I shouldn't have minded the beating so much. Among our people, parents have the right to be severe, and it is better to take a beating from your father than to be punished by the rabbi."

"Your dear father will forgive you in time," suggested Elsa gently.

She felt miserably uncomfortable, and would have given worlds to be rid of Klara. She couldn't think why the girl had stopped to talk to her and Andor: in fact she was more than sure that Klara had come out this evening on purpose to talk to her and to Andor; for now she stood deliberately in front of them both with arms crossed in front of her and defiant eyes fixed now upon one and now upon the other. Andor too was beginning to look cross and sullen; this meeting coming on the top of that lovely walk seemed like a black shadow cast over the radiance of their happiness, and this thin, tall girl, all in black, with black hair fluttering round her pale face, seemed like a big black bird of evil presage: her skirts flapped round her knees like wings and her voice sounded cold and harsh like the croaking of a raven.

But Elsa's kindly disposition did not allow her to be too obviously unkind to the Jewess. Perhaps after all the girl meant no harm, and had only run out now like a released colt, glad to feel freedom in the air around her and the vastness lying stretched out before her to infinity beyond. Perhaps she had only sought the company of the first-comers in order to get a small measure of sympathy. But now, though Elsa's gentle words should have softened her mood, she retorted with renewed fierceness:

"Curse him! I don't want his forgiveness! and if ever he wants mine—on his deathbed—he won't get it—even if he should die in torment for want of a kind word from me."

"Klara, you mustn't say that," cried Elsa, horrified at what she considered almost blasphemy. "Your father is your father, remember—and even if he has been harsh to you ..."

Klara interrupted her with a loud and strident laugh.

"If he has been harsh to me!" she exclaimed. "Didn't I tell you that he thrashed me like a dog, so that I was sick for days. But I wouldn't mind that so much. Bruises mend sooner or later, but it's that abominable marriage which will make me curse him to my dying day."

"Marriage? ... what marriage? ..."

181

"With a man I had never seen in my life until it was all settled. Just a man who is so ugly and so bad-tempered and so repugnant to every girl whom he knows that nobody would have him—but just a man who wanted a wife. The rabbi at Arad knew about him and he spoke about him to father—it seems that he is quite rich—and father has given me to him and I am to be married within a fortnight. Curse them! curse them all, I say! Oh! I wish I had the pluck to run away, or to kill myself or do something—but I am such an abominable coward—and I shall loathe to live in Arad in a tiny secondhand clothes shop, with that hideous monster for a husband—pointed at by everyone as the girl with a disgraceful story to her credit and sold to a creature whom no one else would have—in order to cover up a scandal."

Elsa was silent; her heart now was full of pity for the girl, who indeed was being punished far more severely than she deserved. It was clear that Klara was terribly resentful at her fate, and there was a look of vengeful rebellion in the glance which she threw on Elsa and Andor now.

Overhead there was flapping of wings—a flight of rooks cut through the air and there were magpies in their trail.

"Three for a wedding," said Andor with a forced laugh, trying to break the spell which—much against his will—seemed to have been suddenly cast over his happy spirits.

"One for sorrow, more like," retorted Klara.

"No, no, come!" he rejoined; "you must not look at it like that. There is always some happiness to be got out of married life. You are not very happy in your old home—you will like to have one of your own—a wedding is only the prelude to better things."

"That depends on the wedding, my friend," she sneered; "this one will be a finish, not a prelude—the naughty child, well whipped, sent out of mischief's way."

"I am sorry, Klara, that you feel it so strongly," he said more kindly.

"Yes," she retorted. "I dare say, my good man, you are sorry enough for me now, but you might have thought of all that, you know, before you played me that dirty trick."

"What do you mean?" he broke in quickly.

"Just what I say," she replied, "and no more. A dirty, abominable trick, I call it, and I cannot even show you up before the village—I could not even speak of you to the police officers. Oh, yes!" she continued more and more vehemently, as a flood of wrath and of resentment and a burning desire for getting even with Fate seemed literally to sweep her off her mental balance and cause her to lose complete control of her tongue, "oh, yes! my fine gentleman!

you can go and court Elsa now, and whisper sweet love-words in her ears—you two turtle-doves are the edification of the entire village now—and presently you will get married and live happy ever afterwards. But what I want to ask you, my friend," she added, and she took a step or two nearer to him, until her hot and angry breath struck him in the face and he was forced to draw himself back, away from that seething cauldron of resentment and of vengeance which was raging before him now, "what I want to ask you is have you ever thought of me?"

"Thought of you, Klara?" he said quietly, even as he felt, more than saw, that Elsa too had drawn back a little—a step or two further away from Klara, but a step or two also further away from him. "Thought of you?" he reiterated, seeing that Klara did not reply immediately, and that just for one brief moment—it was a mere flash—a look of irresolution had crept into her eyes, "why should I be thinking about you?"

"Why, indeed?" she said with a wrathful sneer. "What hurt had I done to you, Andor, that is what I want to know. I was always friendly to you. I had never done you any wrong—nor did I do Elsa any wrong—any wrong, I mean, that mattered," she continued, talking more loudly and more volubly because Andor was making desperate efforts to stop and interrupt her. "Béla would only have run after another woman if I had turned my back on him. And then when you asked me to leave him alone, I promised, didn't I? What you asked me to do I promised. ... And I meant to keep my promise to you, and you knew it ... and yet you rounded on me like that. ..."

"Silence, Klara," he cried at the top of his voice as he shook the girl roughly by the shoulder.

But she paid no heed to him—she was determined to be heard, determined to have her say. All the bitterness in her had been bottled up for weeks. She meant to meet Andor face to face before she was packed off as the submissive wife of a hated husband—the naughty child, whipped and sent out of the way—she meant to throw all the pent-up bitterness within her, straight into his face— and meant to do it when Elsa was nigh. For days and days she had watched for an opportunity; but her father had kept her a prisoner in the house, besides which she had no great desire to affront the sneering looks of village gossips. But this evening was her opportunity. For this she had waited, and now she meant to take it, and no power on earth, force or violence would prevent her from pouring out the full phial of her venomous wrath.

"I will not be silent," she shrieked, "I will not! You did round on me like a cur—you sneak—you double-faced devil. ..."

"Will you be silent!" he hissed through his teeth, his face deadly pale now with a passion of wrath at least as fierce as hers.

But now Elsa's quiet voice interposed between these two tempestuous souls.

"No!" she said firmly, "Klara shall not be silent, Andor. Let go her arm and let her speak. I want to hear what she has to say."

"She is trying to come between you and me, Elsa," said Andor, who was trying to keep his violent rage in check. "She tried to come between you and Béla, and chose an ugly method to get at what she wanted. She hates you ... why I don't know, but she does hate you, and she always tries to do you harm. Don't listen to her, I tell you. Why! just look at her now! ... the girl is half mad."

"Mad?" broke in Klara, as with a jerky movement of her shoulders she disengaged herself from Andor's rough grasp. "I dare say I am mad. And so would you be," she added, turning suddenly to Elsa, "so would you be, if all in one night you were to lose everything you cared for in the world—your freedom—the consideration of your friends—the man who some day would have made you a good husband—everything, everything—and all because of that sneaking, double-faced coward."

"If you don't hold your tongue ..." cried Andor menacingly.

"You will kill me, won't you?" she sneered. "One murder more or less on your conscience won't hurt you any more, will it, my friend? You will kill me, eh? Then you'll have two of us to your reckoning by and by, me and Béla!"

"Béla!" the cry, which sounded like a protest—hot, indignant, defensive—came from Elsa. She was paler than either of the others, and her glowing, inquiring eyes were fixed upon Klara with the look of an untamed creature ready to defend and to protect the thing that it holds dear.

"Don't listen to her, Elsa," pleaded Andor in a voice rendered hoarse with an overwhelming apprehension.

He felt as if his happiness, his life, the whole of this living, breathing world were slipping away from him—as if he had suddenly woke up from a beautiful, peaceful dream and found himself on the edge of a precipice and unable, in this sudden rude awakening, to keep a foothold upon the shifting sands. There was a mist before his eyes—a mist which seemed to envelop Elsa more and more, making her slim, exquisite figure appear more dim, blurring the outline of her gold-crowned head, getting more and more dense until even her blue eyes had disappeared away from him—away—snatched from his grasp—wafted away by that mist to the distant land beyond the low-lying horizon.

Something in the agony of his appeal, something in the pathos of Elsa's defiant attitude must have struck a more gentle cord in the Jewess' heart. The tears gathered in her eyes—tears of self-pity at the misery which she seemed to be strewing all round her with a free hand.

"I don't think that I really meant to tell you, Elsa," she said more quietly, "not lately, at any rate. Oh, I dare say at first I did mean to hurt you—but a month has gone by and I was beginning to forget. People used to say of me that I was a good sort—it was the hurt that he did me that seems to have made a devil of me. ... And then—just now when I saw the other folk coming home in the procession and noticed that you and Andor weren't among them, I guessed that you would be walking back together arm-in-arm—and that the whole world would be smiling on you both, while I was eating out my heart in misery."

She was speaking with apparent calm now, in a dull and monotonous voice, her eyes fixed upon the distant line of the horizon, where the glowing sun had at last sunk to rest. The brilliant orange and blood-red of the sky had yielded to a colder crimson tint—it, too, was now slowly turning to grey.

Elsa stood silent, listening, and Andor no longer tried to force Klara to silence. What was the good? Fate had spoken through her lips—God's wrath, perhaps, had willed it so. For the first time in all these weeks he realized that perhaps he had committed a deadly sin, and that he had had no right to reckon on happiness coming to him, because of it. He stood there, dazed, letting the Jewess have her way. What did it matter how much more she said? Perhaps, on the whole, it was best that Elsa should learn the whole truth now.

And Klara continued to speak in listless, apathetic tones, letting her tongue run on as if she had lost control over what she said, and as if a higher Fate was forcing her to speak against her will.

"I suppose," she said thoughtfully, "that some kind of devil did get into my bones then. I wandered out into the stubble, and I saw you together coming from the distance. The sunlight was full upon you, and long before you saw me I saw your faces quite distinctly. There was so much joy, so much happiness in you both, that I seemed to see it shining out of your eyes. And I was so broken and so wretched that I couldn't bear to see Andor so happy with the girl who rightly belonged to Béla—the wretched man whom he himself had sent to his death."

"Whom he himself had sent to his death?" broke in Elsa quietly. "What do you mean, Klara?"

"I mean that it was young Count Feri who was to have come to see me that night. Father being away, he wanted to come and have a

185

little chat and a bit of supper with me. There was no harm in that, was there? He didn't care to be seen walking in at the front door—as there's always such a lot of gossip in this village—so he asked me for the back-door key, and I gave it to him."

"Well?"

"Leopold missed the key later on, and guessed I had given it to Count Feri. He was mad with jealousy and threatened to kill anyone who dared come sneaking in round the back way. He wouldn't let me out of his sight—and threatened to strangle me if I attempted to go and get the key back from Count Feri. I was nearly crazy with fear. Wouldn't you have been," she added defiantly, "if you had a madman to deal with and no one near to protect you?"

"Perhaps," replied Elsa, under her breath.

"Then Andor came into the tap-room. With soft words and insinuating promises he got me to tell him what had happened. I didn't want to at first—I mistrusted him because of what had happened at the banquet—I knew that he hated me because of you."

"It is not true," broke in Andor involuntarily.

"Let her tell her story her own way," rejoined Elsa, with the same strange quiet which seemed now to envelop her soul.

"There's nothing more to tell," retorted Klara. "Nothing, at any rate, that you haven't guessed already. I told Andor all about Count Feri and the key, and how terrified I was that Leopold would do some deadly mischief. He offered to go to the castle and get the key away from the young Count."

"Well?"

"Well! Andor was in love with you, wasn't he?" she continued, speaking once more with vehemence; "he wanted you, didn't he? And he hated Béla having you. He hated me, too, of course. So he got the key away from Count Feri, and later on, after you had followed Béla almost to the tap-room and you had some words with him just outside ... you remember?"

"Yes."

"Andor had the key in his pocket then—and he gave it to Béla...."

There was silence for awhile now—that silence which falls upon the plain during the first hour after sunset—and which falls upon human creatures when destiny has spoken her last word. In the village far away the worshippers had gone back into the church, all sound of chanting and praying had died away behind its walls; there was no flight of birds overhead, nor call of waterfowl from the bank of the stream, the autumn breeze had gone to rest with the sun, the leaves of acacias and willows lay still, and even the turbulent waters of the Maros seemed momentarily hushed.

"Is that true, Andor?"

It was Elsa's voice that spoke, but the voice sounded muffled and dull, as if it came from far away or from out the depths of the earth. Then, as Andor made no reply, but gazed on Elsa in mute and passionate appeal, like a man who is drowning would gaze on the shore which he cannot reach, Klara said slowly:

"Oh! it's true enough. You cannot deny it, can you, Andor? You wanted your revenge on me, and you wanted to be rid of Béla— you wanted Elsa for yourself, but you didn't care one brass fillér what would become of me after that. You left me without a thought, lonely and unprotected, knowing that a madman was prowling outside, ready to kill me or any man who came along. You gave Béla that key, didn't you? ... and told him nothing about Leopold—and you didn't care what became of me, so long as you got rid of Béla and could have Elsa for yourself."

"And now you have had your say, Klara," said Andor, breaking with a mighty effort the spell of silence which had held him all this while; "you have made all the mischief that you wanted to make. Suppose you leave us alone now ... Elsa and me ... alone with the misery which you have created for us."

Then, as for a moment she didn't move, but looked on him through narrowed lids and with a sneer, half of pity and half of triumph, he continued with a sudden outburst of fierceness:

"Well! you have had your say! ... Why don't you go?"

Klara shrugged her shoulders and said more lightly:

"Oh, very well, my friend, I'll go. ... Good-bye, Elsa," she added, with sudden earnestness. "I don't suppose that you want to shake hands with me—and I dare say it's no use asking you to think kindly of me—but I wish you would try and believe that I am sorry I lost myself as I did. I don't think that I ever would have told you if I hadn't seen him looking so happy and so complacent after the horrible, dirty trick which he played me. People used to say that I had a good heart, but, by the Almighty, I declare that I seem to have lost my head lately. That's what I say, Elsa. It's all very well, but what about me? What had I done?—and now, look at my life! But don't you fret about him or any other man. Take my word for it, men are not worth it."

And having said that she turned on her heel and slowly walked away, leaving behind her an ocean of desolation. She walked away—with a slow, swinging stride, one hand on her hip, her head thrown back.

For a long time her darkly-clad figure was silhouetted against the evening sky, a speck of blackness upon the immensity around. Elsa watched her go, watched that tiny black speck which, like the locust which at times devastates the plains, had left behind it an irreparable trail of misery.

# CHAPTER XXXII

## "The land beyond the sunset"

And now the shadows of evening were slowly invading the plains. The autumn wind, lulled for a time to rest with the setting of the sun, had sprung up in angry gusts, lashing up clouds from the southwest and sending them to tear along and efface the last vestige of the evening crimson glow.

Elsa and Andor had both remained quite still after Klara left them; yet Elsa—like all simple creatures who feel acutely—was longing to run and let the far horizon, the distant unknown land, wrap and enfold her while she thought things out for herself, for indeed this real world—the world of men and women, of passions and hatred and love—was nothing but a huge and cruel puzzle. She longed for solitude—the solitude which the plains can offer in such absolute completeness—because her heart was heavy and she felt that if she were all alone she might ease the weight on her heart in a comforting flow of tears.

But this would not have been kind to Andor. She could not leave him now, when he looked so broken down with sorrow and misery and doubt. So, after a little while, when she felt that if she spoke her voice would be quite steady, she said gently:

"It is not all true, is it, Andor?"

She could not—she would not believe it all true—not in the way that Klara had put it before her, with all its horrible details of callousness and cowardice. For more years than she could remember she had loved and trusted Andor—she had known his simple, loyal nature, his kind and gentle ways—a few spiteful words from a jealous woman were not likely to tear down in a moment the solid edifice of her affection and her confidence. True! his silence had told her something that was a bitter truth; his passionate rage against Klara had been like a cruel stab right into her heart—but even then she wanted the confirmation which could only come from

188

his own lips—and for this she waited when she asked him, quite simply, altogether trustingly:

"It is not true, is it?"

Nor did it occur to Andor to lie to her about it all; the thought of denial never for one moment entered his head. The fatalism peculiar to this Oriental race made the man scorn to shield himself behind a lie. Béla was now for ever silent; the young Count would scorn to speak! His own protestations in the ear of this loving, simple-minded girl, against the accusations of a woman of the despised race—jealous, bitter, avowedly half-crazy—needed only to be uttered in order to be whole-heartedly believed. But even the temptation to pursue such a course never assailed his soul. With the limitless sky above him, the vast immensity of the plains stretching out unbroken far away, with the land under his feet and the scent of the maize-stubble in his nostrils, he was too proud of himself as a man to stoop to such a lie.

So when Elsa spoke to him and asked him that one straight and firm question, he raised his head and looked straight into her tear-dimmed eyes.

"What, Elsa?" he asked quietly.

"That you let Béla go to his death—just like that—as Klara said ... that is not all true, is it?"

And as she returned his look—fearlessly and trustfully—she knew that the question which she had thus put to him was really an affirmation of what she felt must be the truth. But already Andor had raised his voice in hot and passionate protest.

"He was a brute to you, Elsa," he affirmed with all the strength of his manhood, the power of his love, which, in spite of all, would not believe in its own misery; "he would have made you wretchedly unhappy ... he ..."

"You did do it, then?" she broke in quietly.

"I did it because of you, Elsa," he cried, and his own firm voice was now half-choked with sobs. "He made you unhappy even though you were not yet bound to him by marriage. Once you were his wife he would have made you miserable ... he would have bullied you ... beaten you, perhaps. I heard him out under the verandah speaking to you like the sneering brute that he was. ... And then he kissed you ... and I ... But even then I didn't give him the key. ... Klara lied when she said that. I didn't urge him to take it, even—I did not speak about the key. It was lying on the table where I had put it—he took it up—I did not give it him."

"But you let him take it. You knew that he meant to visit Klara, and that Leopold was on the watch outside. Yet you let him go. ..."

189

"I let him go. ... I was nearly mad then with rage at the way he had treated you all day. ... His taking that key was a last insult put upon you on the eve of your wedding day. ... The thought of it got into my blood like fire, when I saw his cruel leer and heard his sneers. ... Later on, I thought better of it ... calmer thoughts had got into my brain ... reason, sober sense. ... I had gone back to the presbytery, and meant to go to bed—I went out, I swear it by God that I went out prepared to warn him, to help him if I could. The whole village was deserted, it was the hour of supper at the barn. I heard the church clock strike the half-hour after ten. I worked my way round to the back of Goldstein's house and in the yard I saw Béla lying—dead."

"And you might have raised a finger to save him at first ... and you didn't do it."

"Not at first ... and after that it was too late. ..."

"You have done a big, big wrong, Andor," she said slowly.

"Wrong?" he cried, whilst once more the old spirit of defiance fired him—the burning love in him, the wrath at seeing her unhappy. "Wrong? Because I did not prevent one miserable brute being put out of the way of doing further harm? By the living God, Elsa, I do not believe that it was wrong. I didn't send him to his death, I did not see or speak to Leopold Hirsch, I merely let Fate or God Himself work His way with him. I did not say a word to him that might have induced him to take that key. He picked it up from the table, and every evil thought came into his head then and there. He didn't even care about Klara and a silly, swaggering flirtation with her, he only wanted to insult you, to shame you, to show you that he was the master—and meant to have his way in all things. ... And this he did because—bar his pride in your beauty—he really hated you and meant to treat you ill. He meant to harm you, Elsa— my own dear dove ... my angel from heaven ... for whom I would have died, and would die to-day, if my death could bring you happiness. ... I let him go and Leopold Hirsch killed him ... if he had lived, he would have made your life one long misery. ... Was it my fault that Leopold Hirsch killed him?—killed him at the moment when he was trying to do you as great harm as he could? By God, Elsa, I swear that I don't believe it was my fault ... it was the will of God—God would not punish me for not interfering with His will. ... Why, it wouldn't be justice, Elsa ... it wouldn't be justice."

His voice broke in one agonized sob. He had put all his heart, all his feelings into that passionate appeal. He did not believe that he had done wrong, he had not on his soul the sense of the brand of Cain. Rough, untutored, a son of the soil, he saw no harm in sweeping out of the way a noisome creature who spreads evil and

190

misery. And Elsa's was also a simple and untutored soul, even though in her calmer temperament the wilder passions of men had found no echo. True and steadfast in love, her mind was too simple to grasp at sophistry, to argue about right or wrong; her feelings were her guide, and even while Andor—burning with love and impatience—argued and clung desperately to his own point of view, she felt only the desire to comfort and to succour—above all, to love—she was just a girl—Andor's sweetheart and not his judge. God alone was that! God would punish if He so desired—indeed, He had punished already, for never had such sorrow descended in Andor's heart before, of that she felt quite sure.

He became quite calm after awhile. Even his passion seemed to have died down under the weight of this immense sorrow.

And the peace which comes from the plains when they are wrapped in the darkness of the night descended on the humble peasant-girl's soul; she saw things as they really were, not as men's turbulent desires would have them be—above all, not as a woman's idealism would picture them.

She no longer had the desire to run away—and if the distant, unknown land was to wrap and enfold her out of the ken of this real, cruel world, then it should enfold her and Andor together, and her love would wrap him and comfort him too.

So now—when he had finished speaking, when his fervent appeal to God and to her had died down on his quivering lips—she came close up to him and placed her small, cool hand upon his arm.

"Andor," she said gently; and her voice shook and was almost undistinguishable from the sweet, soft sounds that filled the limitless plain. "I am only an ignorant peasant-girl—you and I are only like children, of course, beside the clever people who can argue about such things. But this I do know, that there is no sin in the world so great but it can be blotted out and forgiven. You may have done a big, big, wrong, Andor—or perhaps you are not much to blame ... I don't know how that is ... Pater Bonifácius will tell you, no doubt, when next you make your confession to him. ... But I am too ignorant to understand ... the plains have taught me all I know ... and ... and ... I shall always love you, Andor ... and not judge what you have done. ... God will do that. ... I can only love you. ... That is all!"

Her voice died away in the soughing of the wind. For a moment or two he stood beside her—not daring to speak—or to move—or to take that cool, little white hand in his and kiss it—for now she seemed to him more pure than she had ever been—almost holy—like a saint—hallowed by the perfect selflessness of her love.

And as he stood beside her—with head bent and throat choked

with sobs of infinite happiness—the darkness of the night fell wholly upon the plain. Nothing around but just this darkness, filled with all the sounds of hidden, pulsating life; overhead the clouds chased one another ceaselessly and restlessly, and from far away the dull murmur of the water came as a faint and rumbling echo.

Andor could no longer see Elsa now, not even her silhouette; but her hand was still on his arm, and he felt the nearness of her presence, and knew that henceforth, throughout the years that were to come, a happiness such as he had never even dared to dream of would be his and hers too, until the day when they would leave the beautiful, mysterious plains for that hidden land beyond the glowing horizon, beyond the rosy dawn and the crimson sunset.

Andor slowly fell on his knees and pressed his burning lips on the small, white hand. Just then in the east there was a rent in the clouds, a lining of silver appeared behind the darkness; the rent became wider and ever wider; the silver turned to lemon-gold, and slowly, majestically, the waning moon—honey-coloured and brilliant—emerged triumphantly, queening it over the plain.

The silvery radiance lit up the vast, silent expanse of nothingness, the huge dome of the sky, the limitless area of stubble and stumps of hemp and dead sunflowers, and where the mysteries of the earth merged in those of the sky—it touched with its subtle radiance that unknown land on the horizon, far away, which no child of the plain has ever reached as yet.

And from the distant village came softly sounding the tinkle of the church bell, tolling for evening prayer.

Hand in hand, Andor and Elsa wandered back to the village—together—hand in hand with memory—hand in hand in never-fading love and understanding and simple trust—hand in hand upon the bosom of the illimitable plain.